The Year of Cecily

The Year of Cecily

A From Sunset Park, With Love Romance

Lisa Lin

TULE
PUBLISHING

Praise for Lisa Lin's *The Year of Cecily*

"Giving a fresh start to former sweethearts, debut author Lin handles complicated family culture and romantic tension by writing passionate, strong-willed protagonists and triumphantly delivers a satisfying second-chance romance."

—Library Journal Review

"*The Year of Cecily* is full of heart and humor with just as much familial drama as witty banter. This is the rom com you've been looking for."

—Sally Kilpatrick, *USA Today* bestselling author

"A delightful debut about finding the courage to go outside your comfort zone and follow your heart. This second chance romance is sweet, breezy, and sure to satisfy. Make it your New Year's resolution to add Lisa Lin to your auto-buy list!

—Lenora Bell, author of *One Fine Duke*

"The Year of Cecily is an absolute delight. You won't be able to put this book down. I devoured it."

—Jayci Lee, author of *Booked on a Feeling*

Dedication

For Eve—one of the best check battle opponents I know.
Thank you for being the first to tell me I could and should
do this, for believing in me, and for being there every step
of the way. But most of all thank you for your amazing
generosity and friendship, it means the world to me.
Love you!

Chapter One

New Year's Eve

S NUGGLED IN BED in her teal fleece pajamas, a glass of white wine on the nightstand, and an aloe sheet mask on her face, Cecily Chang flipped through the TV channels. It was almost 9 p.m., which meant the ball was about to drop in Times Square. Thank God she lived in San Francisco and could go to bed soon. Normally, she'd find the news coverage hokey and cheesy, but some traditions were meant to be observed. So, she'd spend the next half hour watching TV hosts try not to freeze while making inane small talk. She took a glance at her watch. Twenty-three minutes to go. She was getting too old for this shit.

The timer she set on her phone went off. Cecily dutifully got out of bed, went to the bathroom, and peeled off the mask. After chucking it in the trash can, she took stock of her face in the mirror. "Do these things even really work?" she mumbled. As far as she could tell, she looked exactly the same as she did thirty minutes ago when she put the mask on. Maybe it took a day or two to see results. She made a mental note to do more research into the product and ingredients. Even if it didn't give her face a "glowing rejuvenated look" there was still something to be said for self-care and pampering yourself every once in a while. She yawned and padded back to the bedroom, got back in the queen-size sleigh bed, and readjusted the blankets.

Eighteen minutes to go. Damn. As hard as she tried, Anderson and his antics weren't keeping her attention. Maybe some traditions were meant to evolve. Cecily flipped through the channels and saw an old rerun of *Memphis Medical.*

"Oh, this is a good one. Stacey with the plane crash!" She sat back and prepared to soak in the genius of Chandra Rivers for the umpteenth time. She rubbed her hands together in glee. Her phone buzzed, and she opened it to see a selfie text from her best friend Adrienne Arroyo. Who looked like she was having the time of her life, dancing at a rooftop party at Rosemont with a flute of champagne in her hand. Under the picture Adrienne texted:

Ringing in the New Year RIGHT! Wish you were here. Xo

Typical Adrienne. She'd tried to drag her to the party, but Cecily had pleaded exhaustion and a pressing work deadline. The first part was true, the second not so much. She needed some peace and quiet, and a loud raucous party sounded like the last thing she wanted to do. But instead, she was now home alone, and bored out of her mind.

When had she become so dull? It seemed that lately, all she did was wake up, go to work, come home, sleep, rinse and repeat. She had no life to speak of. What a depressing rut. It was time to shake things up.

A loud bang from the TV screen made her jump and pay attention again. Bye bye, Jared. "A hell of a way to go," Cecily muttered with a shake of her head. It was kinda pathetic when the most exciting thing to happen to her in weeks was watching a fictional hot EMT guy get blown up on TV.

"So, do something about it." Cecily sat back on the bed, leaning on the headboard. Inspiration struck. "Of course!"

Maybe what she needed was The Year of Cecily. It was going to be Jan 1 in a matter of minutes, what better time for a list of resolutions and a fresh start? And what better inspiration than Robyn Morgan's *Your Best Life*. She wasn't normally a fan of self-help books, but she hadn't been able to resist grabbing it because it was on sale. Robyn gave great practical tips on setting goals, peppered with personal anecdotes to bring her points home. Mostly, it encouraged women to pursue what made them happy, and not let doubt and fear get in the way. She was definitely here for that.

She nibbled her bottom lip. If she was going to do this, she was going to do it right. She went into her living room to get her new planner from her purse, then a detour to the kitchen to refresh her glass of sauvignon blanc.

Cecily got back in bed and swore to herself she wasn't getting out of it again for the rest of the night. It was 9:05 now according to her watch. She raised her glass of wine in a silent toast to her family back in Brooklyn.

"Happy New Year's, guys. And thank God I'm all the way out here." She loved her family but firmly believed in the adage that absence made the heart grow fonder.

Okay. Back to the task at hand. The first resolution

came easily.

1. *Avoid drama. Not your circus, not your monkeys.*

Spicing up her life was one thing, unnecessary drama was another. Her life was busy enough without dealing with the cray-cray. Blocking her cousin Molly's number would be a great first step. That way, she didn't have to hear about Molly's on-again off-again relationship with her boyfriend Brian every week. On the other hand, that would just mean her mother and Auntie Marcia would be calling and giving her hell ninety seconds later, which seemed counter-productive. Damn. She'd figure something else out.

Right then and there, Cecily also vowed to stop reading the comments when reading the news online. "Do not feed the trolls." They thrived on the outrage and the clicks. Now that one was going to take some self-discipline, but it'd be worth it. Her blood pressure would thank her later.

"What else?" She thought about the pile of work in her office.

2. *Better Work-Life Balance—don't spend all your time at the office.*

These days she was lucky if she got home before 8 p.m. That was just enough time to have dinner, shower, catch the news, watch *Late Night*, and drop dead of exhaustion. Cecily reminded herself that she was on track to make partner, and that this wouldn't last forever. There was light at the end of the tunnel. Once the Yardley deal was wrapped up, she'd have more breathing room. She'd be able to get home at 6 p.m. instead. While still getting to the office at 7 a.m. She just needed to power through this crunch time.

"Maybe I can clone myself. Clone Cecily could go to the office, and I can spend a week at the spa. Or drink mai tais at the beach in Tahiti." She snorted. *Keep dreaming. While you're at it, maybe a cute cabana boy can give you a nice rubdown while you're throwing back the mai tais.*

But if she accumulated some more vacation days, she could probably swing a long weekend in Napa and book herself into a spa there. Considering the hours she'd been putting into the Yardley deal, she had earned a few days of massages, facials, salt scrubs, and lounging by the pool with multiple glasses of wine. It sounded heavenly. And would give her something to look forward to when this was all over.

Her phone buzzed again. It was her sister Gillian.

Mom wanted me to remind you to text a list of goodies you want her to stock up on or make for you when you come home for New Year's next month. See you in a few weeks! 新年快樂!

Oh shit. Cecily let out a groan. Lunar New Year was coming up and she was going to have to go back home to Brooklyn. Skipping the gathering was not an option. It was the biggest holiday of the year in her family, a huge deal. Her attendance was mandatory.

But at least that helped her come up with her next resolution.

3. *Remain calm with family. Don't let them get under*

your skin.

She better start praying for patience now. To whatever deity would work best or was listening. But maybe not. It was only going to be five days. One hundred twenty hours. How hard could that be? Most of the time would be spent eating and doing other holiday-related activities, and she'd have nieces and nephews to spoil and cuddle. She'd also have the built-in excuse of work and could escape when she needed to. She'd suffered through three years of law school, survived and passed the New York and California bar exams. Surely one hundred twenty hours with her family would be a piece of cake in comparison. It wouldn't be that bad.

Cecily then did a mental calculation of how many extended family members she'd be seeing. Not just her immediate family, but all the aunties, uncles, cousins, and "aunts" and "uncles" from the neighborhood.

Maybe asking Adrienne to be on standby in case she needed someone to post bail for her would be a good idea after all.

If you run into him, you will DEFINITELY need bail money.

Shut up, brain.

"What else?" Cecily tapped her pen to her lips. "You have no social life. Time to do something about it." The next two came easily.

4. Make new friends.

Just one or two would do. No need to go overboard. God knows how she'd juggle having new friends in her life with her crazy work schedule, but she'd make it work. Even squeezing in regular twenty-minute coffee breaks once a week with a new buddy was better than nothing, right?

5. *Get out there more. It's been too long since you've had sex.*

She didn't want to think about how long. God she missed sex. A one-night stand held some appeal. Anything to scratch the itch. But she didn't necessarily want to pick up some random stranger for said one-night stand either. At thirty-five, she'd probably missed the window on that particular experience. It didn't feel right. She wore suits to work, had a retirement fund, and the teenagers working at the supermarket called her "ma'am" for God's sake.

That being said, it was high time she got back on the horse. So to speak. However, the idea of dating again, using a dating app, or getting set up gave her hives. Was there a way to have a one-night stand with someone she knew, where she could have some hot sweaty sex with the guy, get it out of her system, but have no emotional strings attached? Some sort of hit it and quit it situation? Unbidden, a face from her past came to mind. *Didn't I just say no emotional attachment? He's the complete opposite of that. Get it together! Snap out of it. What's wrong with you?*

Cecily glanced at her e-reader. It was loaded up with books that she kept meaning to read. But she never got around to it. She was always too busy or too tired. Maybe she needed some accountability. It was time to tackle the To Be Read mountain.

6. *Expand your horizons—join a book club or something.*

Maybe a knitting class? Wine appreciation club? Who knew? Maybe this could be a kill-two-birds-with-one-stone situation. She could make a new friend with one of the other people in the book club, wine club, or knitting store. Cecily had always appreciated efficiency and multi-tasking. Besides, it would be nice to leave the office at a reasonable hour every once in a while, and this would be a good excuse.

It took some time, but Cecily finally came up with the last two resolutions.

7. *Come up with an anniversary present for Mom and Dad that she'll actually like.*

Her parents' fortieth wedding anniversary was coming up. The family was going all out, throwing a huge party slash banquet, despite Ma and Daddy's protest that "they didn't want a fuss". That was Asian parent code for: "We want to be acknowledged and fussed over, but it would be unseemly to ask or appear to be expecting it."

Cecily and her siblings had been planning the celebration for the past six months. But she still needed to come up with a good gift. She was more likely to discover the cure for cancer, but a girl had to try. At least she had until May to tackle this particular minefield.

8. Get out of your comfort zone.

She could go sky diving. Or take salsa dancing lessons. Start hiking on the weekends. The possibilities were endless. She'd been in a rut lately and needed to shake things up. She didn't want to be discovered someday dead in her office on a Sunday afternoon, slumped over a zoning appeal application.

Looking down at the list she'd made, Cecily nodded in satisfaction. Eight was a nice round number and a reasonable amount to tackle in terms of goals. Besides, eight symbolized good luck in Chinese culture, and she was going to take it as a good omen. Even her mother wouldn't be able to find fault with that.

Confident that she'd killed the resolutions-making game, Cecily put away the planner, turned off the lights, turned the pillow over to the cool side, and slept the sleep of the righteous.

Bring on the "Year of Cecily."

"THIS IS NOT how I wanted to start the New Year." Glaring at his agent through his computer screen, Jeffrey Lee crossed his arms. The light coming through the window in his Los Angeles apartment was in stark contrast to his mood.

"What are you talking about? This is good news."

"Sure. This is good news, like appendicitis is good news. They both turn me into a ray of sunshine. I said I needed more time."

Unfazed, Marty Novelli pressed on. "Too late. I already set up the meeting for you. The director and producer are looking forward to meeting you."

"I told you I'm not who they're looking for." He tried not to panic. What Marty was presenting was the opportunity of a lifetime. But was he ready? The script still needed work.

His agent's voice was tough and unsympathetic. "You have until April. It's happening." Leave it to Marty to deliver the tough love like an Asian parent. Is that why he'd signed up with him?

"They're looking at people who have decades more experience than I do! I'll look like an amateur by comparison. A film student going up against Spielberg." He threw up his hands in a frenzied motion.

"The studio is saying they're looking for a fresh new take for the next installment of the franchise. That means you."

Despite himself, Jeffrey began to feel a hum of excitement. Writing the next Ian Grey movie would be beyond amazing. If he could land this job, it would be a career maker. This could mean a chance at some career stability. Plus, it might help get his parents off his back about pursuing a Hollywood career, if he could show he was actually succeeding.

"And besides," Marty continued, "you don't want to know what I had to do to get you this meeting. You owe me."

"You already get your fifteen percent. That's more than enough. As long as it wasn't illegal or unethical, I don't care what you had to do." His lips quirked as his agent's eyes narrowed.

"You make me regret signing you."

"You wound me. That hurts, Marty," he said with a hand to his heart, and a sham forlorn expression on his face. There was a brief pause as Marty looked over his notes.

"But uh, there's a catch."

"I knew it. You're holding out on me." There was always a catch. Hollywood was the ultimate of the axiom: *If it sounds too good to be true, it probably is.*

"Calm down, it's not as bad as it sounds." Marty's voice and demeanor were far too innocent. Like a mom trying to convince her child that this doctor's visit would absolutely not involve needles.

"You know they read your treatment and your script for Act I. They want to see Act II at the next meeting." Marty gave a shrug, like it was no big deal.

"Are you kidding me? I thought I just had to give them a rough idea of the rest of the story, an outline. Now you're saying they want a full Act II." Unbelievable.

"What's the big deal? Don't you have a draft of that already done?"

"No! It's barely started. It's embryonic, not ready to hatch." Now his palms were sweating and his heart rate was picking up. Could he really do this with this little time left?

"Well, looks like there's gonna be a lot of all-nighters in

your future. And oh, wear something presentable." Marty wagged a finger in warning.

"Thanks for the reminder, Marty. I was planning on showing up shirtless with raggedy gym shorts and flip-flops. You know directors and producers love the Bohemian beach bum look." Jeffrey rolled his eyes.

"Sarcasm duly noted and not appreciated."

"The timing couldn't be worse."

"What? You got a job I don't know about? You holding out on me?" Now it was his agent's turn to side-eye.

"I have some stuff I'm ghostwriting. Which means I got deadlines that will give me eyestrain, so adding this on top of all that will just be peachy. I'm going home to Brooklyn at the beginning of February so that week is basically blacked out. I'll barely have any time to prep after I get back." Being a somewhat successful writer in Hollywood was both a blessing and curse in disguise.

"So what?"

"So, I want to make sure I don't go into that meeting making a jackass of myself!"

"You're not going to make a jackass of yourself. And if you do, I'll come over and beat the crap out of you for embarrassing me."

"I appreciate the vote of confidence, Marty. And that technicolor impression of my mother." Despite himself, Jeffrey began to relax. The familiarity of the threat was somehow comforting. Maybe this was going to be doable after all.

His agent's voice turned serious. "Listen, kid. You gotta

stop acting like you're the new kid on the block. You've shown you can write scripts that sell. This is just taking it to the next level. You wouldn't have gotten this meeting if they didn't think you're good. Believe in yourself more. Would I waste my time on you if I didn't think you had what it takes? Get over yourself and just get it done."

Jeffrey gave a salute. "Aye, aye, Captain."

"Anything else?" Marty asked.

"No, but I'm warning you now, I'm going to be working on this while I'm home in Brooklyn. If my parents give me grief about it, I'm throwing you under the bus and siccing them on you. And you'll have no one to blame but yourself."

His agent, oblivious to the gravity of the threat, laughed him off. "You need to calm down. You're going to be fine." Abruptly, Marty cut the feed and ended the Skype session.

"Damn it, Marty," Jeffrey muttered.

He paced around his Echo Park apartment, trying to get his bearings. When that didn't work, he decided to take a thirty-minute jog to clear his mind. He threw on a ratty tank top, gym shorts, put on socks and sneakers, and found the trail near the neighborhood park.

As he did his usual three loops, Jeffrey came up with a game plan. He needed to lay the groundwork now for working while home for New Year's. There was no way his parents were going to let him get away with that. There would be no end of guilt trips if he kept disappearing. Not without an explanation. And God knew Asian parents didn't understand the concept of privacy or boundaries—it wasn't in their vocabulary when it came to their children. He needed backup. Jeffrey decided to recruit the most cunning, strategic, and devious person he knew.

His little sister Bethany.

If anyone could get their parents on board, it was Beth. She could orchestrate a campaign on par with the best political operatives. And she could help make sure Mom and Ba didn't try to fix him up with someone again. Last time, it was Mr. Li's niece's best friend from college. They were really getting desperate and scraping at the bottom of the barrel in their efforts to get him married off and producing grandkids. He was pretty sure his parents wouldn't be satisfied unless he and his siblings popped out a dozen kids each and they all lived in a compound like the Kennedys.

He could've told them to save their breath. Any chance he'd had of settling down went out the window ten years ago when he'd thrown away his chance at happiness. At the time, he hadn't thought he'd had any other choice, but it still haunted him.

As if to prove that point, Jeffrey turned the corner in the jogging trail and saw a couple in their early thirties at a picnic table with their two young kids. The little girl had chubby cheeks, and her hair was in pigtails. Straight out of central casting. The mother was laughing at her son as he smushed a banana all over his face. The image made Jeffrey smile, even as it hit a pang in his heart.

That could've been you and her. Your little girl who prob-

ably would be her mini-me. Now you'd be lucky if she didn't shoot you on sight if she ever saw you again.

The girl, apparently done with her meal, slid off the bench, and made her way to a huge tote bag by her mother. She grabbed a coloring book and crayons. Plopping down on the grass, she opened the book, and started scribbling away. But then a sudden gust of wind blew the crayons away. Instinctively, Jeffrey moved off the path and helped the little girl gather up her things.

With a smile, he handed over the crayons. "There you go. Now you can go back to coloring."

With a solemn nod, the little girl took the crayons back. Just then the dad came over and gave a quick thanks before taking his daughter's hand and leading her back to the family.

Jeffrey shook his head and kept jogging. Even after all this time, he couldn't forget about Cecily, and everything and anything reminded him of her, even random families at the park. She was still there in his mind. He'd screwed things up royally ten years ago, but what was done was done. Even though it had still been the right thing to do, it was time to try to make amends. If she was coming home this year, it'd be the perfect opportunity. He couldn't hope to ask for a second chance, but if he got her to listen, maybe she'd understand. They could be friends again, the way things used to be. She'd always been the Watson to his Sherlock, Bonnie to his Clyde, the soy sauce to his ginger. Though he could picture her now. *"Why do you get to be Sherlock? Why do I have to be Watson? What if I want to be Sherlock, huh?!"*

But first he had to find out if she was coming home too.

He'd ask Beth.

Chapter Two

"HELLO, WELCOME TO Café Versailles." The friendly hostess with Holly emblazoned on her name tag greeted Cecily as soon as she walked through the door of her go-to brunch place.

"Yes, hi. I'm meeting someone here but I'm not sure if she's here yet." She barely got the words out when she saw Adrienne waving. "Oh, there she is."

Holly followed her gaze. "Fantastic. If you'd follow me, ma'am."

She led the way, with menu in hand. Cecily, gritting her teeth the whole time, walked behind Holly, and plopped onto the opposite side of the booth.

"Your waiter will be right with you."

"Yes, thank you."

"Why are you looking so ugly?" Adrienne asked with a raised brow. She was wearing a bright red soft cashmere cowl sweater, gold hoop earrings, and dark wash jeans with adorable ballet flats in a leopard print.

"She 'ma'amed' me." Cecily pouted. She yanked the sunglasses off of her green sweater dress, put them in the case, and stuck it in her bag.

"Oh get over it. You're just hangry," her best friend

replied with a roll of her eyes.

Couldn't argue with that. "I want some eggs Benedict and French toast."

"And a pitcher of mimosas to share?"

"Like you have to ask."

Adrienne signaled for a waiter and gave their order. "I'm so glad you're here. It's been too long since we've done this."

"Way too long," Cecily agreed.

"I haven't seen you since before New Year's, I don't think. I barely even get texts from you as proof of life. If we didn't work in the same building, I'd think you were dead."

Cecily made a face. "I'm swamped with negotiations for the Yardley deal. I'm basically living in the office right now."

"How is it going?"

"Not bad. Except opposing counsel is being totally anal-retentive. At this point, this contract is going to be a thousand pages because he wants to cover every goddamn contingency and what-if scenario. I swear, he's this close to including a clause on what happens to the agreement if the zombie apocalypse goes down in the next six months." Cecily threw up her hands.

"Maybe he's just a *Walking Dead* fan, and there's nothing wrong with being thorough." Adrienne's lips quirked.

"Well, the zombie apocalypse can shove it."

"Now that we've covered how busy you are, I wanna hear about your resolutions. How goes the Year of Cecily? You only gave me the bare bones when we talked on the phone."

She took a delicate sip of water. "Well, there's been a slight change of plans."

"Don't tell me you're throwing in the towel before January is even over? It's only been two weeks, for God's sake." The faux judgment in Adrienne's voice made her laugh.

"No, more like a hiatus. I'm not planning to start on the goals just yet."

"How long of a hiatus?"

"Until February fifth."

"That's random. Why February fifth?"

"That's when the Lunar New Year starts," Cecily explained. "Besides, you know it's the biggest holiday in my family. My parents consider it a bigger deal than Christmas and Thanksgiving combined. So really, that's the New Year's that counts."

Adrienne tilted her head. "I mean, part of me admires your ability to see and exploit loopholes. Nothing but respect for your game, Chang."

"Thank you, thank you." Cecily rolled her hands and took a partial bow. "I didn't suffer through law school and acquire frightening levels of debt to not be on my A-game."

"On the other hand, I can't believe you're waiting until February to get your groove back. Go get laid already."

Cecily turned tomato red. "Adrienne!" she hissed. She whipped her head around to make sure no one else had heard that.

Adrienne gave an unrepentant shrug. "Hey, you're the one who's been saying it's been way too long since you did the horizontal tango, girlfriend. Not me."

Of course, that was exactly the moment Oscar—their waiter—decided to arrive at the table to bring them their food. To his credit, his face gave nothing away, as if hearing two thirty-something-year-old women discussing their sex lives over brunch was just another day at the office and completely normal. Or maybe he was just another struggling actor in California trying to make it. In which case, he had serious skills.

"Can I get you ladies anything else?" he inquired politely.

"No we're fine," Cecily squeaked. The minute he walked away, Adrienne burst out laughing.

She choked out, "You should've seen your face!"

Cecily dropped her face into her hands. "I can't believe you just did that."

"Oh, have some more booze. You'll be fine."

"Easy for you to say. Oscar isn't back in the kitchen gossiping about your love life with the other waiters."

"Objection. Calls for speculation. You have no way of knowing what he's doing back there." Adrienne paused. "Besides, I think most waiters have seen it all and heard it all. He isn't batting an eye. You need to relax."

Cecily huffed out a breath.

"Remind me again why I'm friends with you?"

"You know you love me." Adrienne took her fork and stabbed a slice of bacon. She took the dish and passed it over to Cecily. They always ordered extra bacon to split.

Cecily tried to shake off her embarrassment. "Fine.

Talk about what's going on with you. So I don't feel like I'm hogging this brunch."

Adrienne gave another shrug. "Eh. Same old same old. I just have that price gouging case with Symtech Pharmaceuticals. We're going to trial next month." Being a member of the firm's anti-trust division, Adrienne mostly dealt with pharmaceutical and tech companies, while Cecily dealt with zoning and land use as part of the commercial law division.

"At least it wasn't some oil company after an oil spill. Could be worse."

"Thank God for small mercies." Adrienne made a quick sign of the cross like the good Catholic girl she was. Allegedly.

"So, what else is going on?"

"Stop avoiding. You're the one who called this vent and catch-up session. We can catch up later. Vent."

God bless friends who saw through your bullshit. "I also need to find a good anniversary gift for my parents. I'm drawing a complete blank." Cecily picked up her fork and dug into her meal.

"Can't you just send a nice bouquet of flowers and be done with it? That's what I do, and it seems to satisfy my parents."

Cecily snorted. "As if. I'd never hear the end of it. Nowhere good enough. Especially compared to what Owen is giving them."

"What's his gift?"

Cecily waved a hand. "I have no idea what he's doing.

All I know is he's the baby and the only son in the family, so he can do no wrong. Whatever it is, Ma will think it's the eighth Wonder of the World. And mine will be sadly lacking by comparison."

Adrienne leaned forward and laid her hands on the table. "Then you need to beat him at his game. Claim the Best Child crown from him."

Amused, Cecily crunched a slice of bacon. "Settle down, Arroyo. It's not that serious. I just want to come up with a nice present. Something that shows I put some thought and care into it. That way, I can avoid the guilt trip."

"Well, you can't go wrong with something sentimental." At Cecily's look she huffed a breath. "I know, I know. We're lawyers, and we have black hearts of ice. And no soul. But dig deep."

"Actually, a few years ago Gill, Owen, and I took a bunch of family photos and digitized them. Baby photos, family vacations, birthday parties, stuff like that. We had about two hundred of them and hooked it up to a digital photo frame. Owen set it up on slideshow. They loved it."

"Could you get in touch with your relatives from overseas? Like do a video call or something? I'm sure they'd love to see them on the screen even if they can't be there in person."

Cecily shook her head. "No go. None of them can keep a secret worth a damn, especially Auntie Yi Ting. The next time Ma calls them they'll spill the beans while gossiping. They can't help themselves." She poured another glass of mimosa.

The two of them were silent for a few minutes while they ate and thought hard. Oscar came by to refill their water glasses. And to ask the requisite: "How's everything so far?"

Cecily gasped as the perfect idea came to her. "*Who Are You?* That's it!"

Adrienne wrinkled her nose in confusion. "Huh?"

"You know, that genealogy show with Dr. Jamison. Celebrities come on her show, and she and her team do research on their family history, and present a book and a family tree."

"You're going to get your parents on the show?"

Cecily threw her a look. "No, silly. Maybe I can find a local historian, or genealogist and hire them to do research on our family. I can have them do a fancy family tree, frame it really nicely and they can hang it in the living room. And if they find some photos or newspaper articles in the archives, I can put it in a scrapbook like they do on the show."

Now it was Adrienne's turn to give a look.

"Okay, fine. I'll have to hire someone for that too. But don't you think this will be a good idea?"

Adrienne took a deliberate, thoughtful bite of her frittata. "I gotta say, that sounds amazing. I think they'll love it. How could they not?"

Cecily rubbed her hands in excitement. "I should have enough money set aside to hire someone good. I'll have to Google. Maybe the local historical society can give some names. Or I could call the history department at Berkley and pay a grad student doing research in Asian history or Asian studies."

"You probably should do that ASAP. It's already mid-January, and you've only got till May to do this."

"Oohh, good point." Cecily whipped out her phone and logged in a reminder on her calendar app.

"Well, there you go. Problem solved."

She put the phone away and focused on her friend. "Can we please go back to the catch-up portion of the program? I feel like I'm a crappy friend and monopolizing the conversation. Let's talk about you now."

Adrienne rolled her eyes and waved off Cecily's worries like swatting a fly away. "I don't make time for crappy people, so shut up with that. But, you know my sister Anita is getting married in April right?"

Cecily leaned forward, chin in hands on the table. "Go on."

"Well, she texts me a picture of the bridesmaid dresses and they are hideous. I mean we're talking *Gone with the Wind* pouf. I can't even. Then, it gets worse. She calls Mámi and cries when I tell her there's no way I'm wearing that monstrosity…"

JEFFREY SHOOK HIS head as he read the email he'd just received from Bethany. It hadn't taken his little sister more than three days since he'd asked her to work her magic.

Hey Loser,

You said you wanted an update on the family climate before you came home for New Year's. Ma is still going to give you crap for not coming home last year, and Dad is excited to see you, though he'd never admit it. You know how they roll. The more things change, the more they stay the same. Yadda yadda yadda. Nathan can't wait to see Unca Jeff.

But, I have talked to them, and mentioned that you told me you had a work deadline. (I still think you're better off running off to Starbucks. Just saying.) I convinced them you'll need time to work, and I think they'll be reasonable about it, as long as you don't let them catch you playing Solitaire.

Because I love you, I should warn you Ma is planning on fixing you up with Tracy Du. She wants to invite her and her mother over. Sorry, my powers of persuasion were no match for her desire for more grandkids. For what it's worth, Tracy's not completely vile. You could do worse. And God knows you're in no position to be picky.

Seriously, we all miss you. But if anyone asks, I'm going to deny I said it. Safe travels, bro. We'll discuss how you'll repay me when I see you.

~B

P.S. Before you ask, no I don't know. If you want to know, find her and talk to her yourself!

He had to fight back a grin. The message was vintage

Beth. But she always came through, even if she was about as subtle as the Terminator. Though he should have known she wouldn't make it easy. He wasn't looking forward to finding out what she was going to ask for in return. Knowing Bethany, it could be anything from twenty bucks to a kidney. His little sister's ruthlessness was a double-edged sword. Jeffrey could only be glad that so far, Bethany's powers had only ever been used for good.

His phone buzzed with a video chat request. He grimaced when he saw who it was.

"Seriously, I told you not to call me unless you had news. And I know you're at least two months early. So this better be good."

Greg Tsai's face filled the screen. "Don't start with me. I've been stress eating since I entered the film back in September."

Jeffrey snorted. "Lay off the cha shao baos, man. Besides, it was your decision to enter the NYC Film Festival. Actions have consequences. Like *Jurrasic Park*. Life always finds a way"

In response, Greg lifted a middle finger.

"Is there some reason you called me?"

"I wanted to let you know I'm thinking of having a private screening of *Xiao*. Just friends and family, cast and crew. Gina wants to know what I've been doing for the past year."

"So you're rounding up the usual suspects and throwing a party to keep your wife happy? Going all out like Gatsby?"

"Happy wife, happy life. I don't wanna end up on the couch."

Jeffrey rolled his eyes. "I don't know if I'm up for all that. Besides, I watched the final cut you sent me two months ago." Part of him had been proud of the work he'd help put out into the world. The other wanted to curl up in the fetal position at the prospect of having his baby out in the universe. Made him think of a parent sending their kid off to their first day of school. And he couldn't help picking out lines and scenes he could've improved on. Better dialogue, better pacing. How the writing could've been sharper, smarter. Until he'd texted Greg, who told him to cut that crap out. *You already did your job, bro. Now let the rest of us do ours.*

"It won't kill you to watch it again."

"It just might. You know, I really don't know whether to thank you, or kill you for submitting it to the festival."

"It's good exposure. And the script you wrote was fantastic." Jeffrey bypassed the compliment with a wave. Deep in his heart, he knew it was some of the best work he'd ever done. *Xiao* had been a passion project for him, a small independent film about a twenty-something Chinese-American, Henry, who quit law school to try to make it as a stand-up comedian. Jeffrey was more than happy to ghostwrite to pay the bills, and put his hat in the ring to write the next Ian Grey film to advance his career, but *Xiao* was a story he'd felt compelled to tell. He wanted to make a contribution to telling the story of the Asian-American experience in the U.S. It had food, meddling nagging relatives, tiger parents, and Henry walking the tightrope of navigating his life living in two different cultures. He'd been thrilled beyond belief when Greg got hold of the script and said he wanted to direct. Greg had immediately gotten the vision, showed the material the respect he'd hoped for, and seen the potential.

Besides, it was funny. It was good to remind people that his people could laugh too.

"Either way, we'll know by March. And you know, Sundance, Cannes, Toronto, Venice aren't out of the question either. I've been talking to people."

Jeffrey's heart went through several palpitations as he thought about it. The experience had been a rollercoaster. Hoping for the best, preparing for the worst, like a farmer planting at the beginning of the season. Jeffrey wasn't sure if *Xiao* would end up being a bumper crop, or killed by a drought.

"You know, I was doing a pretty good job keeping all this out of my mind. Thanks for the reminder." He grimaced.

"I don't know why you're not more excited. New York City's in your neck of the woods. Hell, if they decide to air *Xiao*, your whole family could come to the screening. That's a big fucking deal."

Jeffrey scoffed at the idea. "Yeah, no. I haven't even told my parents about this."

Greg's brow rose in speculation. "Why not?"

"They barely understand my job. I'm pretty sure they're convinced I'm secretly waiting tables to make ends meet. I refuse to try to explain film festivals to them." Just thinking about the conversation, and how it'd go, was enough to give Jeffrey a headache. His parents would still be baffled, and he'd have flown over the cuckoo's nest.

"Probably just as well. They probably wouldn't be too happy with the parents anyway."

Jeffrey shook his head. "I have no idea what you're talking about. Any resemblance between Henry's parents and my own are completely coincidental." At Greg's snort he added, "That's my story and I'm sticking with it. To the grave."

Besides, for a long time, he hadn't been sure the film would be made anyway. The process of making a film was harrowing. People said you never wanted to see how laws and sausages were made. That had nothing on filmmaking. The meetings, the egos, the money, the endless waiting. The money. It was demoralizing realizing how 45,017 stars had to align, and how much of it was out of his control.

That being said, it had been a complete thrill seeing the words he wrote come alive on screen. The fulfillment of a dream. Naturally, changes had been made, and compromises were necessary with a film on a budget, but the end result was something he was incredibly proud of. Now it was going out into the universe to be judged and critiqued. God help him.

The last thing he wanted to do was brag to his parents that he was going to get a film made, only for it to fall apart at the last second. No need to reinforce his image as the family black sheep. Again. Which was why he was going to keep quiet about the festival. If it worked out, great. He'd happily shout and brag from the rooftops. If nothing came of it, no harm, no foul. It was an honor just to be considered, et cetera, et cetera. He'd been raised by Asian parents. Stoicism in public was in his DNA. Like Spartacus.

"Whatever. First weekend of March. Mark your calendar. You're coming to my place."

"If I can make it, I'll be there. But only if you have sheng jian boas." Just thinking about the pork-filled buns made Jeffrey salivate. Sheng jian baos were steamed but still came out with a crispy bottom, and the aroma of the pork with chives would perfume the air.

"Deal. In the meantime, we should talk about our next collab. I have an idea about a movie about Iris Chang."

It warmed Jeffrey's heart more than he cared to admit that Greg wanted to work with him again. For all the crap they gave each other, they'd developed a professional respect and rapport. "Let's talk after New Year's. Right now, I'm just focused on trying to survive the week with my family. I'll have aged a couple decades by the time I come back."

Greg chuckled. "I hear you, man. I just stick Sabrina into their arms. It's amazing how a grandkid can cover up a multitude of sins."

The memory of the family having a picnic at the park came to Jeffrey's mind again. He swallowed the moment of envy. "Yeah well, I don't have a cute kid I can use as a shield, thanks very much."

"With you for a father, there's no chance of the kid being cute."

"Whatever. Sabrina's lucky she looks like Gina, not you. Just saying."

His best friend decided to ignore that potshot. "Seriously, it's wild. The hypocrisy is astounding. They spoil Sabrina rotten, and get her all the toys and candy. And tell me I'm being too strict with her while letting her get away with murder. Stuff they would've kicked my ass for if I'd done it at her age."

Jeffrey nodded in commiseration. "Mine are the same with my nephew. I don't even recognize them sometimes. Like who are these people? They aren't the same people who raised me. It's a total outrage."

"We should do a documentary exposé. Call them out on it." Suddenly, he heard crying in the background. Greg craned his head and got up.

"Shit. Sabrina tripped and hit her head on the table. Gotta go." His friend ran off to rescue his child.

Jeffrey ended the call and got back to work. He only had a few days left before heading back to Brooklyn, and he needed to make the most of it. His personal life may be nonexistent, but so far, his professional life seemed to be falling into place. As long as he didn't screw up this Ian Grey meeting. At least something good had come out of his rash decision to come to California all those years ago. A silver lining to detonating his life like a meteor crashing into Earth.

And who knew? Maybe a couple of days with his family could help him whip Act II into shape.

After all, weren't creative types supposed to suffer for

their art to cultivate inspiration? Stuck in a garret some-where, cold and starving and poor? Considering what he was in for, he should be able to produce a script that would rival Sorkin or Coppola.

"LADIES AND GENTLEMEN, this is the last call for flight 2913 to Orlando Florida boarding at Gate 21B."

Jeffrey sat at his gate at LAX, waiting for his flight to board. He had his earphones on, and his laptop plugged in. Revisions were moving apace, and he was trying to squeeze in every minute of writing time that he could. He'd been working for an hour, and he had at least another thirty minutes or so before he had to pack it in. Jeffrey had been too well trained not to show up at his gate two hours early. He'd already texted Beth and his brother Alex to let them know he'd made it to the airport and when to expect him.

He glared at his phone when it pinged. *What now?* It was Alex, who'd sent a video of Nathan riding his bicycle and saying, "Hi, Unca Jeff!" while waving to the camera. He couldn't help the huge smile that stretched from ear to ear while he watched the short clip. His nephew was pretty damn cute. Alex had included a follow-up text.

Just FYI. I'm planning on dumping this monster on you while we're back in Brooklyn. Allie and I need sleep. Have fun, bc he's all yours.

Jeffrey shook his head and fired back a response.

I'm saving this text to show Nate in about 10 years. Something for him to discuss with his therapist. Or on some talk show someday. I can just picture him explaining to the camera. "That's where it all started to go wrong." Great parenting here.

Come talk to me after your toddler plays psychological warfare via sleep deprivation. #sorrynotsorry

What was it with everyone around him telling him to settle down, get married, and have babies? Was there something in the air or water? A gene that activated the minute someone got married or popped out a kid? Everyone expected him to have baby fever. Like there was a memo everyone got that he somehow missed. *Hey, it's time for you to recreate your own Brady Bunch! Tick-tock. Time to get a move on.*

As far as he was concerned, he threw away his best chance at an Asian Ward and June Cleaver scenario ten years ago. It was high time his family faced facts. He wasn't going to be the doctor they wanted, and he wasn't going to provide the next generation of Lees. All he wanted was a chance to try to repair the damage. And if he was extremely lucky, maybe earn a second chance.

Jeffrey put his earbuds back on and started working again. Eventually, his flight to JFK was announced and when his boarding group was called, he gathered his laptop and carry-on bag, got in line, and prepared to make his journey back East.

As he walked through the jetway, he sent up a silent prayer. *Please, please, please let her be there.*

LOOKING AT HER watch for the fifth time in twenty

minutes, Cecily sat at Gate 36 at San Francisco International Airport, conflicted. Part of her (around forty-eight percent) wished it was already time to board so she could get this godforsaken trip over with. The other fifty-two percent was wishing for a weather delay, mechanical issues, *anything* so she could have an excuse to not go home.

She wasn't the biggest fan of flying, and to say she wasn't looking forward to the five-and-a-half-hour cross-continental flight to JFK was an understatement. She sat and people-watched with her Starbucks, while keeping an eye on the departures board and the gate agent behind the counter.

"Ladies and gentlemen, flight 257 to JFK has been over-booked. We are asking for volunteers to take a later flight and are offering a three-hundred-dollar voucher. There is another flight to JFK that leaves in two hours with a layover in O'Hare. You'll arrive at JFK at 11:30 p.m. If any passengers are interested, please see the gate agent at Gate 36."

For a split second, Cecily was tempted. Seriously tempted. Less time with her family, and she'd get three hundred dollars? The only downside was having to navigate the nightmare that was O'Hare. And having to explain to her family why she was suddenly arriving four hours later than previously stated. This was not the way to avoid drama. In fact, it was probably in violation of Resolution 1 as well, because her mother and the aunties would have plenty to say and Cecily wouldn't handle it well. She reminded herself she was supposed to be avoiding drama, not inviting it.

Nix that. Cecily sighed, realizing she didn't have a

choice in the matter, really. New Year's was the one time of year her whole family gathered back in her parents' small Brooklyn brownstone, and she was expected at the appointed time. She had already promised she'd be home to celebrate. It would take an act of God for her mother to excuse her tardiness or absence. Judith Chang ruled with an iron fist, and unless Cecily was in the hospital dying, or in jail, she'd better show up.

She could just hear her mother now. *"I spend all week cooking for you and all the family. Why don't you want to come? You never come home. Are you too busy for us now? A big important lawyer. Or are you ashamed of us?"* No one could dish up a serving of steaming-hot guilt like an Asian mother. Never mind the miracles she had to make happen at work so she could take the time off.

With a heavy sigh, Cecily resigned herself to her fate. She was spending the long weekend with her extended family, and that was that. Bring on the noise, the nosy meddling relatives, and non-stop eating.

Well, the eating she didn't mind so much. There was nothing like home cooking, and she had five days of that to look forward to. And there were certain dishes that only appeared at New Year. Nian gao, jiao zhi, tang yuan. Her favorite was the fried fish. She could practically hear the wok sizzling as the fish hit the pan with the soy sauce, oil, scallion, and fresh ginger. Strong, spicy, pungent aromas that were the staple of any East Asian kitchen. Smells that hit her brain's nostalgia pleasure centers and reminded her of home. Both her parents went all out to celebrate, and truth be told, no matter how difficult it was going to be, there was no place she'd rather be than her parents' Brooklyn brownstone to celebrate the Year of the Pig, her zodiac sign. Though that would be another cue for more nagging.

"Ai-ya, Cecily. You getting so old. You're turning thirty-six this year. Why are you not married yet? By the time I was your age, I already had you and your brother and sister and working full time!"

It was only a matter of time before the comments about her ancient spinsterhood and dried-up expired eggs started up again. She gave it ten minutes tops from the time she walked in the front door of the house. Might as well brace herself and prepare for it now.

Cecily took another sip of her coffee and threw another glance at the counter. There was still thirty minutes until boarding began. Just then she heard murmurs from the person sitting next to her. It was a middle-aged woman, sitting ramrod straight, and her lips were moving as though she was praying. The white knuckles and hard swallows were enough to give her a clue. This woman was a nervous flier.

"Are you okay?" she ventured. Maybe she could try to help calm this woman down. The last thing anyone needed was for a passenger to freak out mid-flight.

The woman turned to her, surprised. "I'm a little nervous," she confessed, clearly a bit embarrassed. "I'm not used to flying."

Bingo. "You know, I usually try to sleep, or bring something to read or watch on my laptop. It'll be distracting and help pass the time."

"I just don't think humans are meant to be hurtling through the air in some metal tube at four or five hundred miles an hour."

Cecily had no idea how to respond to that. But luckily the woman kept talking.

"The only reason I'm flying is to visit my first grandson. Otherwise, I would never do this."

"Well that sounds like a great reason, and well worth it. And congratulations," she offered. Invested, despite herself, Cecily turned to the woman, whose face softened at the mention of her grandchild. She dug out her phone and showed Cecily some photos.

"This is Sebastian. He was born three weeks ago."

Cecily made the obligatory cooing and appreciative noises, which wasn't hard because the baby was very darn cute.

"So what about you? Why are you traveling cross-country?"

Slightly taken aback at the question, Cecily paused. Normally she didn't appreciate strangers asking questions, but she supposed this was on her since she'd made the first contact, so to speak. Besides, it was just random small talk to break the ice right?

"I'm going home to celebrate Lunar New Year with my family for a couple of days," she answered with a shrug.

"Oh that sounds fun. Do you do this every year?"

"Unfortunately, yes." Which apparently was not the answer the woman was looking for.

"Why unfortunately?"

"I mean yes, it's an important holiday and tradition, but it's also a pain in the ass. It's going to be busy and noisy, with everyone underfoot, and I won't have a moment of privacy. Plus, that's not even taking into consideration the well-intentioned nagging, comments about the weight I've gained or lost, and telling me everything I'm doing wrong with my life. And of course, the requisite side-eye because I'm not married and popping out babies for my parents to spoil. It's a real picnic—who wouldn't enjoy all that?" Cecily paused to catch her breath. Man, it felt good to get that off her chest, even if it was to a random stranger. Then she looked at the woman, whose eyes were saucer-wide.

Or maybe not.

"Wow it sounds like your family doesn't respect you or your boundaries. That's really hard. I'm sorry. Have you ever considered going no contact? Sometimes it's the only option if your family is toxic." The woman reached out to give her a comforting pat on the arm.

Cecily furrowed her brows in confusion. Toxic? What was she talking about? Then she mentally replayed what she'd said and realized the disconnect.

"Oh it's not like that," she rushed to explain. "My family is pushy, and it's aggravating but that's how it is. It all comes from a good place, really. They drive me nuts but I love them and they love me. It's all good." Something she'd have to remind herself of periodically over the next few days. She could complain about her family all day long (and had) but that didn't mean she didn't love them.

The woman cleared her throat. "Well it certainly didn't sound that way, from what you described."

Cecily just shrugged. "It's an Asian thing. It is what it is."

"Well I hope you have a pleasant visit," the stranger supplied after a brief awkward pause.

"Same to you." And they both went back to ignoring each other, as God intended in these types of situations.

The American Airlines employee behind the counter finally announced boarding was about to begin. Cecily hoisted her travel bag and carry-on luggage, took a deep breath, and said a quick prayer to whatever deity was listening before getting in line.

Please let me survive the next five days without losing my temper, or wanting to kill anyone. And please, please, please don't let HIM be there.

Six hours later, Cecily was walking through baggage claim, ready to head outside to hail a cab to make her way to Brooklyn. She couldn't help but be smug at all the poor suckers waiting by the carousels while she sailed through with her carry-on. Her phone was blowing up with missed calls from her mother. She rolled her eyes and was digging it out of her purse to call her mother back, when she rammed into a solid wall of muscle. A pair of arms reached out to steady her. Already mumbling an apology, she didn't notice that the wall of muscle had gone still.

"Cecily?" The voice was deep, incredulous, and all too familiar.

No, it couldn't be. Cecily stifled a curse as her fingers dug into her palms. She looked up and sure enough it was him. Damn it all to hell.

All that praying had been in vain after all because there he was. Jeffrey Lee, in the flesh, plain as day. Crap.

Resolution 1—broken. She hadn't gone looking for drama, but drama sure as hell had found her.

Chapter Three

JEFFREY COULDN'T STOP the goofy grin from spreading across his face. It was as if fate had handed him a second chance and dropped it right into his lap. He couldn't have written a better meet-cute if he'd tried. "Of all the gin joints, in all the towns," he murmured.

The deep brown eyes that he hadn't been able to forget for ten years glared at him. Truth be told, Cecily had been glaring at him like that since they were both in diapers, and the familiarity of it all was a soothing balm. He'd always believed the opposite of love wasn't hate, but indifference. If the glare was anything to go by, she wasn't indifferent. It wasn't ideal but he'd take it.

She looked like a little elf bundled in her puffy winter jacket and red pom-pom hat. A scowling elf radiating hostility and aggravation. Definitely not the image one wants of Santa's little helper.

"What are you doing here?" she blurted.

He raised a brow. "I imagine the same thing you are." At her blank expression, he elaborated. "Home for the New Year? Command performance? To play the dutiful son, the epitome of filial piety?"

"I don't remember you being here last year." She'd noticed his absence. He was going to take that as a good sign.

"There were…extenuating circumstances."

"Must have been, for Pam *ayi* to let you off the hook." She raised a brow. Technically there was no blood relationship between their families, but Cecily still called his mother "auntie."

He coughed awkwardly. "Yeah, well." Hoping to avoid that minefield, he quickly changed the topic. "We should head out. My Uber is going to be here in a few minutes."

The same blank expression.

"Jet lag hitting you hard, is it?" he teased.

She frowned. "I never said I was going to share a car with you. I can get my own cab. Or take the subway."

"You're going to take the subway? All the way to Brooklyn? I don't think so."

Cecily bristled. "I am perfectly capable of taking care of myself. I've been doing it for a while now." The unspoken *"You of all people should know, you big jackass"* hung in the air between them. She turned to leave, and he shot out an arm to stop her.

"Well, consider getting a free Uber ride as me paying my penance."

She cocked her head, and gave him the side-eye. "One Uber ride and the slate is wiped clean? Really?"

"A guy's gotta start somewhere. The road to forgiveness can be long—might as well try to navigate it quicker with an Uber ride."

Jeffrey saw her fight a grin and knew he'd won when she let out an exasperated huff of breath. He gave himself a moment to savor the hard-won victory. It was rare for anyone to win against Cecily Chang. He'd consider that as rare as a yeti sighting.

"I want it on the record that I am only accepting your offer under great duress. And because I am too tired and jet-lagged to fight with you about this."

"Always the attorney."

"You bet your ass." Shaking his head at her stubbornness, he grabbed his carry-on suitcase and hefted her bag onto his shoulder. Ignoring her indignant protests, he led them out onto the sidewalk where the Uber was waiting.

After putting their luggage in the trunk, they were finally on their way to Sunset Park. They had a friendly driver named Guillermo who kept up a steady stream of conversation. Guillermo had decked out his Nissan Altima with a Guatemalan flag on the dashboard, and Christmas tree air fresheners attached to the rearview mirror.

Cecily made a point of squeezing herself into the far right corner of the back seat and staring out the window in stony silence. She was ignoring him. Real mature. He turned toward her, and she craned her head even further away. Jeffrey heaved a sigh. Had he thought Cecily was stubborn? That was the understatement of the century.

"There are bottles of water in the side door pockets if you're thirsty."

"Thank you, Guillermo," he replied. Cecily remained silent.

"How was your flight?"

"Good, uneventful. Slept most of the way, actually. I'm

lucky I usually travel well." He heard Cecily's snort.

"And you, miss?" Cecily turned her head to look straight ahead.

"Fine," she clipped out. Silence descended on the Altima.

Unable to take it anymore, Jeffrey leaned over and hissed in her ear. "Hate me if you want, I don't care. But don't take it out on Guillermo. He's trying to be nice. That's beneath you. Stop being a Grinch."

Cecily clenched her jaw. "How dare you?" she whispered back. Jeffrey just raised a brow.

"Yes, I know I'm the scum of the earth, and you're a better person than me. So how about you prove it? Then you can take out a TV ad and broadcast it."

Cecily continued to stare daggers at him.

"You know I'm right."

She huffed out a breath and went back to looking out the window. But her expression and body language was fifty percent less homicidal.

"Sorry, Guillermo. I'm just tired—it was a long flight." She turned and gave him a small smile.

"No problem, miss. I totally understand."

"See? Was that so hard?" Jeffrey murmured.

"Shut. Up." Cecily's expression went back to ninety-nine point nine percent homicidal again.

"So, how long have you two been together?" Guillermo asked.

"We are not together," Cecily growled.

Now Jeffrey frowned. She didn't need to make it sound

that awful, like a fate worse than death. Or like being forced to eat bitter melon soup.

Jeffrey reminded himself Cecily had a right to be pissed at him and take some cheap shots. But still. His ego demanded he defend himself. "You should be so lucky. I'll have you know I'm considered by many to be a catch." Her eyes drilled into him like he was a bug that needed to be squashed, and he knew he was going to pay for it.

"Obviously, they don't know you like I do." With a sniff, she returned to staring out the window, giving him the cold shoulder.

"I'm sure you could give a whole dissertation on my shortcomings. Shouted out from the rooftop for all to hear." He fought to keep his voice low. He didn't want a scene any more than Cecily did. But damn if she couldn't bring out the worst in him sometimes.

Cecily spoke without turning around. "I refuse to have this conversation with you right now. You may be fine with airing your dirty laundry in public, but not me. The least you can do is not embarrass me in front of a stranger. You owe me."

Fine. Two could play that game. The ten years apart made him forget what a pain in the ass Cecily could be when she put her mind to it. He looked out his own window. Damn stubborn, infuriating woman.

"Well, my mistake. You two were whispering back there, so made me wonder. But you two bicker like me and my Marisol. Been married for almost fifteen years next week." Oblivious to the tension brewing in his back seat,

Guillermo sounded way too happy and perky for a man who claimed to have been on duty for almost twelve hours.

"Positive. But congratulations to you and your wife," Jeffrey murmured.

"Gracias." Guillermo beamed. "Marisol is my heart. We were childhood sweethearts. Best thing that ever happened to me."

That sentiment was so touching that even Cecily yielded. "That's lovely, Guillermo." Her face softened, a small smile curving her lips.

"I speak only the truth, señorita. I only wish everyone was blessed with a wonderful marriage like mine to a great lady."

Jeffrey cursed softly as Cecily closed up again. Her posture stiffened, and her voice frosted over like an ice queen's.

"That's a nice thought, but my faith in the institution isn't high these days."

Realizing he'd made a huge faux pas, Guillermo dropped the subject, and they made the rest of the trip to Sunset Park in complete silence.

Jeffrey barely resisted the urge to punch the back of the front passenger seat out of sheer frustration.

SHE NEEDED A serious deterrent. So, Cecily took out her phone to refresh herself on the New York penal code in regards to assault, manslaughter, and homicide. She was reading about murder two when the car stopped. Part of her had been surprised at how upset she was. After all, it'd been ten years. But maybe it was because this was the first time she'd seen Jeffrey since then, and all the emotions had come bubbling back to the surface. Mercifully, the thirty-minute car ride was over, and she was home. Like a pardoned death row inmate running toward freedom, Cecily burst out of the Uber and made a beeline for her luggage in the trunk. Jeffrey came around and handed her her bag. The front porch of the humble brownstone lit up, her mother threw open the door, and ran down the steps.

"Cecily!" Judith made a move toward the luggage before being waved away.

"Ma, I got it." They engaged in a tug-of-war, and Cecily was a heartbeat away from slapping her mother's hand away before Judith saw who else was there.

"What are you doing here with him?" The *him* was said almost with a snarl. Never let it be said that her mother wasn't loyal and a fierce Mama Bear when it came to her cubs.

"We just shared a ride from the airport to save money."

Jeffrey murmured a respectful "Hello, Auntie" in Mandarin before being dismissed with a polite nod. Very Asian mom—showing disapproval without saying a word.

She turned to him. "Thank you for the ride. Be sure to let me know what I owe you for my share. I'll give you the cash for it tomorrow."

"Not necessary. Good night, Cecily. Good night, Auntie Judith." Jeffrey turned toward the car, said goodbye to Guillermo, and made his way two doors down to his family's house.

"Come quick! It's cold." Judith ushered her up the steps, every inch the nagging mother hen Cecily had known her whole life. Quick as lightning, she grabbed Cecily's luggage, and schlepped it with effort.

"Ma, stop it. Put my suitcase down before you hurt yourself," Cecily scolded.

"I don't like your tone." Her mother scowled. It was too early to break Resolution 3, Cecily reminded herself. She hadn't even walked into the house yet. Surely, she could last more than five minutes before being provoked by her family? That would be an inauspicious start to the New Year festivities.

With a heavy, world-weary sigh, she waited for her mother to open the door and entered the foyer. Immediately she was assaulted by a whirlwind of noise and activity. She saw her sister Gillian and brother-in-law Peter, her brother Owen and his girlfriend Sonia embroiled in a vicious game of Monopoly. Her cousin Molly was manning the stove, and a bevy of aunts and uncles, cousins, and nieces and nephews were running around. It was pandemonium and the familiarity and sheer nostalgia of it all hit her like a punch and almost made her weepy.

Cecily took off her shoes, set her luggage by the foot of the stairs, laid her jacket on top of it, and made her way to the kitchen. She could smell daikon, star anise, and chilies. That could only mean one thing.

"Sit down, sit down. I made beef noodle soup for you with a soy braised egg and pressed tofu on the side, your favorite with some bean sprouts. Fan chay chao dan with rice if you want that too. And went to the bakery and got you a bo-lo," Judith said, referring to the classic pineapple bun. Cecily took a deep sniff and started salivating. Her stomach rumbled.

"Molly, get your cousin a bowl of soup. Ai-ya," Judith tsked. "You're too skinny. Before you were too fat and I told you to lose weight but now you're too skinny. Not look good." And right on cue, the nagging, backward compliments, and criticism. Yep, it was good to be home. It was good to know some things never changed—it wouldn't feel like home otherwise.

Just then, her father walked into the room. Paul Chang was dressed in khakis and a sweater vest and looked like the absent-minded professor he was. He blinked in surprise when he saw her.

"Cecily! What are you doing here?" A big smile crossed his face, and he embraced her with a hearty hug. Cecily clung for a beat longer than necessary, savoring the moment.

"Dad. Didn't Mom tell you I was coming home for New Year?"

"Your mother doesn't tell me anything." For which he received a glare and painful swat on the arm from his wife.

"Hey, sis!" Owen shouted. "Come over here and join my team. We're *destroying* Gill and Peter." He was twenty-eight, her youngest sibling, and lived up to the reputation of the annoyingly obnoxious baby brother.

"Only because you're cheating," Gillian huffed.

"You always were a sore loser."

"Enough!" Judith exclaimed. "Leave your sister alone," she scolded Owen. "She just flew across the country. She needs to eat. What's wrong with you?" She then turned to Cecily. "Eat! I didn't spend all day making this for you for nothing."

Ah. There was no place like home.

DESPITE THE ASPERSIONS cast on her profession, Cecily considered herself to be a woman of her word. If she said she was going to do something, she was going to do it. That was the by-product of a strict Asian upbringing. She had the family reputation to consider and God forbid she did anything that would bring shame to the Chang family name.

However, getting out of the house the next morning to run this particular errand ended up being a whole production. She'd tried to sneak out but got caught even before she left her bedroom.

"Where are you off to?" Gillian demanded. She stuck out a hand to block Cecily's path.

"I'm older than you. Knock it off."

After throwing a filthy glare, Gillian gave way.

Relieved, Cecily made her way down the stairs.

"Hey, Ma! Cecily is leaving the house." Cecily whirled back around to see her sister's satisfied smirk.

"Traitor!"

Judith bustled in from the kitchen. "Where you going?"

Cecily heaved a sigh. "Don't worry about it, Ma. I just have to run a quick errand. I'll be right back. Five minutes, promise." She needed to get this over with quick. She'd already blocked out three hours to get some work done finalizing the Yardley deal and looking over the zoning application for Stafford Developers when she got back. The whole work-life balance thing was still a work in progress. But Cecily also rationalized it as keeping her first three resolutions. Sequestering herself in her bedroom would cut down on the probability of getting caught up in family drama.

Judith stayed stubbornly in place. "Don't sigh—it's impolite," she scolded. "Tell me where you're going."

"Fine. Have it your way. I'm heading over to the Lees'." There was an audible gasp from the head of the stairs.

Her mother's eyes narrowed. "Why?"

"I need to see Jeffrey." At Judith's pursed lips, Cecily hastily added, "Nothing like that! God. I need to pay him for my half of the Uber last night."

Judith shook her head. "I don't understand this Uber. Why are you people getting into a stranger's car? How do you know you won't be kidnapped and murdered? *Bai chi*, all of you!"

She didn't have the time or patience to explain to her mother why she wasn't an idiot. "Look, the sooner I leave, the sooner I'm home. Besides, you know I have work to do."

Her mother waved a hand. "Go! Go! I need you to clean the bathrooms when you get back."

Ugh. Having escaped the madhouse, Cecily dutifully made her way down the street to the Lee residence. She knocked on the door and was greeted by Jeffrey's younger sister Bethany. She was dressed in a soft blue sweater and jeans, with a bandana pulling her hair back.

"CeeCee!" Bethany exclaimed as she enveloped Cecily in a hug. Despite herself, Cecily couldn't prevent a grin. She'd always had a soft spot for Bethany.

"You're home for the weekend?" Cecily asked. Last she heard, Bethany was a senior at Columbia, majoring in biochemistry.

"Yep. Where else would I be?" Bethany readjusted her bandana. "Mom needs all hands on deck for the cleaning."

Cecily made a face. "My mom's planning a top-to-bottom deep cleaning today too. I'm on bathroom duty. She's also grumbling because she needs to take me to Walmart later to buy new clothes. But you can't fight tradition." She rolled her eyes good-naturedly. It was a New Year tradition slash superstition to clean the house top to bottom, get a haircut, and buy a new outfit. It was all about out with the old, in with the new and generating good luck and a fresh start for the Year of the Pig.

Bethany had no response, just blew out a breath and looked at her expectantly.

"Oh, right. Is Jeffrey around? I need to speak to him." Speaking of the devil, he appeared behind his sister in the doorway.

"If you're here to pay me for the Uber, think again." He crossed his arms, and a stubborn look came over his face.

All right. If he was going to be a hard-ass about this, then so could she. She had plenty of experience dealing with difficult clients.

"It's out of my hands, Jeffrey. You know that I can't go into the New Year unless I settle all debts. You wouldn't want me to start the Year of the Pig with bad luck hanging over my head, do you? You really want that on your conscience?" She gave her most innocent look and blinked disarmingly.

Jeffrey just scowled. "You always were a spoiled brat when it came to getting your way," he muttered.

Cecily took immediate umbrage. "How dare you!" Such an unfair accusation. Besides, how did he know? They hadn't seen each other in ten years. Maybe she had her moments, but didn't everyone?

Jeffrey just raised an eyebrow. "Who was the one who told our moms I scalped her Barbie doll when she really was the one who decided to give it a haircut?"

"Really with that? I was five years old for God's sake!" Seriously.

An implacable stare from him. "Did you or did you not get a new doll for your birthday?"

"To be clear, the statute of limitations for that has come and gone," Cecily sniffed. "Not fair for you to throw that in my face now. It's been thirty years, and I doubt your ability to accurately recall the event in question.

Besides, whether or not I got a replacement Barbie doll is irrelevant to the current discussion."

"And I was the one who got spanked for something I didn't do."

She continued to glare, and so did he.

Bethany just looked at them back and forth like she was watching a tennis match. "You two are weird," she decided with a shake of her head. She walked away and disappeared back into the house.

Jeffrey ignored her. "But if you insist, it was sixty dollars."

As Cecily dug through her wallet and purse, he added nonchalantly, "Oh and just so you know, Guillermo gave us a four and a half star rating."

Her head snapped up and she stopped searching for the money. "Why didn't we get five?"

"You were always so competitive." He chuckled. He leaned against the doorjamb and put his hands in his pockets.

"Well, why didn't we get five? We did nothing wrong," she insisted, with her hands on her hips.

"Go ask him," Jeffrey suggested, his lips twitching.

Cecily frowned and went back to her purse. Finally, she scrounged up thirty dollars and thrust it at him.

"There you go."

"Glad I could help you start the New Year with a clean slate," he drawled. "Happy now?"

She raised a warning brow. "You're lucky I didn't ask for a receipt."

"Your faith in me is touching."

At that, all her walls and defenses came back up. "When it comes to you, I have no faith." She had the satisfaction of seeing the hit land as he winced.

"Cecily, I am sorry. If you'd let me explain…"

"There's nothing to explain, nothing you need to apologize for. The past is the past." With tears threatening to fall, she willed them back, and gritted her teeth. She refused to unravel. Not now.

He reached out to touch her shoulder. "You don't mean that."

"Oh yes, I do. With every fiber of my being. As far as I'm concerned, there's nothing you have to say that I want to hear." She shrugged his hand off her shoulder. The dam was about to break, so she turned and ran down the steps.

Behind her, she heard a muttered: "Damn stubborn pain in the ass." And the sound of the door slamming shut.

She was going to make him pay for that, Cecily promised herself, blinking back the tears. As soon as she got home, she would escape to her room, have a good cry, and then pull herself together.

So much for avoiding drama today. So far her list was a spectacular fail.

Chapter Four

JEFFREY STOMPED BACK up the stairs, grumbling to himself, battling irritation, aggravation, frustration, exasperation, and guilt. If a hair shirt was available, he'd probably be putting it on right now. As hard-headed as Cecily was, the truth of the matter was that the fault for their estrangement lay squarely on his shoulders. He had no one to blame but himself.

But back then, he hadn't seen any alternative. He had just quit medical school, to his family's horror and consternation. He'd finally worked up the courage to admit that he'd caved to family pressure by applying to medical school, and he was never going to be the doctor they had wanted and hoped for. The Asian trifecta of lawyer, doctor, or accountant was not in the cards for him. He still remembered his mother's tears and his father's grim disapproval.

What are you going to do now? How will you make a living? How could you do this to us?

And that was the problem. He just knew he had to get out of medical school before it suffocated him. He had no idea what the hell he was going to do. He had no plan, no idea how to support himself. He needed time to figure it out, make his own way.

At that point, he and Cecily had already announced their engagement, and their wedding was three months away. Cecily was set to graduate law school that May and was already applying for clerkships and interviewing with the top law firms in the city. The idea of bringing nothing to the table and forcing Cecily to support them both until he got his shit together made him sick to his stomach. He hadn't been able to bear the idea of subjecting her to that. And Cecily had let him know she wasn't here for the fallout and drama. Still, Jeffrey would rather swallow glass than have her look at him with pity, disgust, and disappointment. Call it toxic masculinity, but he still had some pride.

"Instead you broke her heart and ground it under your shoe. Much better alternative," he scoffed to himself.

He'd broken things off, but he'd thought it was for the best, for her own good. She deserved to have someone who was worthy of her, able to be her equal. Not some drop-out loser with no idea what his future held.

He'd left town the day after he'd ended things. He threw his belongings in a bag, and impulsively went on a cross-country road trip. Something compelled him to go to Los Angeles. Once he got there, he worked odd jobs— waiter, receptionist, GAP salesman, construction. He'd even worked as a telemarketer for six miserable months. He'd found a crappy minuscule apartment that he shared with two roommates. One day, he'd seen an ad for a screenwriting workshop, and on a whim decided to check it out. And from that moment on, he knew he'd found his passion, what he was meant to do. For the next year, every spare moment he had was devoted to writing his first screenplay. It was horrible and would never see the light of day, but he'd been bitten by the bug.

He wrote another screenplay, *Judgment Day*, a James-Bond-like action movie, and with lots of luck and perseverance, and about fifty rounds of edits, was able to land an agent, who helped him get it in front of the right producers and directors. Since then, through a magical combo of hard work, sheer luck, and good timing, he'd made a go of it.

Giving himself a shake, Jeffrey reminded himself he needed to get back to work. His second draft of *The War at Home* was due soon and it was nowhere near where it needed to be. The plot felt static, his protagonist wasn't doing what he expected, and he still didn't have an ending. It was a hot mess. His agent had set up a meeting with the producers back in L.A. and he had to be ready. He couldn't afford to blow this opportunity to take his career to the next level. It was his chance to work on a film that would be a major hit, and increase his name recognition. Besides, it'd help take his mind off Greg and the NYC Film Festival.

Though part of him had to admit writing this script was nothing like *Xiao*. *Xiao* had practically flowed out of him—the characters, the voices, it had all clicked. He had banged out a rough first draft in a matter of weeks, which was unheard of for him. Maybe it was because he had so much personal experience to draw from.

Or maybe he was having false misty memories of a past

writing process because he was struggling with his current work in progress.

He sat down in front of his laptop, determined to put his nose to the grindstone. But as fate was determined to curse him, a picture of Cecily stared back at him in his mind.

"You got your work cut out for you," he murmured to himself. But for now, he had to focus. Figuring out how to win Cecily over, so that she no longer hated him with the heat of a nova, was going to have to wait for another day. He resolutely closed out the browser, opened up *The War at Home*, put on his earphones, and zoned in for the next few hours.

Despite the time he blocked out, his reprieve came to an end all too soon. His mother came to the door and knocked. She held up a bucket, a mop and some rubber gloves.

"You go clean the bathroom and mop the floors. Then sweep and vacuum the hallway," she said without ceremony. Before he could catch himself, he made a face. Unluckily for him, it did not go unnoticed.

"Bethany has spent all day helping me clean. You haven't done anything. Just sitting in your room typing. Don't be lazy," she scolded.

Not for the first time, his mother's dismissive attitude rankled. Before he could retort that he was working and was under a massive deadline, she plowed on. "I need to go to the market. The fish your Auntie Alice bought wasn't fresh. And I need to buy banners. We have to go by the community center later. Tuck in your shirt," she tsked. "Why so sloppy?"

She turned around, confident her orders would be obeyed. But not before warning him: "Dinner at seven o'clock. Everyone will be here. Clean quickly. I have to take you to the barber for a haircut before dinner."

What his mother laid out sounded like hell on earth to Jeffrey. But he got up like a dutiful soldier and proceeded to scrub the bathroom. It was going to be an unbearable day.

CECILY RUSHED THROUGH the front door and all she wanted to do was run back up to her room, lock the door, scream into a pillow, and cry. Then she'd set a timer for thirty minutes for her to wallow before she snapped herself out of it. Damn the man for getting under her skin like this, even after all these years. It wasn't fair. She sniffled and dabbed at her eyes angrily with a tissue.

She took a deep breath and told herself to get it together. He wasn't worth it, and she wasn't going to give him the satisfaction of living in her head rent-free. Jeffrey Lee didn't deserve a single tear or thought, period, point-blank, and she'd rather die than let him know he'd gotten any sort of reaction out of her with that stunt. The best thing to do with these stupid irrational feelings was shove them down, way down, and get some work done. The Asian way. Much more productive use of her time and energy. Billable hours beat useless emotions all day every day.

Giving herself a mental head slap, Cecily pushed herself off the bed and grabbed her laptop. She was in the middle of replying to an email from the *Walking Dead* fan attorney—so far, no zombie apocalypse clause had been suggested, thank goodness—when there was a loud knocking on her door. She sighed. There was only one person it could be.

"Open the door! Why is this locked?!" Another round of vigorous pounding ensued. "Cecily!"

With great reluctance, Cecily got up from the desk and opened the door, only to face down a furious Chinese mother with flashing eyes and pruned lips. Judith immediately pushed past Cecily and marched into the room.

"Why did you lock your door? What are you doing in here? Are you hiding something?" Judith craned her neck to look around, her tone suspicious.

Cecily rolled her eyes and quickly closed her laptop. "I'm working. What does it look like I'm doing? I told you I'm busy and my client needs this right away." Her breath hitched, and her eyes must have still been puffy and red because her mother zeroed right in on them.

In rapid Mandarin, she began to interrogate her daughter. "Don't get smart. What's the matter? What happened? Why is your face so ugly?" Literally, the phrase her mother used translated to "Why does your face stink?" but it lost a little something in the translation.

"Nothing, Ma, I'm fine."

Not fooled for a minute, her mother steamrolled on. "It

was him, wasn't it? I told you not to go over there. That boy is trouble, no good."

Damn it. She hated it when her mother had her psychic moments. Judith always had an eerie sixth sense when it came to her children.

"No, it wasn't him. I don't want to talk about it, I'm okay. I really need to work, so can you please go?"

Her mother refused to budge. Because of course she did. "What's more important than spending time with your family? Stop hiding in your room."

"A hundred-million-dollar deal. That's what I'm working on. Not hiding." Cecily had the satisfaction of watching her mother be taken aback at hearing the amount of money at stake. But her victory was short-lived as Judith admirably rallied.

"Well, you can take a break. The rest of us are busy getting ready for dinner tomorrow. You need to help too. Why are you working when you're supposed to be on vacation?"

Cecily heaved a sigh. "Fine. But I'm coming back up after dinner. Get Owen to do the dishes. I need to work."

Judith opened her mouth to protest but Cecily just put up a hand. "A hundred million dollars, Mom. You want me to mess that up?"

Muttering to herself, Judith walked out of the room. "You have ten minutes. And don't go over to the Lees again. Let him pay for a taxi. Least he can do after all the problems he's caused."

Cecily couldn't resist calling out "It was an Uber! And I

thought I wasn't supposed to leave any debts unsettled. I don't want bad luck."

Without missing a beat or turning around her mother responded, "Watch your mouth. Bai chi!" With that she sailed out the door, closing it behind her with a loud click.

Leave it to her mother to always have the last word.

LATER THAT AFTERNOON, Cecily sat at the kitchen table, frantically working away at her laptop.

She had no qualms about being the type of lawyer who defended corporations, the type of lawyer who gave lawyers a bad name. She was damn good at her job, and made no apology for it. Living in the Bay Area was hella expensive, and those student loans were not going to pay themselves. And besides, companies, even evil corporate monoliths, deserved good vigorous representation.

Cecily skimmed through the PDFs her paralegal had scanned for her, checking to make sure she got the dates and times correct in the motion. The devil was in the details. She fired off a quick email to Priscilla Payne, her paralegal, to triple-check a statute citation and to make sure it was on point and applicable.

"What's the point of you coming home if you're going to work the whole time?"

Cecily nearly jumped out of her chair. "Ma! Don't do that! You nearly gave me a heart attack."

Judith dismissed her with a wave. "Why are you still

working?"

"Because this appeal is due next week, and I need to get it done in time."

Her mother frowned. "It couldn't wait until you went home? We never see you, and you're here working all day." She tried to peer over Cecily's shoulders to look at her screen.

Cecily closed her laptop firmly. "Unless you want me to violate attorney-client privilege, don't do that. Don't touch my computer," she warned. "I have sensitive client information in there. I could get in serious trouble!"

Judith rolled her eyes. "I know, I know. You have a big important job. But it's time to go shopping now." Her mother had been fussing all day because Cecily needed a new outfit for the New Year. Even if it was just a pair of sweats from Walmart. So that's where they were headed.

But the fact her mother took no interest in her work, and dismissed it so easily, stung. However, that was nothing new. Ever since she could remember, her mother had always told her she could always push herself harder, do better. To strive for the excellence and perfection that could somehow never be reached, but yet, was the key to her mother's love and approval. Cecily mentally counted to ten and reminded herself it was an excellent opportunity to put her second resolution into practice. Her mother didn't mean to hurt her feelings. As far as Judith was concerned, feelings were probably signs of weakness that she strived to beat out of her children at a young age.

Her mother clapped her hands impatiently. "Let's go. I

don't have all day."

Concealing a huge sigh and a roll of her eyes, Cecily secured and put away her computer, and they made their way to Walmart.

Forty-five minutes later, the two of them were arguing over a black cardigan. Cecily insisted it was the steal of the century at ten bucks, Judith was convinced it was too dark and made Cecily "look too old, like a grandma."

"I think it looks good on you, for what it's worth," a voice said from behind them.

Judith's eyes iced over as she saw Jeffrey and his mother. But she still acknowledged them with a tight smile. Asian manners and passive-aggressive protocols dictated nothing less.

"Hi, Auntie Pam," Cecily murmured quickly.

"Cecily! You're home. What a surprise." Pam Lee's smile was genuine, if a little hesitant. But she too became stiff and proper as she turned to Judith.

"Judith, how are you? Long time no see, ah?"

Translation: *I have made a point of avoiding you like the plague but now you've caught me. Curse you.*

"I know," her mother simpered. "I've just been so busy. We should have tea sometime soon."

Translation: *Too busy for you. And we'll have tea when hell freezes over.*

Well trained in the art of Asian mother one-upmanship warfare, Pam returned fire. "You must be so happy to have Cecily home. I know she doesn't get the chance to come home often."

Translation: *Not like my kids, who come visit me regularly. Therefore, my kids love me more and are better than yours.*

Cecily knew she was supposed to be avoiding drama, but she felt this was a permissible exception. She was watching two experts engage in battle, and she deserved to enjoy herself for a minute or two.

Judith sighed. "I know, she's always so busy. Even when she comes home to visit she's working. Doesn't have time for us anymore."

Translation: *My daughter has a successful career, so I win. She makes a six-figure salary that would make anyone weep with envy. In your face, loser.*

Cecily tried not to take offense that not an hour earlier, her mother was fussing at her for working, but now was using it as a weapon.

Jeffrey came over and whispered in her ear, "If it makes you feel any better, Mom was complaining earlier that I wasn't helping with the cleaning and muttering how you and your siblings wouldn't be so lazy and disrespectful."

Cecily rolled her eyes and bit her lip. The comparison game was classic. According to any Asian parent, when reprimanding their children everyone else's child was better than their own. And any attempts at compliments or boasting to outsiders would be disguised as complaints. It wouldn't do to actually express pride in your offspring's accomplishments. That would be immodest and unseemly. Simply wasn't done.

The kicker was, before The Incident, their mothers had been the best of friends. They'd played cards together every week and were in and out of each other's homes on a daily basis. But things had been chilly since the engagement was called off, and they had been at each other's throats ever since.

It was like the Montagues and Capulets, but Asian style. Instead of a blood feud and tragic deaths, there was passive-aggressive behavior, deliberate snubs, and turned backs.

"How do we stop this? They can keep going on like this for ages," Cecily whispered back. At the moment, she was too amused to remember her ire with Jeffrey. Suddenly, they were fifteen years old again, shaking their heads over their crazy mothers.

"I see no alternative except tackling them and physically separating them." He was just as amused. But mindful of giving even the slightest hint of softening, she walked over to her mother.

She saw him cringe when Judith made a comment about him and medical school. Without even thinking about it, Cecily came to his defense.

"Ma, that was ten years ago. There are plenty of things you can criticize him for without bringing up the past. Talk about why he didn't come home last year for New Year's."

All three of them looked at her in surprise. She shrugged defensively. "Well, it's true." Now she was kicking herself. Stupid brain not stopping her mouth in time. She didn't know what had come over her, but some protective instinct had reared its head. The situation felt so familiar, she couldn't help but fall back into old patterns.

She pretended her phone was buzzing. She gave an

apologetic smile. "Sorry, gotta take this. It's work." She grabbed it and walked a couple of feet away. A few minutes later, Jeffrey casually wandered away too, on his phone. As he walked by her, he whispered, "Thanks, I owe you one."

"Don't worry about it," she said out of the side of her mouth. "It was more a self-preservation thing anyway. I'm still trying to get her to stop talking about how much money she and Dad spent on braces to fix my crooked teeth in middle school."

Judith eyed Jeffrey suspiciously. "Why are you on your phone too?"

Smooth as silk, he threw his sister under the bus. "It's Bethany. She just texted me and said she needs a new scarf and pair of gloves. I was asking if Cecily had any recommendations."

Auntie Pam clucked. "*Chee!* She is always so careless and loses things. I buy her two pairs of gloves every winter. And she loses her sunglasses all the time too."

"I saw a nice red and black hat, glove, and scarf set Bethany might like," Cecily offered.

"I'll get some for her on our way out." Pam continued to shake her head.

"And who are you talking to?" Judith demanded.

"I told you, work." She quickly stuck her phone back in her purse before it could be confiscated. She threw Jeffrey a look.

"Sorry," he mouthed.

She cocked her head. *"You were saying about owing me one?"*

He made a face. *"Fine. A million and one."*

Cecily nodded. *"That's more like it."*

By now the mothers had moved on to throwing shade at each other's culinary skills.

"Are you going to start cooking tonight?" Judith's voice dripped with faux concern. "I know last year, your dumplings were still raw, so make sure you give yourself enough time."

"I will. I want to make sure they don't end up greasy, like yours," Pam retorted.

Okay. Enough was enough. The expression on their faces told Cecily they had passed the point of no return. They were both in it for the long haul now. Cecily grabbed Judith and their shopping cart. "Ma, let's go. We have to get home and avoid rush hour traffic."

"And we still need to grab the stuff for Bethany," Jeffrey reminded Auntie Pam.

With massive reluctance, her mother made her way to the checkout line, complaining the whole time. Cecily saw Jeffrey still trying to reason with Auntie Pam, trying to calm her down.

The only thought running through her head was *"Better him than me."* And she would be the bigger person and not rub it in his face. Probably.

THE NEXT MORNING, Cecily was a woman on a mission. She had to get out of the house before she lost her god-damned mind. Cecily pulled on her thick winter coat, gloves, scarf, and hat. Sometimes she considered just storing heavy winter clothing here in Brooklyn to save valuable closet space, because she almost never wore it in San Francisco. But it wasn't worth the nagging she'd get from her mother.

She cracked open her bedroom door like a fugitive and checked to see if the hallway was clear. Cecily had hit her quota of family togetherness and she needed out. She was over the shopping, the cleaning, the noise. All of it. Luckily, it was still relatively early, so the house was quiet. She tiptoed down the stairs, being careful to avoid the spots that creaked, and hallelujah, escaped unnoticed. Maybe she should look into becoming an escape artist. It would be a useful skill and may even count as a new hobby. Definitely an option worth exploring.

Cecily took a deep breath and made her way to the Sunrise Café, a typical New York corner coffee shop. The café was a neighborhood institution, and Cecily had been going there since she was a kid. All she needed was an hour of peace and quiet, a cup of coffee, and some eggs, pancakes, and sausage. And the free Wi-Fi.

She opened the door, and the bell rang. It looked the same as it always had—the vinyl booths, Formica tables, laminated menus. All of the signs of a tried-and-true greasy spoon. Cecily looked around for a spot where she could tuck herself into the corner. She found her way to her spot when she spotted a man tapping away on his laptop, intensely focused, oblivious to his surroundings. Cecily took a moment to appreciate the broad shoulders, and black-rimmed glasses. He was wearing a navy blue sweater, and had his earphones in, so she could ogle in peace and privacy. Very nice, intellectually sexy. Probably some starving artist who was trying to catch a break, she mused. She walked closer and then realized who it really was.

Of course it was him. Fate hadn't listened when she asked for help avoiding Jeffrey on this trip, so why wouldn't she run into him at every turn? What was he doing here anyway? Cecily quickly turned around and made a beeline for a table on the other side of the shop.

"Coward."

His voice froze her and she slowly turned around. There was a mocking gleam in his eye, and her chin rose at the challenge. There was no way she was going to let that stand. She walked over to his table.

"You looked busy. I didn't want to disturb you." She injected as much haughtiness as she could.

In response, he crossed his arms and leaned back in his seat. "Liar. You were trying to avoid me, and I think that's beneath you. I've never known you to cut and run."

Her eyes flashed at the insult. "No, that's more your style, isn't it?"

Jeffrey heaved a sigh and turned away from his laptop. "Touché," he acknowledged. He gestured toward the other side of the booth he was sitting at. "Please."

"No thank you."

He raised his brow.

"Proving that I'm not avoiding you does not mean I

need to sit and eat with you," she insisted, increasingly desperate to get out of the situation. This was what she got for trying to avoid her family. The ancestors exacted swift and brutal vengeance.

Jeffrey shrugged. "Suit yourself." He put his earphones back on and went back to work. Provoked and irked, Cecily sat down across from him with a bad-tempered huff.

"I better not see even a hint of a smirk," she warned.

"I wouldn't dream of it." Setting his work aside, he gave her his full attention, and signaled for a waitress.

"What brings you here this early?"

"I needed to get away from the house," she admitted.

"Same here." He chuckled in commiseration. "I came here to get in a couple hours of work in peace and quiet."

Curious despite herself, she had to ask. "What is it you're working on?"

Before he could answer, their waitress came to the table. A buxom platinum-dyed blonde with her hair in a messy bun, bright red lipstick, and a name tag that identified her as Roxy. She flashed Jeffrey a bright smile, which dimmed considerably when she saw Cecily.

"Oh." She made a passable attempt to conceal her disappointment, much to Cecily's amusement. "What can I get you?"

Cecily placed her order and Roxy took her menu. The waitress then turned to Jeffrey and turned on the charm. "Can I get you anything else? Freshen your coffee?" She practically simpered the words and Cecily wondered if a tornado was brewing, she was batting her eyelashes so hard.

"No thank you. I'm fine," Jeffrey muttered. He was busy putting his laptop away.

"Well, be sure to let me know if I can get you anything else." Then she turned to Cecily. "I'll put your order right in, ma'am."

"Thank you," she murmured. She shook her head as Roxy turned away, coffee pot in hand. "That poor girl."

"What are you talking about?"

Cecily was incredulous. "She was hitting on you shamelessly."

He blinked. "What are you talking about? She was just being friendly, probably hoping for a good tip."

"Oh trust me, she wanted more than a good tip. She was ready to offer you a free sample, and I don't mean the coffee cake." She smirked.

"You're totally off base here. Plus, she's barely out of college. I would never."

"No interest in being Roxy's sugar daddy?" She cackled at the look he threw at her. This was too much fun. He was making it too easy. "Anyway, how do you know how old Roxy is?"

"I heard her talking to another waitress. She's taking a year off before starting graduate school. Practically a baby." He wagged a finger at her. "Call me all the names you want, throw the book at me, but one thing you can't say is that I'm a cradle robber."

At that she had to laugh. "Fair enough," she acknowledged. "Now, what are you working on?"

Jeffrey shrugged. "The sequel to *Scars and Souvenirs*."

She barely contained a squeal. "The Ian Grey series? Oohh, I love those movies!"

"Really?" Pleased, he leaned back with a smile.

"I didn't know you were a screenwriter."

He nodded. "For a few years now. Even sold a few."

She gave a low whistle. "Good for you. That is one tough cut-throat industry."

"Takes one to know one." Jeffrey saluted with his coffee cup.

"You have a very cool job. I watch the Ian Grey movies the day they come out. I keep hoping they'll cast Daniel Henney. That is one gorgeous, sexy, swoon-worthy man." She gave a dramatic sigh with her hand to her heart.

Jeffrey threw her a dirty look and muttered that Daniel wasn't British. Cecily responded with a cheeky, unrepentant grin.

"I had no idea that's what you'd decided to do." She was intrigued. Before they lost touch, he'd been in his third year of med school. This was quite the change.

"It took me a while to figure it out."

"But still. I can't imagine Auntie Pam and Uncle Martin took it well."

He gave her a long speaking look. "They're still hoping I go back to medical school."

Cue the awkwardness.

Chapter Five

THE TENSION DESCENDED on the booth like a thick, dense blanket of fog. Trying to lighten the mood, Jeffrey quipped, "Hey, it isn't all bad. Who knew I would be the one who'd end up being the black sheep, bringing shame on the family?"

Cecily wasn't distracted. "I can't imagine how difficult that must have been."

"Yeah, well. Bethany is on track to graduating and applying to med school. So they can live vicariously through her."

"Maybe it's like a Highlander thing," she suggested. "You know, only Bethany is destined to be Dr. Lee. A 'there can only be one' type deal."

"You've known my parents all your life. You really think they'll buy that explanation?" He scoffed and rolled his eyes.

She made a face. "Probably not," she admitted.

"But thank you. I appreciate you trying to help." He smiled. He took a breath and delved into trying to apologize and explain when Roxy came to the table to drop off Cecily's food.

"Here you are. Guess someone's hungry this morning,"

she said in a syrupy tone.

Cecily, to her credit, was having none of that nonsense. "As a matter of fact, I am." With no shame or guilt, she dug into her food.

Her ploy having proved unsuccessful, Roxy left them alone with a slight pout.

"You're lucky if she didn't spit in your food."

Cecily didn't miss a beat. "If I find out she did, I'll sue her ass, and the restaurant, and bleed them for every penny."

"You're ruthless." He shook his head in admiration.

She shrugged. "Lawyer."

They sat in companionable silence while she ate and he sipped coffee and checked his phone. He was due back at home shortly to help cook the night's meal. He was on dumpling duty and had about two hundred dumplings to help make.

Cecily cleaned her plate and pushed it to the side of the table. He looked up.

"You ready to go? You want anything else?"

"No, I'm good." She reached into her purse for her wallet and he waved it away.

"Your money is no good here," he informed her as he signaled for the check.

"That's not necessary," she protested but he ignored her.

"And don't even think about fighting me for the check. We've both had a lifetime of training, but I outweigh you by at least fifty pounds and I know all the tricks." Fighting over who paid the check was a time-honored Asian tradition, and akin to two MMA fighters in a no-holds-barred death match. It could get loud, physical, and potentially violent. There was a whole list of stratagems one learned through osmosis to employ to ensure you got to the check first. Like pretending you had to use the restroom halfway through the meal, but instead you sneak over to the waitress and hand over your credit card.

She narrowed her eyes. "But I know how to fight dirty." The simple phrase conjured up images he had no business conjuring. He had firsthand knowledge of how well she could play dirty and wouldn't mind a refresher.

Thanks to Roxy, he was able to prevail in the battle of the check as he handed over the cash. He gave her a smile and turned to Cecily. They had both stood up and were ready to leave.

"Ready, sweetheart?" He turned adoring eyes at Cecily; she gave him a look like he'd lost his mind. He mouthed, *"Go with me on this."* He draped his arm around her and gave her a quick kiss on the cheek. The move was intimate and proprietary and meant to send a message.

"We have a busy day ahead of us," he reminded her.

With a blink, Cecily finally caught on. "Right you are, dear," she intoned. She made a show of lacing her fingers with his as they walked toward the exit.

He wasn't going to lie—Roxy's palpable disappointment and slack-jawed expression were amusing, but he had bigger fish to fry at the moment. He threw his arm around Cecily, and guided them both out of the restaurant. They walked the five blocks home until they were standing in front of his parents' house.

Finally, she was able to speak. "Why did you do that?"

"Because I wanted to." It was the simple truth.

"You felt compelled to put on a show in a coffee shop full of patrons because you felt like it?" She was always too smart for her own good.

Now he took offense. "It was hardly a show. And unless you've suffered a momentary memory lapse, you were a full and willing participant too."

Cecily just pursed her lips and stared at him, drilling him with her gaze. Stared so long that it became uncomfortable.

"What?" he asked defensively.

"You did it on purpose," she said as the pieces of the puzzle fell into place. Her eyes narrowed.

"I believe we've already covered that," he hedged.

"No, it wasn't just because your hormones got the better of you."

He snorted derisively at that.

"You did it to send Roxy a message didn't you."

Caught, he came clean. "It was ninety-five percent me wanting to kiss you, and five percent letting her know she was better off pinning her hopes on someone else. And that I am very much off the market."

She just shook her head. "You are such a piece of work, you know that? And such a jackass."

"Stipulated."

She started walking ahead of him.

"And for the record, you are a hundred times more gorgeous than she is."

She turned around and rolled her eyes. "Now I'm going to have to call you the liar."

He came up to her and stroked her cheek. "No lies," he whispered. He studied her oval face, ebony hair, delicate brows, berry lips, ivory skin, etching every detail into his memory.

"I'm thirty-five years old," Cecily scoffed. "Like I can compare to some perky bouncing twenty-something cheerleader type. And what do you mean you're off the market? Do you have a girlfriend? Never mind. I'm really going to have to kick your ass if you just turned me into the other woman."

He spoke, pretending not to have heard her. "You are strong, frighteningly smart, driven, with a big heart and sharp tongue." His voice was a caress. "You have eyes that bore into a man's soul and can bring him to his knees. And lips more tempting than sin. You're right. There's no contest."

"Wow," she whispered. "That was damn good." She laughed and shook her head.

"Told you. And I meant it."

"You always had a way with words."

"I've gotten even better with non-verbal communica-tion." He saw the spark in her eye that told him she knew exactly what he meant.

"Maybe I should give you a chance to prove it," she teased.

"Anytime."

Cecily looked at her watch and faked a yawn. "What the hell. I don't have to be back home for at least five minutes. I have time to kill."

Challenge accepted, he cupped her head with his hands, yanked her close and lowered his mouth to hers.

The minute their lips met, it was like time stood still and spun back to ten years ago. He still remembered the curves of her face, the lushness of her lips, the way their bodies melded together so perfectly. He savored the moment, wanting to commit it to memory. He held her close, and cradled her neck. Jeffrey felt the moment Cecily began to relax and lose herself. She tilted her head and he took the invitation to deepen the kiss.

It was familiar, but new. Comforting, but exciting. It was as if the past ten years had flown by, and they were just getting reacquainted. Like two old dance partners who had found their rhythm together again. Jeffrey forgot about the cold, the prying eyes and ears, and just indulged in the pleasure of being connected with Cecily. He knew how unlikely it was that he even had a shot of getting a second chance with her, and he wasn't about to blow it. So he poured every ounce of emotion he could into this kiss, trying to communicate what he could without words.

A loud, rude honk from a passing truck broke him out of his reverie. And suddenly, those prying eyes and ears took on a much bigger significance. The last thing he wanted was for the two of them to be the object of neighborhood speculation and gossip. Cecily would never forgive him for that.

He broke off the kiss and stepped back. He wasn't ashamed to admit that Cecily's flushed cheeks and glazed eyes gave him a sense of pride. A man liked to know he hadn't lost his touch.

Satisfied he'd made his point, he left her standing there as he went up the front steps. But he had one last piece of business to clear up.

"And yes, I am off the market. I have been since the day I proposed to you. I was an idiot and it took me too long to realize we belonged together no matter what. And I'm determined to get you back." With that, he went inside and left her there open-mouthed and frozen like a statue.

He opened the door. "Go home before you freeze to death from exposure." Then closed it again.

That should be enough to keep her off her game and maybe give him the edge and advantage he needed to get through her defenses.

Hey girl. Wanted to check in on you. Hope you're surviving. Remember, I got bail money for you if you need it. Just send up the Bat Signal.

She quickly fired back a reply. *So far so good. No need for bail $ yet.* She included a fingers-crossed emoji and an upside-down smiley face.

Remember, no one looks good in prison orange. She couldn't hold back a snort. This was typical Adrienne.

Really, Arroyo?

Just looking out for you. Also, you're bringing me back food right?

I'll see what I can do.

Good. You spent so much time talking about the noodles and dumplings and spring rolls. I wanna eat ALL THE FOOD. But I'm gonna pass on the fish. It sounds like a lot of food though.

It's all symbolic! Must-haves at New Year's. Fish in Mandarin is "yu" and that sounds the same as the word for "abundance", which hopefully means prosperity in the New Year. The noodles are for longevity. The dumplings represent wealth. We have rice balls for family togetherness. The irony of the last item didn't escape Cecily.

Adrienne sent back a drooling emoji. *Pics please! That all sounds amazing!*

I'll let Ma know you want some extras. She'll probably pack an extra cooler for you. God knows how I'll be able to bring all of it home. She got praise hands in response. Her time was probably up. She picked up her head and saw Auntie Marcia's pursed lips. Yeah. Time to go.

My reprieve is over. Once more unto the breach.

Honestly, who needed a new friend when she had Adrienne? She was making her way back to the kitchen when another text came up from Bethany. Cecily was surprised. They hadn't spoken much since The Incident, but they exchanged texts on occasion.

Making sure you got home okay.

I'm...fine? she replied. *The hell?*

No sign of food-borne illness? Roxy didn't poison your food?

The sneaky bastard.

Really? You've resorted to impersonating your sister? That's low, even for you. She included a side-eye emoji and the poop emoji.

I think we've already established my low moral character. Besides I doubt you'd have answered a random number or if you'd known it was me. Shrug emoji.

Does she even know you took her phone?

What she doesn't know won't hurt her.

You are a real piece of work. Cecily fought back a grin as she typed. She tried to stay mad, but she couldn't help but be amused. Jeffrey had always known how to get through her defenses.

…You've already said that. Negative points for repetition and lack of originality.

Oh, now it was ON.

SERIOUSLY??!!

The text bubbles were moving, and she found herself waiting for his response. He didn't disappoint.

I'm a writer. Calling out sloppy word choices and bad writing is what I do. Don't hate the player, hate the game. If you can't handle the heat, get out of the kitchen. Not my fault if you can't handle it.

She arched a brow. *A writer who just resorted to a litany of clichés.*

His response was a grimacing-face emoji.

She walked back out to the staircase for more privacy.

Truth hurts, huh?

What was I thinking, trying to argue with a lawyer?

Her lips twitching, she typed back. *Give Bethany back her phone.*

Does this mean I can use my own phone now? You won't block me? She shook her head as he sent her his number. Give the man an inch, and he took a mile.

The court has not yet reached a decision on the matter.

An eye-roll emoji was his response.

Gotta go! I hear Ma calling. Needed in the kitchen.

She put her phone in her pocket and made her way back to the kitchen.

"Who were you talking to?" Molly asked. She was standing at the kitchen counter, chopping a mountain of vegetables for tomorrow's dinner. Cecily joined her and picked up a knife to deal with the ginger, garlic, and cilantro. Auntie Marcia was at the stove arguing with Judith over whether or not the noodles were overcooked, and other relatives were making the fish and dumplings and other dishes.

Besides all the dishes she'd mentioned to Adrienne, there were also lobsters in the fridge ready to go, along with the rice cakes, and chicken, and tomorrow her father would heat up the wok to deep-fry the spring rolls. And there were about five other dishes to be prepared. Gillian and Peter were keeping an eye on the kids along with Auntie Karen.

The whole house would be a mess of cooking and noise until New Year's dinner. It was tradition, and Cecily loved it.

"Just someone from work," she said to Molly. She tried to be as casual as possible so as not to give anything away.

"I thought it was Jeffrey," Owen teased, strolling into the kitchen for a snack.

The whole kitchen fell silent. Cecily bit back a curse as she glared at her younger brother. The smug look on his face told her he knew exactly what he was doing. Thank God she had remembered to secure her phone in her pocket so it couldn't be stolen.

"Jeffrey? Why him?" their mother demanded.

"Oh, I heard a rumor that they were spotted at the Sunrise this morning, and they looked very cozy," Owen said, using air quotes on the last two words.

Cecily flushed, recalling the events of the morning. That kiss had melted her knees, and his words to her before they parted ways made her heart thump, and all sorts of girlish, romantic notions started running through her head again. Thankfully, she reminded herself, she was older and wiser now. He'd broken her heart ten years ago, and she wasn't going to give him another chance to do it again, no matter how intoxicating the man's kissing skills were. No way was she going to make the same mistake. Maybe they'd had a fun text conversation and shared a brief steamy kiss, but that was as far as it was going to go.

"Yes, we had breakfast together," she managed. "Not a big deal."

"What were you doing with him?" Auntie Marcia demanded.

Uncle Ray piped in. "What do you mean cozy?"

Judith said nothing, but still managed to send off vibrations of disapproval.

Wanting to put an end to it, Cecily decided to make it quick and painless. "I went to the café to get some coffee and food. He was already there. He offered to have me join him. He paid. So I got a free meal. That's it. End of story."

Owen opened his mouth to contradict, but Cecily nailed him with a look. *So help me God, if you say a word I will end you.*

Luckily, her brother had a strong sense of self-preservation and kept his mouth shut.

"I hope you ordered the most expensive food on the menu," Molly said.

"That boy is a disgrace," Auntie Karen muttered. "I haven't spoken to Pam and Martin since."

"I saw Jeffrey the other day. He's hot." This from her cousin Theresa. Before she could help herself, Cecily glared.

Theresa shrugged. "I speak the truth."

"Hot? He treated your cousin like trash, and you call him hot?" Judith demanded. As expected, Theresa cowered and quickly offered an apology.

That done, Judith turned to Cecily and with a pointed finger declared, "You stay away from him. He's bad news. You understand me?"

As always, Cecily's back went up, and her "Don't tell me what to do" button was triggered.

"I am thirty-five years old, Ma. I can decide who I can and can't talk to. If I want to speak to him, I will." Good God. If anyone would have told her she'd ever be defending Jeffrey, not once, but twice over the course of the weekend, she would have told them they needed a psych eval. Once again, she was failing at two resolutions on her list at once. Maybe she was over-reaching trying to avoid drama and keep peace with her family. Cecily was a strong proponent of multi-tasking but even for her, this was too much.

Judith put down the kitchen cleaver she was wielding and started to speak, ready for battle.

Thankfully, her father waded in to keep the peace. "Judith, calm down. It's New Year's. Let's not fight." Grudgingly, Judith listened, but her expression was still stormy. They were definitely going to revisit this at a later date.

She could hardly wait.

SHE DIDN'T WANT to do this. It was Lunar New Year and Cecily felt cheated. She really didn't want to do this. But at this point, she was backed into a corner and had no choice. The hundred-million dollar-deal she was working on was going down the toilet. Fast. Stafford Developers just got hit with an SEC inquiry and now the Planning Department was freaking out. She was in a time crunch and couldn't wait until she got back home to handle this. She needed a financial expert to help make sense of the filings and paperwork. And of course, there was only one available choice.

"You should ask Rachel," her father suggested. *Et tu, Dad?*

Rachel Bai. Her middle and high school nemesis. Ever since she could remember, she heard: "Why can't you be more like Rachel? She's such a good girl. Always listens, gets good grades and never gives her parents trouble like you. Do you think she back talks?" She would never ever live up to the perfect Rachel Bai. There were times she was convinced Rachel was part robot. It was the only explanation that made sense. And now instead of celebrating New Year's and stuffing her face with all the food, she had to meet with her nemesis.

"I haven't seen Rachel in ages. It would be wrong for me to call her out of the blue and ask for help. Besides, I don't even know her number."

"Rachel Bai?" Judith's ears perked up at the name. Of course they did.

"Yes. I need some financial help with a client."

"Oh, I'm sure Rachel won't mind. She was always such a good girl. Got good grades. Went to Harvard. Auntie Rose says she's working for Merrill Lynch, or some big company." *Yes I know. I only went to Columbia, a lesser Ivy.*

"Ma, I don't want to bother her." This was what she got for letting Resolution 3 slip. The things she did for her job. What work-life balance?

But Judith was already on the phone. Cecily looked over at her father. Paul just shrugged and went back to his newspaper. *You know how your mother is.*

"*Hao, hao.* Cecily will call Rachel right away." With a satisfied smile, Judith hung up the phone.

"All done," she declared. She ripped off the top sheet on the notepad next to the phone and gave it to Cecily. "That's Rachel's number. Call her."

"I'll do it later."

Her mother frowned. "No, you said this was an emergency. Call her now. Don't be irresponsible to your client. Besides, you've been working all weekend. Daddy and I have barely seen you. Just finish this before dinner." As she went back upstairs, she heard her mother's voice. "Aren't you going to say thank you?"

SO NOW IT was 3 p.m. and she was meeting Rachel back at the Sunrise Café for a coffee and quick consult. With a deep feeling of dread, she walked inside and saw Rachel right away. Of course Rachel was already there. Early and prepared. Wearing a bulky white cable-knit sweater, cargo pants, Ugg boots, thick glasses, pageboy haircut, and a frown of concentration. She had a stack of paper before her that she was studying intently.

Cecily walked over to the table, gave a cough to announce her presence. With an owlish blink, Rachel looked up. "Oh, you're here."

"Sorry I'm late."

"No it's fine. I'm still looking over all this material you sent over. You didn't give me a lot of time."

She winced. "Sorry about that."

"Well, not your fault. These things happen. Are you going to sit?"

She took a deep breath and sat down on the opposite booth. And of course, because the universe had it out for her, it was Roxy who came over and dropped off a menu. With a side of death glare.

"Get whatever you want; put it on my tab," Rachel murmured, her nose back in the stack of papers.

"Oh no. I'm the one asking you the favor here," Cecily

protested. "The least I can do is buy you coffee, or pastry or something."

Rachel looked up again. "Don't worry about it."

"Are you sure?"

"Positive. Besides, we're both saving our appetites for the New Year meal tonight. The least you can do is buy me an actual meal. So next time."

Did she make a joke? The perfect Rachel Bai has a sense of humor?

"Sounds fair."

"Besides, you got me out of the house. I should thank you for that."

Am I in some alternate universe? I have something in common with her?

"Well I really appreciate your help."

"Sure, no problem. Besides, my mom wouldn't have let me refuse." When she saw the look on Cecily's face, she gave a little sigh.

"I didn't mean it like that. I'm sorry. I have a vicious headache. I'm happy to help. Seriously."

Roxy came back to the table and slapped down a chocolate chip muffin and coffee for Cecily, and a cinnamon bun and hot tea for Rachel. Which she was much more gentle with.

"Still, I know it's a huge ask. And a lot to wade through."

"Eh, nothing I haven't dealt with before," Rachel said as she bit into the sticky, gooey pastry. "Besides all this is public record or stuff you can get off the SEC, so you're fine. Nothing that can get me thrown in jail or anything."

Okay, that was definitely a joke.

Maybe she's not so bad after all.

"I definitely owe you a meal. Let me know when you want to collect." Cecily took a fortifying sip of coffee.

"Will do. I'm surprised you asked me for help though."

Yikes. "What do you mean?"

"The great Cecily Chang coming to little ole me for help? Who would've thought?"

She frowned "What does that mean?" This girl was out of her mind.

"Come on." Rachel took off her glasses, put them down on the laminate table, and leaned over the table. "You were student council president, got a scholarship to college, and now you're some big-time lawyer out in San Francisco. Do you know how many times my mom guilted me, asking why I couldn't be more like you?"

Cecily stared at her bug-eyed. Rachel's eyes widened too as the implications of their statements sank in. "You've got to be kidding me."

"Son of a…"

"I should've known. Do you know how much grief I got as a kid, and even now?" Cecily imitated Judith's voice. "Why can't you be more like Rachel Bai? She didn't move all the way across the country like you did. She comes home every weekend, sees her family. Like a good, obedient daughter."

Rachel rolled her eyes. "Well, I got: 'Did you hear Cecily graduated top of her class at law school? And on a scholarship! Auntie Judith said she's going to make partner soon. When are you going to make partner? And she calls home. We never hear from you.'"

"Incredible." Cecily leaned back on the booth, her mind blown. "All this time."

"Yes, our parents engaged in the age-old Asian parents comparison game and pitted us against each other. Everyone else's kid is better than you, you rotten spoiled ungrateful child." The gleam in Rachel's eyes was equal parts humor and annoyance.

"Now I feel guilty about hating you," Cecily murmured. She winced as soon as the words came out.

"I hated you too, so we can call it even." Rachel's smirk took the sting out of the words.

"Deal." The two of them went back to their food and beverages, with Rachel asking questions, and Cecily answering, filling in gaps.

"These numbers make no fucking sense," Rachel muttered out of the blue, rifling through an earnings report. "I'm going to have to take a look at these more closely."

Gobsmacked, Cecily's jaw dropped open. Rachel peered up over her glasses.

"Yes, I just dropped the f-bomb. I curse. Get over it." Her mild tone just made the experience all the more surreal.

"All righty then."

"Can I get you ladies anything else?" With a scowl in Cecily's direction, Roxy came by to top off her coffee.

"No, we're good. Just the check."

"Right away," she said, giving Rachel a bright smile.

When she walked away, Rachel arched a brow. "What's up with that?"

"Long story, don't want to talk about it," Cecily mumbled.

"It wouldn't have anything to do with you having breakfast with Jeffrey Lee here the other day would it?" Cecily narrowed her eyes.

"What do you know about it?"

"Just that. And people are still wondering what happened ten years ago. You two could barely keep your hands off each other. We all thought he'd have gotten you pregnant on your honeymoon and you'd be on baby number ten by now."

"Really? TEN kids?" That was terrifying.

A shrug. "I'm sure you would be one of those uber soccer moms. You know, in court in the morning, then running over to the soccer field in the afternoon. Minus the Botox and plastic surgery of course. Like a good old-fashioned sitcom mom."

"I don't know what I ever could've done in a past life to deserve a fate like that."

Rachel began to reply, but something in Cecily's expression told her a change of topic was in order.

"Anyway, you know what it's like in this neighborhood. Everyone is in everybody else's business."

"Which is why I moved to the other side of the country," Cecily said wryly.

"Can't say I blame you. I gave you the basics, so that should be enough to get you started, right?" Rachel grabbed a twenty out of her wallet and put it in the folder.

"Yes, for sure. Seriously, you went above and beyond, and I totally appreciate you helping me out like this."

"You're welcome," Rachel said with a small smile. "But let's check in in a few weeks once I get a better handle on all this stuff. We can go over it in more detail. That work for you?"

"Definitely." The two of them got up and put on their coats. "If you're ever out in San Francisco, let me know. Dinner and drinks on me." To her surprise, Cecily found herself not just saying it, but meaning it. This meeting had not turned out the way she'd expected. At all.

"Guess you've decided I'm not that bad after all."

Starting to understand Rachel's humor, she replied with a grin, "We'll work on making each other friendship bracelets later."

She was well on her way to keeping Resolution number 4. An old acquaintance still counted as a new friend, right? And the month wasn't even over yet.

SITTING IN HIS childhood living room, surrounded by dozens of relatives, Jeffrey tried to block out the noise and focus on the football game. Absently reaching for the bowl of potato chips, he grabbed a handful and stuffed his face. Just then his nieces and nephews ran up to him.

"Happy New Year, Uncle Jeff!" they said in the cutest chorus ever. He gave each of them a high five.

"Where's our money?" Nate demanded. Jeffrey's lips twitched but he tried to keep his expression neutral.

"Nathan Lee!" Alex scolded. "Who taught you to be so rude?" Nate looked at his father with wide innocent eyes.

"But Baba, Uncle Jeffrey is supposed to give us red envelopes. It's New Year!"

"Keep acting this way I'm taking away all the money."

"New Year's? Is that what today is?" He pretended to scratch his head in confusion. Really, it was too much fun.

"YES!"

"Well, I guess that's why I have these." He reached into his back pocket and pulled out a stack of red envelopes stuffed with cash. *Hong baos* symbolized blessings and good luck for the New Year and was given from elders to those of the younger generation.

With great ceremony, he passed them out to each one of the children. Who promptly tore them open and grabbed the twenty dollars inside.

"Oh my God. This is like a million dollars!" All the kids scampered off to revel in their newfound fortune after showering their benefactor with hugs and kisses and very loud thank-yous.

"God, don't you miss those days?" Alex asked with a chuckle. "Remember that one year when everyone was here and we made two hundred bucks in fifteen minutes?"

"For real. We used to be the ones getting the money, now I'm out almost a hundred bucks. You and Becca and your other halves need to stop having kids."

Alex snorted. "A hundred bucks once a year versus half

a million a year to put those kids through college. Sorry if I don't feel bad for you at all."

"Time to eat—dinner's ready!" his mother called. Like moths to a flame, the whole family descended on the dining room table, which was creaking under the weight of all the food. His dumplings were on a giant platter, and they looked pretty damn good, if he did say so himself. Jeffrey could feel his mouth drooling. He couldn't wait to dive into his mother's noodles and the chicken and bamboo shoots. The whole family quickly sat down and proceeded to dig in. The next hour was lots of noise, eating, and toasting. There was clinking of classes and *"Gan bei!"* even from the kids who got juice instead of alcohol. He loved it and he wouldn't want to celebrate New Year's any other way.

Two hours later, Jeffrey sat back on the couch, stuffed to the gills. He wasn't ashamed to admit he had pigged out. His mom was cleaning up the kitchen, Bethany was wrapping up the leftovers, and his father was doing the dishes. His brother Alex had taken his family back to the hotel so was excused from cleanup duty. The aunts, uncles, and cousins had already gone home. It had been a fun and noisy night, but now he was ready for some peace and quiet, and maybe getting an hour or two of work in before bed. He felt guilty not pitching in, but Deadline Hell loomed.

"Ba," he called out to his father, "I'm going up to my room to work. Do you need any help?"

He saw his parents give each other a look. This did not

bode well. His father cleared his throat, and pulled a red envelope from his pocket.

Jeffrey frowned. "What is this?"

His father passed him the envelope. "For you."

"Dad, I'm too old for this!" Indeed, once a child became an adult, and became self-supporting, they generally stopped receiving the envelopes. "I should be giving you and Mom envelopes. Bethany should get one, not me."

"We know how hard you work. California is expensive. Mom and I want to help."

Jeffrey softened. "Thank you, but I'm fine." He opened the envelope. He shook his head and immediately gave it back. "This is too much." There was two hundred dollars inside.

"Don't be rude, Jeffrey," his mother scolded.

Martin pushed the hong bao back into his hand. "Take it. If you don't need it, save it. Maybe you can save enough money to go back to school."

And the shoe finally dropped. Jeffrey resisted the urge to grab the envelope and rip it in half. From over his father's shoulder, he saw Bethany wince and cringe. His mother's hopeful face was like a punch in the gut.

He opened his mouth, then closed it again. It took every ounce of willpower to keep his calm and not say something he'd regret or couldn't take back. Instead he put the money on the coffee table, turned to the front door, put on his coat and shoes, and left the house with his parents' protests ringing behind him. He barely resisted the urge to slam the door, but that would only serve to make them even more pissed at him.

Jeffrey walked blindly for three blocks, not even cognizant of where he was going.

"Damn it. Damn it!" Just when he thought it was safe, his parents had to remind him how much he had disappointed them and let them down. They were not going to be happy until he caved and followed their prescribed life plan.

Screw that. He kept walking, hoping that he could blow off some steam and walk it off. Literally. Fifteen minutes later, he found himself at a local park. Before he knew what he was doing he found himself on the swings. For the first time in twenty-five years, he began to swing.

Chapter Six

"SCREW IT," CECILY muttered. Without another word, she pulled on her boots and went out into the cold crisp dark night.

She couldn't help beating herself up as she walked out the door of her parents' home. Dinner had been going so well and then suddenly the aunties and uncles got involved, and kept asking questions she had no interest in answering. It had all come to a head when Auntie Karen had offered to set her up with her hairdresser's neighbor's nephew. There was only so much button pushing a person could take and she'd exploded. While she hadn't exactly used any profanity, as far as the family was concerned, she pretty much had, in terms of the level of disrespect. The things she'd said were definitely considered beyond the pale and she would have a lot of apologizing and atoning to do. But right now, Cecily couldn't bring herself to care. She just needed to get out.

She didn't know why but something led her to the park. Maybe she needed the solace and reminder of a simpler and more innocent time. Her boots crunched through the snow and slush as she made her way there. But someone had already beat her to it.

At this point, she'd stopped questioning fate and why she and Jeffrey seemed destined or cursed to run into each other at every turn. The Serenity Prayer applied here. Accept the things you cannot change or go stark raving mad.

He was on the swings, pumping his legs like an elementary school boy. The image was sweet and brought back nostalgic memories. How many times had they played together in a park or playground like this as kids? Too many to count. And if she was reading the scene correctly, Jeffrey was in search of some peace and calm as well.

She walked up to him and sat down in the other swing without a word. For a few minutes the only sound was the noise of the swings moving back and forth.

Finally, she broke the silence. "Hope the cops don't catch us. We'd have a lot of explaining to do."

He smiled, but his eyes were still troubled, and his expression grim.

"Wanna talk about it?" she asked softly.

"Not particularly."

"All right then." They had stopped moving their legs and were now just sitting still in the swings.

Eventually he spoke. "Mom and Dad made it clear again what a bitter disappointment I am to them."

The sympathy and empathy were instant. "I'm sure that's not what they meant." She reached out to lay a hand on his shoulder, but stopped herself.

He scoffed. "Dad gave me money. To help me go back to school."

"Ouch."

"Exactly."

"I'm sure they meant well. Were just trying to help," she ventured.

He gave her the evil eye. "Good intentions doesn't make it suck less."

Too true.

"If it helps, Mom said that Auntie Pam told everyone at the community center when your latest movie came out last fall. It was all she could talk about. She said it was sickening." It had surprised her. She hadn't been able to resist the urge to Google, and it turned out he was becoming well known in Hollywood.

"No one ever told me that." He frowned.

"Me neither. I overheard the gossip earlier today. The relatives don't tend to…discuss you in front of me."

"I can imagine," he drawled. He gave a big sigh. He reached out to squeeze her hand. "I am sorry about that. More sorry than I can ever express."

Cecily quickly extracted her hand. The gesture did not go unnoticed, but Jeffrey didn't comment on it.

A few moments later, he asked, "So why are you here?"

It was her turn to sigh. "My mom, the aunts and uncles were driving me nuts about why I'm not married with a husband and kids and I kinda snapped." She winced.

He raised a brow. "Now that I would have liked to have seen."

"I basically cursed out Auntie Karen."

"You what?" His eyes went wide as saucers.

"Asian-style," she clarified. "I was pissed, but I didn't have a death wish. I didn't actually use any four-letter words."

Jeffrey let out a breath. "I was going to say."

"She wanted to set me up with her hairdresser's nephew. Or was it her neighbor's son? It just devolved and spiraled out from there." Cecily shook her head.

"Does she even know the son? Why are they setting you up with strangers?" Jeffrey sounded peeved.

"That's not the point," she snapped.

"Fair enough. Go on," he encouraged.

"No, I'm fine. Honestly I'm not sure why I'm dumping on you like this."

"Hey, I volunteered, and you did the same for me."

"Old habits die hard, I guess," she said with a sigh.

"Something like that. Come on, get it out of your system—it'll make you feel better."

"No offense but I'm not sure you're the one I want to vent to about all this." She slid him a look and he acknowledged the hit.

"Who better? I'm a safe target, I won't judge, and I already know all the players. Think of it like confession—cleanses the soul."

"So what, we're Catholic now? You're going to tell me how many Hail Mary's I'll need to do afterwards?"

"CeeCee."

"Okay fine." He had a point. He of all people would understand.

After a few minutes, and a deep breath, she dove in.

"Why won't my family believe I like my life as is? That I'm happy? That I love my life in San Francisco with my job and my friends? But no. Instead, I get told it's high time I moved back to New York and settled down. Like it would be that easy for me to find another job and pick up my life and move back. They just made this decision for me without even consulting me or asking what I actually wanted. Decisions about *my* life. Instead, they decide they know what's best for me, and I should just get with the program. They're my elders, they know best, right? Just do what they say and thank them later. I'm over it." Getting worked up all over again, her words began to come out in a tumble, her breathing quickened, and her pulse elevated.

"It's like no matter what I do, it's never good enough. Ever since I was a kid. There's always something else I could be doing, or do better. I practiced the piano for hours every day. Why wasn't I playing Mozart already like Vivian Wu? I graduated with honors from college. Why wasn't I the valedictorian? I get an amazing job offer, they complain about the hours I work and that they never see me anymore. I'm on track to make partner next year, and all they want to know is when I'm going to give them grandkids to spoil. I'm tired of always trying to make them happy, make them proud, and coming up short every time. I'm tired of not being good enough no matter how hard I kill myself to live up to their expectations for me." Her voice rose with every word, and tears were already running down her cheeks like rivulets.

Jeffrey just sat there silently, letting her vent and get it out of her system.

Cecily took a few deep breaths. "I'm just tired," she whispered. For a moment, she dropped her head and stared at the ground.

He reached for her hand again, laced their fingers. She looked up at him. In for a penny, in for a pound. She gathered her courage.

"And then there's you."

"Me?"

She took another breath. This could potentially be the most difficult thing she'd ever done. What the hell, she'd already gone through the emotional wringer once tonight, what was one more. Besides, she'd been wanting an answer for ten years and now was her chance. Might as well rip off the Band-Aid and get it all over with at once.

"You left town the day after you broke our engagement. You broke my heart. I never understood what I did to make you do that. I thought we were happy. I was so happy, so in love. And then I found out it was all a lie. What did I do wrong? Why did you change your mind?" She looked at him beseechingly. "That's what kills me. I never knew why. Please help me understand."

THE PAIN IN her voice was breaking his heart. How could he make her understand that it had nothing to do with her?

"I was an idiot. You did nothing wrong." His voice was fierce in an effort to make her believe. "It was me, not you." The trite line slipped out before he knew it. Even before he finished speaking, he knew it was a mistake.

"You're resorting to clichés now?" she demanded.

"It's the truth. I walked away because I was a mess, and I was trying to protect you. Stop beating yourself up for something that wasn't your fault. You have every right to hate me. Please go on hating me. I'd rather that than seeing you like this."

Cecily gave a watery chuckle. Taking that as a good sign, he plowed on. "And another thing, stop thinking you aren't good enough. You are more than good enough and it's not your fault if your family can't see that because they view things through a different cultural lens. You are an amazing woman, Cecily Chang. Don't you ever forget it."

A short pause. "You know, if you had one of your characters say that, I guarantee they could get any woman they wanted. They'd be putty in his hand."

He shot her a look out of the side of his eye. "I meant it."

"I know. And that's why it worked. Thank you," she said with a wobbly smile. "It's good to have someone to talk to who understands how frustrating the whole thing can be."

"Anytime."

"For once, I just want to feel like I'm good enough. That I don't have to prove myself to anyone. Someone who doesn't constantly find me wanting."

He raised his hand. "I already told you. To me, you are more than enough. Frankly, you've always been way too good for me. I lived in fear of you figuring out you could do so much better." His voice lowered. "And if you need someone to help take your mind off things, and to show you they find no aspect of you lacking, I am more than happy to oblige."

Her face was a red splotchy mess, but to him, she had never looked more fragile, beautiful, and precious. She was so eaten up with self-doubt, beaten down by her family, he was desperate to do something, anything, to ease her pain. If that meant taking her somewhere where he could ply her with tea, blankets, and Netflix, so be it. Or if she wanted to go to a batting cage to work off the excess energy and emotions, they could do that too. Whatever she wanted.

Oh what the hell. He was offering her sex and they both knew it. No point in pretending otherwise, or that he was that noble. He was a man after all, and to his mind, some hot sweaty sex could definitely help take the edge off. But really. If the batting cages or Netflix were what she wanted, that's what she'd get. The ball was in her court.

She let out a shaky breath. He tensed, waiting for the verdict. When she spoke, her voice was low, but firm and resolute.

"I want you to take me away. Take me somewhere where I can take my mind off all this. And hell, maybe for you too. I want to go somewhere where we can tear each other's clothes off and have a couple of screaming orgasms. That's what I want."

Well all righty then.

CECILY'S SKIN PRICKLED as she waited for Jeffrey's answer after her declaration. Part of her was dying of mortification. She had never spoken that brazenly or boldly before, but there was a first time for everything. But still, she forced herself to not look away. This was her decision and she was going to own it.

And honestly, the prospect of a few amazing orgasms sounded pretty good right about now. Like the perfect way to end a wretched day.

A slow sensual smile curved his lips. "At your command," he murmured. He took out his phone and started typing away.

She grew impatient. "What are you doing?"

"Finding us a hotel for the night. Something tells me you don't want to have these screaming orgasms within earshot of anyone you're related to." He raised a pointed brow.

Cecily blushed furiously. "You make a good point." She hopped from foot to foot, trying to keep warm. "Can you hurry up?"

"How do I not remember you being so impatient?" His eyes were hot as he looked at her.

"I don't mean that. I'm cold." The wind chill was biting but his gaze was like a warm brandy heating her from the inside out. A slow liquid yearning pooled in her belly.

He put his phone away. "Don't worry. I'm more than happy to keep you warm." The innuendo was unmistakable. What was it about this man? Normally, she would shut down any man who used lines like that on her. But coming from him, it made her toes curl.

Jeffrey took her hand and walked her to the corner. "I got us a reservation at the Lannister Hotel. It's about fifteen minutes away. They're expecting us."

Wordlessly, they hailed a cab and got in. Unlike their last car ride together, there was no lingering tension in the air. Or more accurately, this was an entirely different kind of tension. And this time, she wasn't pretending to ignore him.

The phone in her purse buzzed. "Oh crap," she muttered.

"What is it?"

She held up her phone. "My family."

"Oh." He breathed a sigh of relief.

"Don't worry, I haven't changed my mind."

He threw her a look.

"I guess I better respond before they call the police and report me as a missing person."

Gillian's text popped up first.

WHERE. ARE. YOU? Answer your phone. Mom is FREAKING. OUT.

Cecily's reply was quick and to the point.

Tell everyone I'm fine. I found a place to stay for the night. I'll see you guys in the morning.

But her sister didn't find it satisfactory.

What?? What do you mean? Where are you going? Are you wandering around the city alone?

Gill included a hair-pulling-out emoji and a cross-bones-and-skull emoji.

No. I'll see you in the morning. She turned off her phone to put an end to the discussion.

She looked over at Jeffrey who was typing away on his phone too. He caught her eye.

"I'm texting Bethany to cover for me. So they don't call the police either."

"Ah. Hopefully she won't ask as many questions. Gill was about to give me the third degree."

"She and I have an understood 'don't ask, don't tell' policy."

"Convenient."

Luckily, their cabbie was pretending not to hear a word, much to her relief. He dropped them off at the front of the hotel.

Out of nowhere, he told her to go into the lobby and wait. "I'll be back in fifteen minutes," he promised. What in the world?

Seeing the look on her face, he explained. "One of us needs to go to the pharmacy, or a bodega." As she understood his meaning, she blushed furiously. He looked a bit uncomfortable too. But they were two grown adults here. If they couldn't even talk about sex, they should not be having it. Just her opinion.

"That's a good idea."

"Listen, I can't claim to be a monk since the last time we were together, but I haven't been with anyone in a little over a year. So we don't have anything to worry about there. Too busy with work." He shrugged.

She couldn't say she liked the idea of knowing that he'd been with other women while they'd been apart. But if she was forced to be mature about this, she couldn't blame him. He had a life to lead, and so did she. And she expected him to show her the same consideration.

"Same here, but more like eighteen months for me. No risk of infection, but better safe than sorry. And I'm on the pill." And that was all she was willing to share at this particular moment.

"I'll be back," he promised as he jogged away. Leaving her with nothing to do but pace the front of the hotel like a hooker looking for her next high-class trick.

True to his word, he was back fifteen minutes later, purchase in hand. She raised an eyebrow as he ushered them inside.

"Did you buy two packs? Aren't we the optimist?" She took a breath to jettison the nerves.

"Let's just say I have a lot of time to make up for. And from the sound of it, so do you."

Well. All right then.

The Lannister was a richly appointed four-star boutique hotel. Cecily felt underdressed and outclassed. They stood in the lobby of the hotel and looked at each other for a moment.

"Well, this is certainly an improvement from that night our freshman year of college," she joked, trying to lighten the mood. That night had been a first. For both of them.

"You know better than anyone I've learned some things since then. Sounds like you need a reminder," he said out of the side of his mouth. Cecily laughed, then kept back a yelp as he gave her a light slap on the butt. She stayed silent as Jeffrey went to the reception desk and checked in. He grabbed their keycard. She flushed as she caught the knowing smirk of the concierge—Derek. Hopefully he wouldn't be there in the morning as she did her Walk of Shame.

That was the problem with last-minute assignations and booty calls. One never gets the chance to pack properly to avoid rousing suspicions from hotel staff.

The two of them rode up the elevator to the fifth floor. They still didn't speak a word until they entered the room. The minute he closed the door behind them and they took off their coats, hats, gloves, and scarves, Jeffrey backed her up against the door and kissed her like his life depended on it. The bag containing the condoms clattered to the floor.

"Slow down, we got all night," she said, her voice throaty.

"And I plan to make the most of it," he growled. He grabbed her tight and flush against him. There were a few more minutes of frantic kissing and by the end they were both panting and aroused beyond belief. Jeffrey gave her a boost, and she hiked up the long thick skirt she was wearing and wrapped her legs around his trim waist. He tried to make it to the bed but only made it as far as the desk. He plopped her down and cleared the desk. He gave her a dark hungry look and scooted her to the edge of the desk. Before she knew what he had in mind, he pushed her legs apart and dropped to his knees in front of her. He shoved the skirt up to her waist.

"Hold this." She shouldn't find his commanding tone sexy, but it was shifting her into overdrive. She had the presence of mind to wish she was wearing some sexy silk or lace panties instead of plain serviceable cotton hip-huggers.

But judging by Jeffrey's hungry gaze and the way he was licking his lips, he didn't seem to mind. With a slightly rough pull, he had those panties off and flung away. Cecily kicked off her shoes.

With a breathless laugh, she unhooked her skirt, lifted her hips, and tossed that aside too. She reached out to unbutton his shirt, but he pushed her away.

He tsked. "I'm a gentleman. Ladies first." With a wicked grin, he got down to business. He placed a trail of hot kisses up her thigh.

"How chivalrous," she gasped. Her skin felt hot, and she gripped the front edge of the table for purchase. Part of her mind realized what a sight she must be at the moment. Half dressed, head thrown back, lips open, and a man kneeling between her spread legs. How brazen. How wanton. And right now, she loved it. There was nowhere else she'd rather be.

He shook his head. "I must be doing something wrong if you can still talk." He redoubled his efforts with devastating effect. She gasped again as he blew a hot breath against her now wet sex. Her nipples tightened, and her legs opened wider to give him more access.

"I've been dreaming about doing this ever since I saw you again," he murmured. With that, he began to lick her feminine folds, leaving no bit unexplored. He was driving her crazy with slow languorous strokes of his tongue. The rough brush of slight stubble was a delicious counterpoint. His ministrations were setting off fireworks all over her body, but there was still something missing. Too lost in sensation to be embarrassed, she grabbed his head and brought him where she needed him most. Her primal instincts kicked in and her hips started to move to meet his motions.

He chuckled at her impatience and the vibrations only served to pull greedy, needy groans from her. She grabbed the table again and looked down, mesmerized by the sight in front of her. His dark hair between her legs, his tongue working magic against her most intimate places. His eyes glinting dark as the night sky outside their window. The way he applied himself to the task almost felt reverent, like there was nowhere else he'd rather be. Like there was nothing as important to him in the world as the pleasure he was bringing her.

"Ohhh," she panted as he finally lavished her clit with the attention it had been craving. Gripping her ankles to keep them apart, he kept licking and rubbing and kissing until she was ready to burst. She began chanting his name over and over, almost like a plea, a prayer.

And just as she had requested, when she came, she came with a great shout as the orgasm ripped through her in crashing waves. She was wrung out, and her heart was pounding out of her chest.

Jeffrey rose to his feet, and his smile was smug. At the

moment, she was too limp from the climax to care. He'd earned it. She'd thought he'd been good before, but the man had become a virtuoso.

"I believe I delivered on the screaming orgasm," he said with a smirk. He looked around the room. "And the ripping of the clothes." She gave a chuckle.

"I believe I requested multiple." With a saucy smile, she jumped off the table, and closed the drapes while he sat at an armchair. Maybe she didn't care in the heat of the moment, but the way she figured it, she'd already given the neighbors an earful. No need to give anyone more of an eyeful.

She turned back to Jeffrey. "Now where were we?" Her smile was sly and coy.

"It's up to you. Tonight's all about you." Taking him at his word, she tossed back her hair, walked over to the doorway and picked up a discarded scarf. Knowing that his eyes were glued on her every move, she consciously added a sassy sway to her hips with every step.

Cecily made her way back to him, put the scarf around his neck, and used it to bring him closer to her.

Using the momentum, she turned and pushed them toward the bed, both of them shedding articles of clothing as they went. Suddenly, he scooped her up and carried her over to the bed and unceremoniously dropped her on it. He threw the scarf aside and quickly grabbed a condom.

She bounced on the bed with a laugh but stopped as she got a good look at him. She shamelessly devoured his sculpted chest.

"Like what you see?" he asked, amused. In answer, she cupped his face and gave him a deep kiss, then pushed him back onto the sheets. Straddling his hips, she gave him a smile full of feminine secrets and power, leaned down and gave him a hard kiss. Cecily's hands reached out to grab the headboard for balance. She rolled her hips, her sex grinding against him, just where she needed it most, just the way she liked it. She closed her eyes as she settled into a rhythm. Her breath quickened as need and excitement built. Then suddenly, he grabbed a hold of her and stopped.

"Enough," he growled. "You're driving me crazy. I need to be inside you. Now. Right now." To emphasize his point, he leaned up and started torturing her nipple.

With a breathy moan Cecily readjusted and repositioned herself as she helped him put the condom on. Taking his cock in her hand, she placed it at her entrance. Her eyes never leaving his, she sank down, taking his cock into her, savoring it inch by inch. It felt like coming home. God, she had missed this, missed this man. Once she was fully seated to the hilt, they both groaned in mutual pleasure.

Then finally she moved. She rocked, trying to find the right rhythm and angle. She raised herself up slightly and the change made all the difference. He met her stroke for stroke. He seemed to be hitting some secret place inside her that set all of her nerve endings ablaze. And every time she pressed down, it gave her just the pressure and friction she needed against her clit. The combination was delicious and irresistible. Jeffrey was on his back, his eyes glazed.

Closing her eyes again, Cecily's hands went up to her breasts and she started playing with them experimentally. Her movements became more erratic the closer she got to the peak.

"Open your eyes," he ordered. Surprised, she looked at him.

"I want to see you. I want to see your eyes, your face when you come." His voice was harsh and guttural and knowing he was as lost in pleasure as she was excited her even further.

His hands came up to grip hers and intertwine as they continued to move together in perfect harmony.

"Gorgeous," he rasped. "The most beautiful thing I've ever seen."

Those words unlocked the dam, and Cecily came with a loud cry, spasms of pleasure racking her body, moved beyond words.

Jeffrey's climax came shortly after, and with a shout, he emptied himself inside of her, and was there to catch her when she collapsed on top of him, overcome.

HUMMING WITH PLEASURE, Cecily lay cradled in Jeffrey's arms, exhausted, sated, and blissfully relaxed. She burrowed deeper into the blankets and stretched, warm and happy. He was stroking her hair, making her purr. She turned to him and smiled.

"Happy?" he asked, his voice gravelly. Besides him getting up to remove the condom, they hadn't left the bed.

"Very." With a tender smile, Jeffrey leaned down and kissed her again.

"Enough screaming orgasms for one night?" he asked.

"Maybe, maybe not," she said with a raised brow. "But you were right about one thing."

He raised an inquisitive brow in turn.

"You have definitely learned a thing or two since the first time we did this." She gave him a cheeky grin.

He burst out laughing, deep from his chest.

"That was fifteen years ago. God." He shook his head.

Her hands snaked up his chest, drawing lazy patterns over his taut skin.

"I like to think we helped each other learn and improve." She brushed her lips over his.

"I still remember college graduation." They'd gone to the shore to celebrate for the weekend with a group of friends. They'd barely left the rental house.

"Ma did ask how I managed not to get sunburned," Cecily said with a grin.

Jeffrey shuddered. "We're naked in bed together. Please don't mention mothers."

She snickered. "Poor baby," she mocked.

In retaliation, he flipped her over and captured her hands above her head. "As much as I hate to say it, we are going to have a lot of explaining to do tomorrow."

She heaved a sigh. "I know. But I don't want to think about that. For right now, I just want to enjoy the rest of the night."

He shook his head. "But, CeeCee…"

Her heart squeezed at the use of the nickname.

He was not to be dissuaded. "At least tell me you no longer hate me. I'm not asking for forgiveness. That's too much. But I want to at least start earning your trust back. And the non-hate," he said with a self-deprecating smile. He let go of her hands and cradled her face with his hands.

At that Cecily melted. "I don't hate you. I never could. That's always been the problem," she whispered. Maybe at this particular moment her emotions were a messed-up jumble: she'd just made love with the man she had never been able to put out of her mind, she still had to face her family in the morning, and she had no idea how she was going to deal with any of it.

But for right now, she was going to enjoy this oasis, this temporary escape from real life. She'd earned it. And she was beyond grateful that she was with a man who understood that because, thank the Lord, he didn't push her any further.

Maybe she couldn't articulate how she felt, but she could show him. She wound her hands around behind his neck and brought him to her.

"I want you. I need you." It was the closest she could get to speaking her heart. As if he knew just what she needed, he gave her a slow deep kiss. Within minutes she was panting with want and desire again. She tilted her hips, impatient. He entered her slowly, and with deep strokes and soft caresses and murmured endearments, made love to her so thoroughly that her soul shattered from the beauty of it. When it was done and they both fell into a deep sleep cradled in each other's arms, she didn't know where she ended and he began. It was as if fate had put them together tonight and made them one again.

Chapter Seven

THE HARSH MORNING sun cut through the windows and into Jeffrey's eyes. He opened them with a groan. But that wasn't what woke him up. What woke him up was the sensation of Cecily's lips trailing kisses up his chest. Still foggy from sleep, part of him wondered if it was all a dream. If it was, he never wanted to wake up.

Cecily smiled at him, her expression as wicked and tempting as a witch. "I wondered how long it'd take you to wake up."

"I assure you, you now have my full attention," he said, his voice thick.

She hummed. "It occurs to me I never returned the favor last night. Allow me to make it up to you."

Before he realized what she had in mind, she slithered down his body, kissing him all the way down. Past his neck, past his chest, past his navel, past his hips. Then he understood. And every inch of his body approved. One body part in particular that was already awake and at attention.

Jeffrey scrounged up enough decency to put up a token protest. "You don't have to do this."

She looked up at him. "If you like, I can stop." She

raised a brow in challenge.

"Oh hell no," he burst out, before he could help himself.

Cecily smirked. "That's what I thought." She went back to work. When she finally used her hands to stroke his cock, he let out a grunt of pleasure. Cecily worked him with slow, sure strokes until he was ready to burst.

"God you're too good at this," he groaned.

"I'm only just getting started," she promised. She let go of him, and his body protested the loss. But then she replaced her hand with her mouth and it was even better. Never in his wildest dreams had he imagined he'd ever be with Cecily like this again, and the reality was better than any dream. He struggled to keep his eyes open so he didn't miss a moment. He watched his length disappear into her soft wet mouth and her tongue work him over, bathing every inch until he was rock hard. Her eyes sparkled with mischief and fun as she continued to torture him.

Before he knew it, he knew he was close, and he tried to warn her. But Cecily ignored him, and continued to stroke, lick, and suck, until he came long and hard, the spasms rocking his body. When he finally came back to earth, there was only one thing he could say.

"Best. Wake. Up. Call. Ever."

Cecily gave a rich laugh, and collapsed back on the bed.

Ready to take advantage of the light mood, he gathered her close to him, and then helped flip her onto her side. She craned her neck, gave him a quizzical look.

He smiled and leaned over to whisper in her ear, "I

think we're done with the loud portion of the program. I think it's time to play the 'Let's See How Quiet We Can Be' game."

The gleam in her eye told him she was more than game. She flipped her hair over her shoulder, gave him a saucy smile, and laid her face on the pillow. If her breathing, her flushed face, and her gleaming sex were any indication, she was already well on her way to being wet and aroused. He just needed to get her the rest of the way there. He lay on the bed behind her and forced her legs apart a few inches. He reached over and placed his hand on her nipples, rolling and teasing them until they turned into stiff peaks. Before he knew what she was doing, Cecily's hands came down to her sex and she started working her clit in quick feverish circles. It was the hottest sexiest thing he'd ever seen. She bucked against him as his hands and hers were working her most sensitive erogenous zones. He could smell her arousal, and her sex was dripping wet. Before long, she was whimpering with need. In a silent invitation, she opened her legs wider to grant him better access. Her breathing was now in pants and so was his.

"Please," she said in a whisper, still playing the game, and that was all it took. He grabbed a condom, rolled it on, and entered her quickly with one rough stroke that had her gasping. She grabbed the counterpane as he pumped into her from behind, both of them working together to create the perfect rhythm.

Lost in sensation, neither expected the climax that came over them both, and they rode the storm together, in perfect harmony.

After it was over, he went to the bathroom to remove the condom, then joined her back in the bed. But even after being so thoroughly pleasured, Cecily still had to have the last word. "I won," she said drowsily. Jeffrey laughed and gave her a light bite on her shoulder in retaliation.

"I'll settle for a tie," he said.

"We can negotiate later," she decided as they both fell asleep again, content and happy.

WHEN JEFFREY OPENED his eyes again, Cecily was dozing peacefully next to him. A burst of tenderness welled up inside him. He brushed her cheek and pulled up the blankets under her chin. She gave a soft sigh and snuggled in deeper. He was tempted to doze off again himself when he glanced at the clock on the nightstand. Crap.

He gave her shoulders a light shake. With a grumble, she batted his hand away. He gave a wry smile. Cecily never was and never had been a morning person. It was good to know some things never changed. He gave her a firmer shake. She cracked open one eye.

"What?" she growled, sleep coating her voice.

"As much as I would love to lounge around in bed with you, it's almost eleven. Checkout is noon."

"Oh shit." Cecily threw back the blankets and jumped out of bed. She ran into the bathroom, and for the next ten minutes he heard the water running. She came back out wrapped in a towel and immediately started bustling around the room, grabbing her clothes.

Jeffrey yawned, stretched and grabbed a sheet. He wrapped it around his waist and stood up. "I'm going to take a shower," he announced. Cecily ignored him, still gathering up her belongings. She came across the scraps of cotton that once constituted her panties. She threw him a look.

He shrugged unrepentantly. "Bill me." He left her to it and disappeared into the bathroom. The shower was just what he needed to clear his head. As the water cascaded over him, he tried to think about the next step. It was one thing for them to sleep together again, but it was a far cry from getting back to where they were, and earning back Cecily's trust to give him another chance.

She'd told him she didn't hate him and that was a good start. But what was the next step? He didn't have a lot of time left. So he better figure it out soon. He toweled off and opened the door. Cecily was sitting demurely at the edge of the bed, dressed and ready. Her hands were folded in her lap, and she was biting her bottom lip. A sure sign she was nervous and unsure of what to do or say.

"Everything okay?" He saw that his clothes were placed in a neat pile by the pillow. He grabbed his shirt and pulled it on, followed by his boxers.

"Can we talk for a minute?" He didn't like the sound of that.

She patted the spot next to her. "First of all, thank you for last night. I needed someone and you were there for me."

What the hell? "You're going to piss me off if you're going to act like I was doing you a favor by letting you use me for sex."

"No, that's not what I meant." She closed her eyes and groaned in frustration. "God. This is why I hate doing this. Talking about stupid feelings." She dropped her head into her hands. Typical Cecily.

He lifted her face by placing a finger under her chin. "Talk to me," he said softly. "What's going on in that head of yours?"

"First: no, I wasn't referring to you as a manwhore gigolo, okay? Let's get that out of the way first." *Manwhore gigolo? How did she come up with this stuff?*

"Duly noted," he said with a quirk of his lips.

"My feelings are a mess right now," she said bluntly. "But last night meant something to me. I don't know what, but it did. Obviously our history makes this complicated but those are the facts."

He felt encouraged. "I agree. It meant something to me too. I am not averse to taking this slowly, and seeing where it goes. You're going back to San Francisco, and I'm in L.A. At least we won't be across the country from each other."

"How did you know where I live?" Her voice was suspicious.

He gave her a look. *Really?* "I Googled you." The *duh* was implied.

She gave a dirty look in response. "My work schedule is crazy, and I am not looking for a relationship right now."

She held up a finger to ward off any argument. "That being said, I am also not going to ignore the fact that whatever is between us is still there. I'm stubborn but not stupid." She ignored his snort. "We can't go back to where we were," she warned. "But maybe I'm not averse to seeing where this goes either."

Cecily looked up at him through her lashes. "And I wouldn't be averse to more screaming orgasms in the future either." She bit her cheek.

He chuckled. "Glad to be of service." He stood up, grabbed her hands and lifted her until she was standing too. He took one of her hands, lifted it to his lips, and brushed it with a soft kiss. "I agree to your terms." But before she could be too relieved, he went on. "But I feel it's only fair to warn you that I intend to do everything in my considerable powers to get you back, like I said. So be prepared to be swept off your feet." With a wink, he quickly grabbed the rest of his clothes, and got ready to go. "And eventually, maybe we can even figure out a new living arrangement. It'd probably be easier for you to transfer to your firm's L.A. office, but we have time for that." He didn't miss the quick frown that crossed Cecily's face, and decided it was best to pump the brakes.

"But one problem at a time. Right now our biggest obstacle is sneaking home and not getting killed by our parents." To his relief, she shook her head in amusement, and grabbed her things.

With one hand on the small of her back, he raised his other hand to point the way. "Shall we?"

"Dear God. What have I gotten myself into?" she said as the door slammed shut behind them. But she couldn't hide the smile.

Jeffrey considered that a major win.

THIRTY MINUTES LATER, the taxi dropped them off two blocks away from their street. She looked at Jeffrey questioningly.

"You're the one who wanted to take things slow. Besides I figure we're both dead men walking. No point in making things worse by having them see us together."

Cecily nodded. "Good thinking."

"I have good ideas on occasion," he said drily. He paid and tipped the cabbie, and they got out. "You go on ahead. I'll duck into the bookstore and browse for ten minutes. I'll take the long way around and walk in the opposite direction."

"You are way too good at this."

"Writer," he reminded her. "This is the kind of stuff I think about all day."

"If you say so." Before she made her way to walk home, she gave in to her instincts and grabbed him for a long kiss.

"I'll see you soon," she whispered. She was gratified by the goofy grin on his face.

But the good feeling didn't last long. Every step she took toward her parents' house felt like one step closer to Judgment Day. A feeling that was confirmed when she opened the front door and was accosted by Gillian.

"You owe me. Big," she hissed, her hands digging into Cecily's arm like claws. She dragged them both down the hall into the kitchen.

"Ow, Gill!" she complained.

"Don't even, sis. Do you know what it took to keep Ma from calling the police last night?"

"I told you I was all right."

Her sister shot her a dirty look. "You're not stupid enough to buy that. And what the hell, CeeCee?"

Before she could explain, her mother came into the kitchen. Judith's eyes landed on her. Her eyes cooled, her lips pursed, and she turned around and left the room without a word.

Cecily would take a knock to the head, a half hour scolding and guilt trip over being iced out like this. When it came to waging emotional and psychological warfare, Judith Chang was a four-star general. A clear master who mowed down anyone in her path.

"Damn it," she muttered.

"You thought I was kidding?" Gillian shot her a *get real* look.

"I'll be lucky if she speaks to me before I leave."

With a shake of her head, Gillian left her to the wolves, and shouted at her daughter Diana to put down the bag of cookies.

Oh yeah, there was going to be hell to pay later.

DESPITE ALL HIS bravado, Jeffrey wasn't looking forward to facing his family any more than Cecily was. But there was no way to avoid it. He put the key in the lock, opened it as quietly as he could.

Any hope he had of returning unnoticed was shot to hell when his nephew Nate sounded the alarm. "Unca Jeff! Unca Jeff!"

He leaned down and scooped him up. "Hey, buddy." He tickled Nate's ribs and set off a storm of giggles.

Without a qualm, he decided to use his beloved nephew as a shield. They likely wouldn't do him bodily harm or ream him out in front of a small child. He heard noise in the living room and headed there. All eyes in the room turned to him. His siblings, cousins, and aunts and uncles galore. Fan-fricking-tastic.

"Hey, everyone," he said, deciding to brazen it out. Maybe if he pretended nothing was wrong, they'd follow his cue. Maybe they'd decide not to bring up such an awkward topic of conversation in consideration of the holiday.

He looked at the expression on his parents' faces. Yeah. No such luck. Jeffrey gave an inner sigh and braced himself for the worst. He put Nate down, who promptly scrambled away to join his cousins in the playroom. Traitor.

He saw one unexpected face in the crowd. "Becca!" His sister Rebecca was here all the way from D.C.? And she'd brought her kids too. Her husband Ryan must be around somewhere as well.

She came over and gave him a hug. "Hey, bro."

"What are you doing here?"

"Tradition, remember? What kind of daughter would I be if I didn't come back home to visit the day after? I managed to rearrange my schedule and come up for a few days." Ah yes.

She leaned into his ear and whispered, "Good luck." Then she whacked him across the back of the head.

"What was that for?" he demanded, as he soothed his stinging scalp. A former champion soccer player who was now a proud stay-at-home mom, Becca could still make him double over in pain, even while being under five feet tall.

"You're such an idiot," she muttered as she scooped up the kids and left him to face the wrath of the parents and aunties and uncles.

Auntie Lois was the first to speak. "Jeffrey." She was his mother's younget sister, and his favorite. Auntie Lois had always taken his side and stuck up for him, right or wrong.

"Hi, Auntie." He swallowed as he sat down next to her.

"Where did you go last night?" his father demanded.

"I found a hotel for the night."

"A hotel?" his brother Alex interjected. His younger brother was an IT guy living in Boston with his family. He pushed up his glasses and stared at him, fascinated.

"You ran out of here, and wasted money to stay at a hotel?" his mother asked.

He firmed his jaw. "It was my money to waste."

"Why are you acting like this?" she demanded. "What did we ever do to make you disrespect us like this?'

"I'm sorry I ran out of here last night," he gritted out. "And I didn't mean to be disrespectful." Good God. What was it about being back at home and around his family that regressed him back to being a sullen ten-year-old being called out on the carpet?

"We taught you better than that." The disappointment in his father's voice was more than he could take.

"Yes I know. I'm sorry I'm such a failure and disappointment," he bit out.

Auntie Lois took a look around the room. "Out," she commanded. In short order, the room emptied except for the four of them.

His parents looked shocked. "What are you talking about? We never said you were a failure or a disappointment."

Jeffrey scoffed. They had to be kidding. "You say it every time you bring up medical school. It's obvious you don't like what I'm doing and want me to give up the life I've chosen and live the way you want. I'm sorry I'll never be the doctor you wanted."

"Why do you think we're trying to control your life? We're just giving advice. We're trying to help." His mother's baffled expression would be laughable under other circumstances.

"By telling me to do things the way you want," he ground out.

"What's wrong with that?" his father demanded. "We're your parents. We're entitled to give you advice."

"They just worry about you, Jeffrey," Auntie Lois said

softly. "You live so far away. They never see you." That was the problem with Asian parents. They never talked about feelings or spoke directly. You were supposed to read the subtext to gauge their true intention. Oftentimes actions spoke louder than words. Jeffrey knew his parents loved him and showed it in their own way. The long hours they put in at work to provide for their family, the nagging, the feeding. It was just frustrating as hell when they refused to see his point of view.

"What happens if you can't get another writing job?" his mother asked. "Do you have a backup plan? If you go back to school, you have a backup plan. People always need doctors."

"I am doing fine, I already have three other projects lined up. If they don't work out, I'll figure out my next step. You raised me to be resilient and independent. I'm thirty-five years old. Don't you think it's time to trust me to make my own decisions? If you're worried about me moving back home, trust me, that's not going to happen." He crossed his arms.

His mother got up and wagged her finger at him. "I don't care how old you are. You will always be my child—that will never change. I will always worry about you. Show some respect."

This was going nowhere fast. He was about to bail again, when Auntie Lois ran interference, bless her. She turned to his parents. "He's always been like this. The more you prod, the more he digs in his heels. Stop trying to push him." Then she turned to him. "You know they mean well, so stop being so defensive." There was a three-way standoff as they stared at each other, seeing who was going to be the first to break.

Finally his father spoke. "I don't like it, and I'll never understand it, but I suppose I can stop pressuring you about going back to school." He let out a heavy sigh.

His mother implored, "Won't you at least consider it?" She crossed her arms defensively at the looks she got in response. "Fine." It was as close to capitulation as he was going to get.

Jeffrey let out a sigh of relief. This wasn't as bad as he thought it was going to be.

"Well maybe this is okay. Doctors work hard, long hours. Don't have much time for family. Maybe you'll have more time to meet a nice girl. I'm not getting any younger and I want more grandchildren."

Jeffrey resisted the urge to face-palm. His mother was relentless.

Martin looked at his watch. "Didn't you say you have a deadline? You should go back upstairs and work. You don't want to be late." So typical. They may accept that he wasn't going to be a doctor, but the sky-high expectations were still intact. He'd lay odds that before long, they'd be asking if he'd won any awards yet, or how many screenplays he'd sold that month.

"Actually, I was going to take a nap and work for a few hours before I pack to go home tomorrow."

"Don't nap. Go work!"

Jeffrey shook his head at his father's words and went up

the stairs.

His parents would probably never understand his work and would probably always wish he'd finished medical school, but at least this was a small step in the right direction.

He'd take it.

CECILY PACED AROUND her childhood bedroom, trying to figure out what to do. How was she going to explain where she was last night? Her family was going to insist on answers. And no way in hell was she going to tell them the truth. Then she flopped back onto her bed.

There was a perfunctory knock on the door, and her mother came in. Great. She should have known her reprieve would be short-lived. This was exactly what she needed: to face off against her mother when she was down and vulnerable and nowhere near her best, and her mother was clearly loaded for bear and ready to go.

Without ceremony, Judith stood at the edge of the bed, looming over her. "What is the matter with you?"

Cecily groaned. This was so typical of her mother. She sat up on the bed and assumed the proper shamed, repentant posture. She had a feeling she was about to fail Resolution 3 big time.

"I'm sorry, Ma, okay? I'll apologize to everyone before I leave."

"I don't care about that. But yes, you need to apologize.

I want to know why you ran off all night without telling us where you're going."

"It was fine. I was fine."

"Do you know how worried we were about you?"

"I'm sorry," Cecily said through gritted teeth.

"Where did you run off to?"

Her head reeling, she scrambled for a cover story. There was no way in hell she was telling the truth.

"I was at Rachel's." She said a quick prayer to the gods and the ancestors that she wouldn't be struck down for her lie. And for bringing poor innocent Rachel into her web of deception.

"What?"

"I went over and stayed at her place."

"Why? And why didn't you tell us where you were?"

"Don't want to talk about it," she muttered.

"Stop mumbling and answer my question. And look at me when I'm talking to you. Who taught you to speak to your elders like this? I know I taught you better. What is wrong with you?"

Most times her mother's tirades were mere annoyances. The easiest strategy was to tune her out and roll your eyes without getting caught. Let Judith vent and get it off her chest then move on.

Other times the ball of frustration, chaotic emotions and sheer unfairness were too much to bear and she couldn't take it anymore. Times when she hit the wall, because no matter what she was never going to be heard, much less understood.

This was one of those times.

"I need you to leave my room."

Judith's eyes widened in shock. "What did you just say to me?"

"I'm telling you to please get out. As respectfully as I can. I don't want to talk about this right now, and if you push me, I'm going to say something I can't take back. Please don't make me do that. I need some peace and privacy and want to be left alone. I *need* to be left alone. We can talk later."

"No child of mine acts like this." Judith's tone was one of disbelief, as if wondering where she'd gone wrong. She held on to one of the bedposts for support.

Cecily clenched her fists and forced her voice to remain calm. At the moment, that was a Herculean task. "Yes, I know I'm horrible and selfish. You can sue me later." Her mother's other hand rose, as if to slap her. And in that moment, Cecily probably would have taken it as her due. Especially if it would have gotten her mother out quicker.

Instead, the hand went back down, and her mother just shook her head. There was a flash of emotion in Judith's eyes that she couldn't identify, but it went as quickly as it came.

"All right, if that's what you want. We hardly ever see you, but if you want to be by yourself, fine. It's better than you ruining New Year's for everyone else with your attitude."

Judith let go of the bedpost and silently left the room, closing the door behind her with a soft snap.

Cecily sat on the bed, frozen. This should be a cause for celebration. She'd stood up to her mother and prevailed. She'd set boundaries and enforced them. So why did success feel so hollow?

Leave it to her mother to snatch victory from the jaws of defeat. Judith Chang always won. When would she learn to accept that?

Chapter Eight

AN HOUR LATER, Cecily stared at her phone like it was radioactive. She knew what she had to do, and she didn't want to. But she had no choice. Cecily bit her lip and took the plunge.

Hey, so I know we just had our bonding moment and we agreed we no longer hate each other, but I need your help with something.

If she had any hope of getting out of this latest predicament alive, she had to get a hold of Rachel stat and get her on board. Which was going to be a huge ask.

Thankfully, Rachel responded quickly. *Okay. What? I still haven't finished going through the paperwork you gave me.*

"Oh God. She's going to hate me." *It's not like that. This is more...personal.*

If you're asking for money, the answer is no.

Cecily gulped. *No. I just need you to cover for me. I got into a thing with my family last night, and it went south. I left for the night and just came home. I would prefer they not know where I was.*

And where do I come in exactly?

I was hoping I could tell them I was at your place? You offered to let me crash at your apartment for the night?

This is very weird.

I know, but I wouldn't ask if it wasn't urgent.

How would this even work? When would I have seen you? How would you even have known where I live? There is no record of you calling or texting me last night. You need a better plan.

She took a deep breath. *Okay. I know this is a big ask.*

Where did you really go last night? Why don't you want your parents to know?

I really don't want to talk about it. Please. And I promise I'll do my best to keep my family from calling you and prying. Or getting your parents involved. Maybe we can just tell them we were doing more work stuff.

Now you're making promises you can't keep. Damn Rachel Bai was a tough nut to crack.

My firstborn child?

Yeah, no.

Okay. Well thanks anyway.

Cecily threw the phone on the bed and sighed. Well, she'd given it her best shot, and she really couldn't blame Rachel for not agreeing to this crazy idea. She began to work on a Plan B. How feasible was it for her to sneak out of the house undetected and head back to California early? Now she really wished she'd taken up escape artistry as a hobby. That would have come in handy as Resolution 6.

She glanced up at the ceiling to make sure Confucius himself hadn't come down to smite her for even considering it.

A few minutes later, her phone pinged again.

Okay, I've thought about it. I'll help.

Oh my God. THANK YOU.

I figured you must be hella desperate to be coming to me. And offering up a hypothetical not-yet-born first child.

I promise I'll make it up to you, since you declined my firstborn. Thank goodness. Legally it probably wasn't enforceable but better safe than sorry. Her mother would seriously never forgive her otherwise.

I still don't know what this is about, but what the hell. What's the worst that could happen? This whole James Bond thing could be kinda fun.

You are a lifesaver, Rachel. THANK YOU. My next step was to pack, head back to JFK and beg American Airlines for mercy to get on an earlier flight.

Shit. You really must have been desperate.

You have no idea.

Okay. We'll talk at the community center. We can compare details, get our stories straight.

Great!

But I'm warning you now, if this goes sideways, I am throwing you under the bus without a second thought.

Fair enough.

This is Bai, Rachel Bai. Over and out.

Ha ha. Very funny.

You really want to mock the person you just begged for a lifeline?

Sorry. That was hilarious.

That's better.

Cecily decided it was safe to cross Resolution 4 off the list. Mission accomplished. If plotting and scheming, and threats weren't a sign of friendship, she didn't know what was.

JEFFREY WAS IN his room, immersed in the world of his screenplay. A light switch flipped in his head, and he was in the zone. The words were flowing out, almost faster than he could type. The protagonist finally made sense, and he had an ending in mind that wasn't trite and lackluster. It was just like the moment in *Xiao* when he finally figured out how Henry was going to come clean to his parents about his stand-up career and invite them to his next gig. He lived for days like this when the writing was going well. It made up for the days when he wanted to bang his head against the wall and writing five hundred words was like pulling teeth.

He was in the middle of writing a kick-ass fight and chase scene when his phone lit up with a text message. He told himself to ignore it and focus. Whoever it was could wait.

But eventually, curiosity got the better of him.

I just wanted to know if you were coming to the community center.

Their local community center always held a New Year's celebration for the entire neighborhood, complete with food, music, and dragon dances. And as many fireworks as local ordinances would allow.

Glad you're anxious to see me. I'll take it as a good sign. He grinned.

Never mind. I take it all back. Always with the sassy retort.

It'll be good to see you before we head out west.

There was a long pause before the text bubbles started going. Eventually, she responded.

I just wanted to give you fair warning. The families will be there and I didn't think it was fair for you to be ambushed.

I appreciate it. He really did. There was a time Cecily would have thrown him to the wolves without a qualm. He took this as a good sign.

Anyway, I'll see you tonight. There was another brief pause. *And maybe we can compare schedules and find a weekend for you to come up to San Francisco. I can show you around the city.*

Jeffrey resisted the urge to fist-pump. He didn't dare hope for total forgiveness or trust, but he would take whatever he could get.

Sounds like a plan. See you there. He tried to keep it cool and casual, though he felt anything but. He looked at his watch. He didn't have much time left.

He threw on his jacket and made his way downstairs. Screw work. He had more important matters to attend to.

Cecily: *Thanks again for covering for me, Rachel. It was great seeing you at the community center tonight. And for the photos of your apartment so we can sell the cover story if we need to.*

Rachel: *If I'm going to engage in espionage and covert activity, I want to do it properly.*

Cecily: *Well your thoroughness is appreciated.*

Rachel: *By the way, I meant to ask, what were you and Jeffrey Lee talking about? I saw you two in the corner together before you found me.*

Cecily: *Oh nothing...*

Rachel: *It looked serious. Pretty sure you weren't re-marking on the weather.*

Cecily groaned. Damn it, Rachel was too observant for

her own good. She thought she and Jeffrey had managed to be stealthy enough to escape notice but apparently not. They had spent a good half hour laughing at the adorable kids doing a dragon dance and just enjoying each other's company. And that was before he'd given her his New Year gift. Somehow he had found an old photo of the two of them as kids celebrating New Year's and framed it along with a single rose. The cuteness and nostalgia had almost been too much. Luckily she'd been able to stick that in her bag to avoid detection. When she'd protested that she didn't have anything for him, he'd just raised a brow and given her a devious look. And proposed she make it up to him back in California. The sneaky jerk. She wished she didn't find this as appealing as she did but Jeffrey had always known how to get to her. For better or worse.

Cecily: We were just talking about how cute the kids were doing the dragon dance. That's all.

Rachel: Yeah, right. Does this have anything to do with where you really were the other night?

Cecily: I will literally give you a hundred bucks if you drop the subject.

Rachel: Have it your way. I'll send you my PayPal info.

Cecily: Done.

Rachel: If there's nothing else I'm going to say good night. I have an early day tomorrow.

Cecily: And I need to get back to work. So, night!

It took another hour but Cecily was finally able to wrap up her last email and call it a night. And now she was starving. She made her way down the stairs when she heard voices coming from Owen's old bedroom. Unless she was mistaken it was Auntie Marcia, who'd apparently decided to stay the night.

"Judith, you need to be careful." Cecily's brows furrowed. Was her mother trying to move furniture around?

"I'm just moving your suitcase to the corner so no one trips and gets hurt."

"That's not what I meant."

"Then what?"

"Judith, you need to ease up on Cecily. I heard you two talking earlier and it wasn't right." Frozen on the landing, Cecily could only stay still as a statue as she shamelessly eavesdropped.

"What are you talking about? I was just doing my job." Cecily rolled her eyes. A typical response from her mother.

"I'm telling you, you are too hard on her. She's already an adult, let her be." Cecily had to marvel that it was Auntie Marcia of all people who was sticking up for her. Auntie Marcia was her mother's youngest sister, and had always been quieter and more reserved.

"A child will always need their parents' advice and guidance." Despite everything, Cecily had to admire her mother's ability to constantly channel the swagger and confidence of a mediocre straight white man. It was an enviable skill she was still working on herself.

Auntie Marcia gave an inelegant snort. "You keep telling her how to do her job, what she's doing wrong, every time she falls short. All criticism. If that's all she hears, that's not healthy."

It felt like the wind was knocked out of her. How did Auntie Marcia *know*? She would suspect her aunt of bugging her apartment, phone, or email or something, except she knew that her aunt was technologically challenged at best.

"Marcia, you're talking nonsense. I'm not criticizing, I'm helping. I push because I care. If I didn't think she could be better, why would I bother? You make it sound like I'm being cruel for no reason. Kids these days who get participation trophies instead of having parents to teach them to work hard and come back from failure—now that's cruel." Cecily stood there, riveted. Part of her understood where her mother was coming from, but that didn't mean being on the receiving end of that tough love wasn't hard. And as for that last bit, it sounded nice in theory except for the fact that failure was not an option in the Chang household growing up.

"You really don't see that you're doing to her what Ma did to you? And look how that turned out. You rebelled and lashed out, and Ma clamped down even harder, which just made you angrier. You hated how hard Ma was on you. You two were barely on speaking terms for a few years. All I'm saying is don't make the same mistake. Trust that you and Paul did a good job raising her and let her be. Do better. Talk to Cecily, damn it."

Cecily let out a small gasp of shock and quickly covered her mouth. This was totally mind-boggling information. As far as she knew, her Amah was the sweetest, kindest person in all of creation, always ready to spoil her grandchildren with food, toys, and treats whenever they visited her in Taiwan. Amah always fussed over them and lavished praise and affection. In fact, Cecily would be hard pressed to remember a single incident of Amah raising her voice. After all this time, to realize the apple had not fallen far from the tree. At all. It was near impossible to wrap her mind around the fact that Amah had been just as much of a hard-ass as her mother. Consider her gobsmacked.

"Oh please," Judith scoffed. "That's totally different. Ma was all stick, no carrot, and I was a stupid teenager. That doesn't count. Of course Cecily knows I love her—that goes without saying." Cecily did know that but it was still nice to hear every once in a while, among all the pushing, nagging, criticism, and "help".

"That's just my advice—take it or leave it. But don't come running to me if she decides you're holding too tight and you lose her for good." Auntie Marcia's voice was skeptical.

And suddenly Cecily couldn't breathe and her knees almost buckled. This was too much to process at once. It almost felt like she'd been looking at her relationship with her mother through a kaleidoscope and had settled in on one familiar pattern, and with one small tilt, she was getting a completely different image. An image made of the same colors but rearranged as if it was brand new and totally different. On a deep fundamental level, part of her knew everything her mother was saying, and where Judith was coming from, but good God sometimes it was hard to remember.

That didn't mean she should let her mother run rough-shod and always get her way. As Auntie Marcia said, she was a goddamn adult now, and she had every right to establish some boundaries and expect a modicum of respect. But she could do a better job of extending some grace and remembering that even if the way it came out drove her up the wall, her mother's intentions were good and she only wanted the best for her.

"Right now, the only problem Cecily and I have is that she's locking herself in her room and won't see or talk to anyone. I don't care how busy she is with work, or how important she thinks she is now that she's some big-shot lawyer. That's not okay. She needs to spend time with the family."

She heard Auntie Marcia heave a big sigh. "I don't even know why I bother. It's late and time for me to go to bed. I'll see you in the morning."

Cecily took that as her cue to dash back into her room before she got caught snooping. Closing the door as quietly as she could, she leaned back against it and put a hand to her chest.

The Lunar New Year had barely begun, and the ancestors were already conspiring to make her work for her list of resolutions. She wasn't built to handle all these emotional bombshells. She liked dealing with facts, not messy human emotions. Stupid feelings. Now she was going to have to sit with this and reevaluate a bit. Life was much simpler when she could just be frustrated with her mother; now she really had to consider all the nuances and shades of gray. Ugh.

But she was still starving and wanted a snack. She put her ear to the door and listened for any sound. After a few minutes, she decided it was safe and tiptoed back downstairs.

Cecily heard a rustle behind her and turned her head to see her father coming down the stairs. She'd just finished raiding the fridge and was stuffing her mouth.

"What are you doing up so late? Couldn't sleep either?" he asked.

"Nope," Cecily said over a mouthful of spicy noodles.

"What are you eating?"

"My feelings." Normally she'd be ashamed to admit to such a weakness and be seen in such a low moment. But this was her father. She'd always been able to tell him anything.

"What?" With a puzzled frown, Paul looked at his daughter. "Who eats feelings? That makes no sense." Wearing worn twenty-year-old pajamas, her father shuffled into the kitchen. His eyes were alert, not bleary, meaning he'd been staying up late too.

Cecily gave a sigh and pushed the bowl of noodles away. "Never mind. I don't think I'll be able to explain it properly."

"Why aren't you eating the ice cream like a normal person?" After grabbing a carton of Breyer's Butter Pecan out of the freezer, her father put it on the kitchen table, and in his methodical way, got two bowls from the cabinet, and the ice cream scooper, and spoons. He scooped a generous portion for each of them and slid one bowl over to his daughter, and they both dug in.

"I'm sorry about last night, Daddy," she confessed. "I know I shouldn't have run out or talked the way I did. I just couldn't help it. You know how Ma is."

Paul nodded slowly. "Yes, I do. I've been married to the woman for almost forty years." He gave her a look. "And I also know you."

"What does that mean? And why are you taking her side?"

Her father cleared his throat and she felt ten years old all over again.

"I'm not saying your mother is perfect. But she's still your mother. She doesn't always do it the right way, but she's showing she loves you and she cares, the way she knows how. You need to meet her halfway. She's trying, honey." Deep down she knew her father was right. It was just hard to remember when her mother inevitably reduced her to a flaming ball of rage and frustration.

"You're right, but it's so hard. She gets under my skin and I just want to scream," Cecily muttered through a gulp of ice cream.

"I know. And you know why that is, don't you?"

She saw the look on her father's face. "Don't say it," she said with a wag of her spoon.

Her father just chuckled. "The two of you are too much alike for your own good," he persisted. "That's why you two butt heads. Neither of you want to listen. It's been like this since you were a baby. I still remember when you were three. You didn't want to eat your spinach. The two of you sat at the kitchen table until midnight." She groaned, the words stinging her ego.

"I don't want to listen to any more slander." Cecily pouted. "That could be the meanest thing you've ever said to me, Daddy."

With a chuckle, Paul walked over and dropped a kiss on the top of her head.

"The truth hurts, honey. You feeling better?" he asked in Mandarin. She nodded. Her father had always been her calm in the storm. She always felt better after talking with him.

"Good, I'm heading up to bed," he said. "Take care of this before you go upstairs, will you?" He gestured toward the mess they'd made.

"Sure. Night, Daddy."

Before he left the kitchen he casually tossed over his shoulder, "And by the way, in the interest of maintaining the peace, I suggest you make sure your mother doesn't find out you're seeing Jeffrey again."

She gasped in horror. How did he know? They'd been so careful. But apparently not careful enough.

"Who told? How did you find out?"

Paul rolled his eyes and shook his head. "I told you, you're my child. I raised you. Don't you think I know you by now? You have no secrets from me."

That was comforting and horrifying at the same time. All Cecily could do was continue to stare at her father wide-eyed.

"Don't worry, I won't tell your mother," were his last words before he disappeared upstairs.

Well crap.

Chapter Nine

S HE WAS BACK at JFK airport. One hundred twenty hours. She'd survived. Barely by the skin of her teeth, but she'd survived nonetheless. Her whole family had insisted on accompanying her to the airport and she'd had to deal with the noisy goodbyes and her mother's fussing before ditching them to go through TSA security.

As much as Cecily hated to admit it, she was glad she'd come back home, messy drama and emotional upheaval and all. So what if Resolutions 1 to 3 fell by the wayside a bit? She never claimed to be perfect. She may not have avoided drama, had overworked, and lost her cool with her family, but she'd made a new friend. So it wasn't a total loss.

She was more than ready to get back to her life in San Francisco, but it was good to see her family again. And of course eating all the food. In fact, she was schlepping a ton of it back home. Her fridge would be stocked and she'd have leftovers for days.

Cecily sighed and leaned back in her seat as she waited at her gate. There was still one dangling loose thread she had to contend with.

Jeffrey.

In a million years Cecily had not expected to sleep with her ex again. The ex who had done her super wrong and super dirty. But somehow it had happened. It had been a mistake. The sex had been amazing but still a mistake.

Clearly, he was sorry and was hoping they could start over, and initially she'd been open to the idea. She'd even suggested showing him around San Francisco. But now she wasn't so sure.

In a way it was good that she'd run into him even though it was the last thing she'd ever wanted. Like she'd told him, the worst thing about what he did was that she had no explanation, and the question of why had been nagging at her the past ten years. Now, finally, she'd gotten an answer from him, of sorts. Now she had closure and could move on with her life. Chalk up the night at the Lannister as a random crazy fluke brought on by stress and excess emotions. She could totally plead mitigating circumstances. She shouldn't be held liable for one moment of temporary insanity.

Maybe she was ready to start letting go of the hurt and resentment she held toward Jeffrey, but that was a long way from agreeing to pick up where they'd left off. She had too much on her plate right now to handle navigating a complicated relationship with her ex on top of it all. It would be smarter and more sensible to avoid that particular land mine. She didn't even want to think about how her mother would react. Cecily gave a small shudder.

The best thing to do was to forget about the sex and embrace the fact that she was starting the process of moving past what happened ten years ago. Cecily wasn't sure if she was capable of forgive and forget, but for sure letting go of that emotional weight would be fantastic. She no longer had to boil over in fury at the thought of Jeffrey and wish all manner of ills on his head. If they ever ran into each other back in Brooklyn again, they could be polite and cordial in public.

As polite and cordial as anyone could be with someone who they'd been naked with. Multiple times.

UGH. Cecily gave a small shake of her head and tried not to face-palm. It was already too complicated. It would definitely be easier to make a clean break. Wish Jeffrey well and let him know that she really didn't think it'd be a good idea for them to try to restart a relationship.

As she got up to board her flight, she started forming the email/text in her mind the next time Jeffrey tried to reach out to her.

It was for the best. For everyone involved. Really.

She perfected the wording in her mind as she made her way past the gate agent down the jetway and found her seat. She heaved her carry-on into the overhead compartment and settled into her seat.

Instead of waiting to respond to Jeffrey, she should just do it now. There was no point in prolonging the inevitable. Before she lost her nerve, she grabbed her phone, and quickly typed in the text, like ripping off a Band-Aid. It was best to get it over with before she gave herself too much time to think and second-guess herself.

Once she was done, Cecily gave it one more pass to

make sure there were no typos or errors then nodded. Then she pressed send before she could take it back. Thankfully the captain announced that the plane was ready to taxi and take off so she turned off her phone.

Now that that was done, she grabbed her jacket, turned it into a makeshift pillow, and slept like the dead for the rest of the plane ride.

You have got to be kidding me.

Reading Cecily's text with a sinking heart, Jeffrey shook his head in disbelief. He couldn't believe she'd done such a one-eighty on him in less than twenty-four hours.

I know I said I was open to giving whatever this is between us another shot, but I think I was just caught up in the moment. Now that I've had time to think, it's way too complicated. I really don't see how it could work. But I'm glad we could clear the air, and now we can move on without all that baggage. Let's just go back to giving each other our space. No hard feelings, okay? Good luck with your new script.

He couldn't blame Cecily really. She was probably right when she said the whole thing was too complicated and was best left alone. But he'd thought they'd made some progress over the holiday weekend, and it sucked to know he was back to square one.

The question was, what now? He wished there was a way to change her mind without coming across as stalker-y and too aggressive. The last thing he wanted was to have Cecily think she was dealing with a *Fatal Attraction* situation. The ball was in her court and that's how it had to stay.

It was going to be a tricky line to walk. But it was obvious that what had been between them ten years ago was still there or they wouldn't have ended up in bed together, and he was loath to give up on it quite yet. The problem was how to convince Cecily, while respecting her boundaries.

Nothing ventured, nothing gained. The first step would be to simply ask her if there was any way she would possibly change her mind. Based on her answer, he'd take it from there.

CECILY SHOOK HER head. The man was as persistent as hell. She was looking at an email from Jeffrey, where he'd asked her to "state the terms under which she would change her mind and consider going out to dinner with him." It was less than twenty-four hours since she'd sent him the text and he was already back at it.

Her response was short and to the point. *I said what I said. I don't think it's a good idea, and that won't change, even if you offer a million dollars.*

Obviously, she had been joking about the million dollars but she was serious about her decision, and resolved to stand firm. Though she couldn't deny part of her had been curious to see how he'd respond.

His reply was lightning quick. *Is that a challenge?*

Cecily rolled her eyes and shot back a reply. *NO.*

Within seconds her email pinged again. *Too late. You've thrown down the gauntlet and I must respond. A million dollars it is.*

Are you telling me you have a million dollars lying around?

I do all right for myself, but…no. I'm going to have to look into black market organ donation. All for you. I hope you appreciate the lengths I'm willing to go to here.

Is that supposed to sway me? She sent along a YouTube link of Shania Twain's "That Don't Impress Me Much". She was never going to let him know how amused she was.

If things go wrong, I could name you as my main beneficiary in my will. And life insurance. So either way you get something out of it.

Then you better get busy. Changing wills and life insurance policies takes time.

Wow. That's cold.

You're the one who suggested it, not me. Just stating facts here.

I get no credit for risking my life and being willing to go under the knife for you?

So far all I see is talk. Come back to me when you follow through with some action.

Will do. Do I need to hire a lawyer to write my will, or can I use some online templates?

Oh for God's sake. You're impossible. How did he always do this? She'd sworn to cut off all ties and now they were emailing back and forth. And damn if she wasn't having fun.

Does this mean you've changed your mind?

NO.

You really are a tough nut to crack.

Then save your time and give up.

I didn't say you weren't worth it. If organ donation to raise money won't work, I'll have to figure out what will.

Good luck with that.

Thanks, I'll need it. Stay tuned.

Cecily left the last email unanswered. Really, what was there to say? The line about her being worth the effort was a sneak attack against her defenses. And she'd be lying if she said she wasn't curious about what Jeffrey was going to do next. She better be prepared for anything. It sounded like he was preparing to pull out all the stops. Forewarned was forearmed.

A FEW DAYS later, Cecily was buried under a pile of work, papers spread out all over her desk, her eyes glued to her monitor, when she heard a knock on her door. She looked up, slightly annoyed.

"Yes?" This was her first day back at the office after being away for New Year's and she was already horribly behind. She couldn't afford to waste time with interruptions. She had taken two days to work from home and was still jet-lagged.

Her assistant Priscilla poked her head in. "Hey. Don't shoot the messenger."

Cecily sighed and rolled her eyes. "Sorry didn't mean to bite your head off. It's been a very Monday type of day."

"Well maybe these will cheer you up." Priscilla ducked out and came back with a huge bouquet of variegated tulips. The red, orange and yellow was like a beautiful sunset. Before she could stop herself, her heart gave a little flutter.

"These just came for you."

Priscilla walked over and placed the vase on the side table in her office. "Let's just leave this here for now."

"That works. I'll have to find a nice vase to put them in at home." She walked over to examine the blooms more thoroughly. Her fingers ran over the soft petals. Then she began to poke around for a card. Who could have sent her the flowers? This wasn't a typical thank-you gift from a client, it wasn't her birthday, so she was at a complete loss.

"Is there a card?" she murmured, still staring.

"As a matter of fact, yes." Priscilla walked back outside and came back. "This also came with it," she said, producing a card and a small white cardboard box. Her eyes were wide and curious.

Cecily took the card and box and went back to her desk. Priscilla remained standing, with an expectant look on her face.

"Is there anything else?"

"Aren't you going to open it?" her assistant demanded.

"Not right now, no. I'm busy."

"You're no fun," Priscilla complained as she marched back out of the room.

"Get back to work," Cecily called out. "And close the door."

With a sniff, Priscilla did as she was told. The door closed with a smart click.

Cecily gave it thirty seconds to make sure she wouldn't

be caught, then tore the card open. The note was short and simple.

> *Flowers are classic, and they say the quickest way to someone's heart is through their stomach, so here's hoping it works. Stay tuned for part 2.*

The card wasn't signed but it didn't have to be. It could only be one person. Impatient, she also opened the rest. The cardboard box contained half a dozen gourmet red velvet cupcakes and another envelope. Tearing the envelope open, she came face to face with a huge stack of Monopoly money.

Before she could stop herself, she let out a hearty laugh. This was so typical.

The bastard was on a charm offensive.

And damn if it wasn't working.

The fact that he'd turned her words around on her by sending Monopoly money appealed to her sense of humor, and she had to be impressed by the creativity. She was willing to bet he'd printed out a million dollars' worth of fake money. He'd even used an array of different colors, to complete the effect. As much as she hated to admit it, he was earning points.

However.

Just because they'd slept together didn't mean she was ready to forgive and forget. She'd told him she was hesitant, and had reservations, and she meant it. No way was she going to let him back in and give him the chance to rip her heart apart again. No matter how good he was in bed.

But the fact that he still remembered her favorite flowers and her favorite cupcakes even after all these years had to mean something. And he was trying.

Cecily looked over at the flowers again and couldn't help smiling.

She gave herself a stern talking-to. "Stop mooning and get back to work. You know better than to fall for something like this. It's just flowers. And cupcakes. And fake money."

Except apparently she didn't.

She was in serious trouble.

There was a knock on the doorway and her head shot up. Adrienne was in the entrance.

"You ready?"

"Yeah, come on in."

Adrienne came in and rubbed her hands in glee. They finally managed to sync up their schedules to have lunch. Cecily had lugged in a ton of New Year's leftovers for them to share, and she couldn't wait to dig in. Once her mother had found out Adrienne was deprived of New Year's goodies, she'd gone overboard. Her carry-on suitcase coming home was basically all food.

"I don't know about you, but I'm starving." Then her best friend's eyes caught the flowers and other gifts.

"What's going on here?"

"Nothing."

"A large bouquet of flowers is not nothing. And are those cupcakes I spy?"

"Keep this up, and I won't share." The threat was empty and she knew it, but it was all she had at the moment.

Adrienne's brow rose as she saw the manila envelope full of money.

"What's this about? You're holding out on me."

"I don't want to talk about it," Cecily mumbled.

"This is a violation of the Girl Code."

"Don't bother. I couldn't get anything out of her either," Priscilla's voice cut in. "I'm heading out to lunch. Just wanted to let you know."

"Okay."

Pris then turned her attention to Adrienne. "If you manage to pump any information out of her, let me know."

"You got it."

Priscilla closed the door again and left the two of them alone.

"Why don't you go grab us a couple bottles of water while I set everything up?" Cecily walked over to the mini fridge she'd put in the corner and brought out the plastic containers of food.

"Nice try." Her best friend dug into her huge tote purse and pulled out two large bottles of water.

"Great, that will save us time. I just need to go nuke this in the microwave."

Adrienne shook her head. "You really doing this?"

There were times she hated that her best friend knew her so well, and this was one of them. Cecily blew out a breath. "This right here is why I'm glad I'm looking for a new friend."

Her complaint was dismissed with an eye roll and a flick of the wrist. How rude.

"You know you wanna tell me. Come on, give it up."

"Let's do an exchange. Six months ago, you stopped talking to Noah over in Governmental Affairs. Why is that? You go first."

The two of them had a silent standoff. With a shake of her head, Adrienne barked out a laugh.

"You play dirty, but fine."

"So how about we both keep our mouths shut and enjoy this food?"

"Deal."

JEFFREY WAS ENJOYING a rare night off. He was on the couch, watching the basketball game. Home-team loyal to the last, he was a Knicks guy all the way, despite the pain and misery that entailed. He was shoveling in a double order of samosas and lamb tikka masala as he yelled at the screen.

"Why do I do this to myself?" he grumbled at halftime. It wasn't going well. He was tempted to turn off the TV, but as a glutton for punishment, or someone with a slight masochistic streak, something compelled him to wait and ride it out to the bitter end.

Just then, he got a text. When he saw who it was from, he grinned. After he sent the flowers, cupcake and fake money last week, he'd been wondering what to do next.

He'd only gotten a quick thank-you text from Cecily, and she hadn't engaged since.

The idea he'd come up with for his next move was pretty inspired if he did say so himself. He'd drawn on his lifelong knowledge of Cecily and used it to his advantage. Her favorite foods, books, places, et cetera.

As usual, Cecily didn't disappoint.

You bastard.

The usual response in this type of situation is "Thank you".

Thank you. You bastard.

If you don't like it, you can always send it back. I can always give it to someone else.

Wow. You really trying to piss me off right now?

He could just picture her furrowed brows and wrinkled nose as she texted in annoyance.

I admit it wasn't the EXACT version of Little Women *you had, but it still looked nice. And I went to a lot of trouble to track down a signed copy of* The Joy Luck Club. *If you don't want it, I can donate it to a charity fundraiser.*

Even he had to admit sending a copy of *Little Women* had been a stroke of genius. She'd blamed him for tripping her when they were racing home from school one day and the book had flown out of her backpack and into a nasty rain puddle.

He still maintained innocence, but he figured it would be a good gambit to help soften her up.

There was a pause as he waited for a reply.

You're really reaching right now, aren't you?

Don't you like Amy Tan's books anymore?

That question is disrespectful.

Don't I get any points here? I mean, it was as close as I could get to a Hawaiian tropical getaway. I thought you'd appreciate it. Do you know how expensive mangoes and pineapples are this time of year? Not to mention the Kona coffee and macadamia nuts.

Ever since they were kids, Cecily had been obsessed with Hawaii, so he knew he couldn't go wrong there.

What possessed you to do this?

You know why.

When he didn't get a response, he felt compelled to ask. *Is it working?*

No comment. He was going to take that as a yes.

You know, most women would salivate at a gift certificate for a weekend at a spa. Part of the getaway vibe. It may have been overkill, but he figured in such cases as these, it was go big or go home.

I'm not most women.

Why do you think I'm doing this?

The guava candy was really unfair though. And the Pocky sticks. That was a low blow. He'd sent along two pounds of her favorite guava hard candy. They were Cecily's favorite candy growing up, and he had been betting that was still the case. They weren't always easy to find, even in Asian markets, so tracking them down was a real coup. It looked like his gamble had paid off. Big time.

Like I said, if you're really unhappy, you can give it back.

You'll have to pry my candy from my cold dead hands.

Wow that's violent.

You deserve it.

He paused. *Harsh but fair.*

But you've convinced me to not physically hurt you.

Color me relieved.

It wouldn't be worth it. Too much evidence. But to be clear, verbal insults are still in play.

Understood.

And maybe I hate you 20% less than I used to.

That's progress. I'll take it.

Make that 15%.

Jeffrey decided to stop while he was ahead. Fifteen percent? He could work with that.

Now the question became, what was his next move going to be? Whatever it was, it had to be good.

CECILY LOOKED AT the email sitting unread in her inbox like her computer had gone radioactive. She was waiting for documents from opposing counsel when it popped up. The minute she'd seen who the sender was, her body had gone on full alert.

The subject line said *Important Message*. With great trepidation, she opened the email. The only thing in the body of the email was a link to a YouTube video.

Cecily turned her neck left and right before she clicked on it. Then she made sure the volume on her speakers was turned down as low as possible. Whatever this video contained, she didn't want Pris or Adrienne, or anyone to hear it. It had been a week since he'd sent her that "care package" and she'd been on pins and needles wondering what his next move would be and when the other shoe was going to drop.

It was a short thirty-second video, marked *private*. Which also raised red flags. But she forgot all about it the minute she saw who it was on the video.

There was Daniel Henney in the flesh, in jeans and a dark T-shirt and sneakers. Looked like he was on set somewhere. Still ridiculously handsome. He gave a small wave and started talking.

"So hi, Cecily? It's Daniel. I'm not sure who you are, but I was asked to do this video as a favor for a friend. I also don't know who Jeffrey is, but I'm told he's a nice guy? So please go out with him. Give the guy a chance. And thanks so much for being a fan, really appreciate it. Okay bye." The clip ended there, and Cecily sat at her desk in shock and awe for at least five minutes.

How had he managed to pull this off? And what was she going to do about it? She had to admit, this gesture was checking all of her boxes, as ridiculous as it was. That, plus the flowers and gift basket. A girl could only hold out for so long. It was the peril of being involved with someone who'd known you since birth. They knew all your weak spots. And even after ten years, Jeffrey still hadn't lost his touch. Sigh.

If he was going to these lengths, the least she could do was give him a chance and hear him out. After all, she'd only be committing to a date. How hard could that be? What's the worst that would happen? It's not like she was agreeing to walk down the aisle again. Just a date. A civilized meal between two people. She could milk this for a while and let him grovel and keep trying to make it up to her. She deserved some perks for what he'd put her through, right? Never let it be said she wasn't a forgiving and charitable soul, allowing someone who'd wronged her deeply to make amends.

She could even work on Resolution 2 with this—getting out of the office at a reasonable hour to have dinner had to count.

But for now, she was going to let him twist in the wind for a bit. It would serve him right. She wasn't going to let him know he'd won that easily.

It was no one's business but hers that she favorited the video and bookmarked it so she could access it whenever she wanted.

And if Priscilla and her coworkers wonder why she was smiling like an idiot the rest of the day, well that was her business too.

JEFFREY LOOKED AT his phone and laptop, willing it to ping with some sort of response from Cecily. Unbelievable. The woman was as stubborn as a cantankerous mule. Or an Asian mother determined to break her children's spirit through sheer force of will. It had been two days since he'd sent the video and he had yet to hear a word from Cecily.

If she had any idea what he'd gone through to make that video happen, she wouldn't be so cavalier. He'd called in just about every favor he could, and made an idiot of himself in the process. Swallowing his pride and admitting to Greg what he needed and why, and having his best friend laugh until he cried was something he never wanted to do again.

But he thought it would be worth it. If the video wouldn't soften her up and win her over, nothing would.

His phone rang and he almost sprained a muscle grabbing at it.

"Hello?" he asked, his voice out of breath.

"Hey, loser."

"Oh, it's you."

"Try to contain your enthusiasm," his sister drawled.

"Sorry, was just hoping it was someone else."

Beth gave an inelegant snort. "No shit. Let me guess. Would this someone happen to be about five foot four, an attorney, and have the initials C.C?"

"Shut up. What do you want?" he muttered.

"Is that any way to talk to your beloved sister?"

"You always want something."

"Well now that you mention it, I could use your help with a thing."

"You want a kidney don't you?" Jeffrey knew the bill would come due someday, but it always managed to take him by surprise whenever Bethany cashed in her IOUs. Now he was going to have to go all John Q and find a black market kidney because of his devious kid sister.

"What? No, you weirdo. Who would ask for a kidney?"

"Name your terms," he said with a deep sigh.

"Don't be like that. All I need is some help moving when I head down to Johns Hopkins for med school. I found an apartment and I'm gonna need you to help pack, schlep, and move boxes. Not until the end of July, but I'm staking my claim now. Put it on your calendar."

That didn't sound too bad. "Done. Anything else?"

"No, that's it. What's going on with you? Why are you so pissy?"

"I'm not pissy."

"Whatever. Why are you waiting to hear from CeeCee?"

"I don't want to talk about it."

"Spill," Bethany ordered.

"I'm older than you, you know."

"Look, do you want my help or not?"

"Who said I was asking for help?"

Bethany let the silence hang and speak for her.

As always, when it came to Beth, Jeffrey crumbled.

"Okay, fine. Maybe I could use your help." He briefly explained the situation, how he was trying to convince Cecily to go to dinner with him, and why they were currently at an impasse.

"I can fix this." Bethany's tone was confident.

"How?" he asked suspiciously.

"I don't think you should ask too many questions. The less you know, the better."

"You sound like a mobster—you know that right?"

"It's better this way," she assured him.

"I'm already regretting it, but okay." He sighed.

"Excellent. And this means you also buy the beer and pizzas for us for the move. And the rental for the U-Haul and gas. Thanks, big bro." Bethany clicked off, leaving him staring at his phone in bemusement.

How did she always do this?

BUT BETHANY WAS as good as her word. Not even forty-eight hours later, he heard from Cecily.

So I was talking with Bethany. She had a great suggestion.

I'm officially scared.

I propose we have dinner at Tokaido.

A quick Google of Tokaido revealed that it was a Michelin-starred restaurant and considered one of the most expensive restaurants in San Francisco. He blinked at the prices.

You have a craving for Japanese?

More a craving for draining your wallet. Your sister suggested I take it as an opportunity to get a first-class meal for free. To live it up, and I can't say I disagree.

So my sister gave you this recommendation, did she? What would I do without her? He made a mental note to thank Bethany later. Like by letting their parents know what time she really got home from homecoming when she was in high school.

I was leaning in that direction before she contacted me. Besides, I've wanted to eat there forever, but it's way out of my price range.

But not mine?

That's a you problem, not a me problem. And bear in mind, I will be trying the sakes too.

Fine. You can eat. I won't. That's the only way I'll be able to afford this.

Those are my terms. Do you accept or not?

You drive a hard bargain. Deal.

Good. I made a reservation for next Saturday night. 7 p.m. Don't be late.

What would you have done if I'd said no?

I'd cancel the reservations and go on with my life. And continue to avoid you like the plague. Not sure what answer you were expecting.

I'm your literal meal ticket?

I think I'm entitled to a little fun and payback don't you? I don't think a nice meal is too much to ask.

See you next Saturday.

Dress appropriately.

Yes, Mom.

Cecily sent back an unamused-face emoji. Sensing he was pressing his luck, Jeffrey left it at that.

It was going to cost him, dearly, but he was going to take this opening. Cecily was worth it.

Chapter Ten

CECILY STRODE THROUGH the restaurant with a casual confidence he envied. As an attorney, she was probably accustomed to high-end places like this and dealing with movers and shakers, but a part of him was still a Brooklyn boy at heart. Even though he'd been to his share of Hollywood events, he couldn't help feeling a bit out of place. It was so in-your-face upscale. Give him a hole-in-the-wall restaurant with cheap but delicious food any day.

She was wearing a red and white floral wrap dress that looked incredible on her. And skyscraper heels that made him wince just looking at them.

"Nice dress," he commented.

Cecily raised a warning brow. "I'm dressing appropriately for the venue. This has nothing to do with you."

"Noted." So that was how she was going to be.

She sat down opposite him and opened her menu.

The waiter came over to their table and discreetly poured them both a glass of ice water. Then he saw Cecily and immediately beamed.

"Ms. Chang, how lovely to see you again."

"Hi, Kenji, how are you? I told you, call me Cecily."

"I'm good, thank you. Are you ready to order?"

"I think I may need another minute to look over the menu and specials." Kenji then turned to Jeffrey.

"And for you, sir?"

"Just water for now, thank you." Kenji gave a slight bow of his head and walked away. Jeffrey then turned to Cecily with a raised brow and a *You are so busted* look.

"What?" she asked defensively.

"I've always wanted to come here but it's out of my price range?"

"It's technically true. I was here only once before but it was for a work thing, so I didn't pay. I can't afford a meal here, and I've always wanted to come back."

"I call bullshit. You're on a first-name basis with the waiter."

"That's different. I helped Kenji out with a landlord tenant thing, pro bono."

As if out of thin air, Kenji came back out and set down a plate of food. With a beam he announced, "Grilled abalone and green bean tempura with ponzu sauce. On the house."

To Cecily's credit she had the grace to look a bit cha-grined.

"Thank you," Jeffrey replied drily.

"Are you ready to order?"

"I'll have the king crab sunomono and cucumber sal-ad."

"Just the appetizers, sir?"

"For now."

"Order something else," Cecily insisted. "You'll finish

off both in two bites each. You'll starve."

"You said you were going to order the menu. I'm just preparing my wallet."

Cecily rolled her eyes. "You know I was kidding. I'm not that evil."

"I don't know. I've seen you. You've had your moments."

She just gave him a look.

"Why don't you order for us? I trust you."

With a shake of her head, she did. Then she turned back to him and laid her hands on the table. "Well, you got me here. Now what?"

"I thought we could have a nice meal, get to know each other again."

"I'm going to need a lot of sake for that," she muttered.

"Oh come on. Ten years is a long time. This could be fun and interesting. Am I really that bad?"

Her head poked up over the top of the menu and she just gave him a look.

"I'm making a good-faith effort here," he said in an appeal to her sense of fairness.

"Fine. You're right." She put down the menu and sized him up. "You go first," she said with a wave of her hand.

"What do you want to know?"

She shrugged. "You asked for this. Whatever you want. Entertain me."

He thought for a moment. "I rented an apartment with a bunch of other guys when I first came out to California. I slept on an air mattress in the living room."

Cecily raised a brow. "You couldn't afford your own bedroom?"

"The two guys living there were renting out space to save money. It was within my budget."

"Sounds cozy."

"It's not a period of my life I look back on fondly. Plus, the landlord was a jackass."

"All they want is to be paid on time. And for you to not trash the place or disturb the neighbors." At his narrowed eyes, she shrugged. "I defend landlords. They're not all evil bastards."

"Well this one was. He was also a plumber. Old, cranky, dirty son of a bitch. Hated his guts. Totally unreasonable, refused to make or pay for any repairs. Dabbled in conspiracy theories."

"He sounds great."

"Didn't believe in flu shots, so of course, he ups and dies of it."

"Holy crap." Cecily's eyes widened.

"I know. Twist surprise ending right? The guys and I went downstairs to his unit to pay the rent and saw the police and ambulances there—that's how we found out. Apparently he'd been dead for a few days before the body was discovered. Hell of a thing." He took another drink of water and a bite of the appetizer.

"That must have been creepy. Especially if you saw the body."

"Eh, he had it coming. And I didn't see the body. But I'm still considering working it into a script someday. Use what you know and all that."

Cecily took a sip of the sake. "When I asked to be entertained, I thought you'd go the comedy route. Didn't think you'd pick horror."

"More of a revenge flick sort of thing. Karma is real and vicious."

"I've seen enough evidence of that at work not to doubt it," she said with a smile and shake of her head.

"What do you mean?"

"My first year at Harmon Burke, I went to a hearing with one of the partners. Guess he was having a bad day or something because he was harassing Judge Jimenez's clerk who was in the courtroom. A week later, he was in another courtroom and caught hell from Judge Boyle. Every objection was overruled; she was nitpicking everything."

Jeffrey leaned forward as Cecily indulged in a dramatic pause.

"And?"

"It turns out the clerk was Judge Boyle's cousin, and Her Honor was not happy when she heard about the partner's behavior. I will never forget the look on his face when he found out what he'd done."

He stared for a moment dumbfounded before he burst out laughing. "That's amazing."

"Well you know what they say. It's not what you know, it's who you know."

"Seriously."

"As you said, karma is real. He kinda had it coming though. But if anyone asks, I never said that." Her eyes sparkled with amusement.

"My lips are sealed."

"See? This is how you behave at a dinner. You tell funny, entertaining stories. You don't go macabre and mention dead bodies."

"It'd work on Morticia Addams. And Wednesday."

"Do I look like Morticia or Wednesday?"

Jeffrey's lips twitched. He'd forgotten how fun it could be to wind her up sometimes. "Besides the black hair, no. But you can be kinda bloodthirsty like Wednesday. You definitely scare people."

Cecily's eyes narrowed, but he could tell she was fighting a laugh.

"I'm going to take that as the compliment as I'm sure it was meant to be."

"Absolutely."

The waiter came by and dropped off their meal. The two of them ate in companionable silence for a few minutes before she spoke again.

"Okay, I have to ask. How did you make that video happen?"

"Well, since you asked for a funny, entertaining story…"

Cecily put down her chopsticks and looked at him expectantly.

"I asked my agent, and one of my good friends in the industry to see if any of them knew Daniel. Turns out my friend Greg met him at a benefit event and made a few phone calls. But that didn't really pan out. My agent hung up on me when I called to ask."

"That was rude of him," Cecily said, hiding a smile.

"Tell me about it. Talking about how if it has nothing to do with my work or career he doesn't want to hear it. Anyway, I struck gold when Greg found out he and Daniel go to the same barber."

"You're kidding me."

"Nope. So the barber had to get involved. He played intermediary. Conversations were had, terms were discussed, favors were exchanged, and voila. Here we are."

"Another case in point of it's not what you know, it's who you know." Cecily chuckled.

"So I have a barbershop full of guys who think I'm a crazy idiot, and Daniel Henney is also probably out there telling all his friends about this fool who asked him for this weird favor and how he got conned into it by his barber offering him free cuts for six months."

"Ahh so that's what you had to do in exchange for the video."

"Greg and the barbershop also demanded their cut of the deal. I don't want to talk about that right now."

"I can't be a part of anything illegal or suspect," Cecily said, lips twitching. "So let's leave it there."

Before he knew it, the meal was over and it was time to pay the check. He peeked and did his best to hide a wince. But he gamely broke out his credit card and put it on the sleeve and prepared to hand it over to the waiter.

"Oh no. Let me pay half at least," Cecily protested. She made a grab for the check but he managed to keep it out of her reach.

"I believe the terms of the deal were that I pay."

"C'mon. Don't be stupid. You know I never meant for you to pay this by yourself. It wouldn't be fair."

"A deal's a deal. It's okay. I should still be able to pay my rent next month. Probably." He couldn't resist teasing her.

"Stubborn ass," she muttered. "Now you're making me feel guilty."

"You can make it up to me by going out with me again."

She narrowed her eyes.

"You jerk. That was your plan the whole time, wasn't it?"

"I can neither confirm nor deny." He flashed a winning smile. She folded her arms and glared at him.

"Come on," he cajoled. "You had fun tonight—admit it."

"I admit nothing."

Kenji came back with the credit card slips. Without a word, Jeffrey figured out the tip then signed the slip.

He saw her digging in her purse and warned, "Don't even think about it."

Cecily's head shot up and she gave him a snippy look. "Let me give you some cash. At the very least, I can cover the tip."

"Forget it. Look, the dinner is over, and you got a free meal. And now you never have to see me again. Win-win right?"

"This is ridiculous."

"My dropping this much money on a meal is ridiculous, I agree."

"Hey! No one forced you to."

He threw her a look.

"I never expected you to be a stubborn ass and actually pay for the whole thing. I was always going to pitch in," she protested in response.

"So now you feel guilty."

She huffed. "Yes, and it's all your fault."

He tilted his head as he considered the situation.

"How about we compromise? Next time, you can cook. That way, our eating-out budget won't resemble the national debt."

Cecily crossed her arms and stared at him for a moment. "I still don't think you should get off that easy. You cook."

He smirked. "You want me to cook?"

"Only seems fair. You want to spend more time with me, you gotta work for it."

"If you insist. But I'm going to need a written statement that you won't sue if I accidentally give you food poisoning. I'm making no promises."

"That is not inspiring confidence. And don't try to bring the legalese. Leave that to the professionals."

"Do we have a deal or not?" he demanded.

"You know what? What the hell. Sure. I could always use a homemade meal and an excuse to sue someone if it goes badly. I'll call you." With a cheeky smirk of her own,

Cecily turned on her heel and left him in her dust.

"I am a poor writer trying to make it in Hollywood. Good luck trying to squeeze any money out of me!" he called out behind her back. But on the inside he was giddy.

Game on.

CECILY ZOOMED AROUND her living room, trying to make it look presentable. Or at least the area that would be captured on her laptop's camera. That meant the magazines tossed on the coffee table had to go, the pillows plumped and organized, and dust bunnies had to be chased away. She had a Skype appointment with Rachel in ten minutes and appearances must be maintained. It wouldn't do for word to get back to Brooklyn that her apartment was a pigsty. Not that she thought Rachel would dime her out, but the Asian mother network and sensors were powerful and not to be underestimated. If anything was out of place, her mother would hear about it and be giving her grief within the next twenty-four hours.

She threw a worried look toward her bedroom. She'd left Jeffrey crashed out in bed, and he'd always slept like the dead. It had been a month since their dinner at Hashiri and they were taking things slow. Well maybe not that slow. But they'd been seeing each other on the weekends and getting to know each other again and so far it was going well.

She figured she had a good solid hour before he stirred

and made his way out of the bedroom in search of food. That should be enough time for her and Rachel to go over everything. She glanced at her watch. Three minutes left. She took the tie off of her wrist and threw her hair into a quick sloppy ponytail. Settling herself on the couch, she opened her laptop, and organized her files and notepad. Cecily took a deep breath to calm her nerves.

Her laptop beeped and she accepted the chat request. Rachel's face filled the screen.

"Hey, can you see me? Can you hear me?" Clearing her throat, Cecily tucked a stray tendril of hair behind her ear.

Rachel blinked owlishly behind her glasses. "Yep, loud and clear. We're good." She looked like she was in her office, her desk cluttered with files and tchotchkes. Stand-ard-issue industrial gray file cabinets were in the background.

"Thank you for giving up your weekend like this," Cecily began. "I appreciate this so much."

"No problem. It's eleven my time—you're the one who agreed to get up at the crack of dawn for this. Besides, I had to come into the office anyway to catch up on some things, so it was no big deal."

Well what would you know? Rachel was a fellow work-aholic. Yet another thing they had in common.

"And I should thank you for that gift basket you sent me. The wine, sourdough, and chocolate were really nice. I liked all the local artisanal goodies too." Rachel gave a small smile as she pushed up her glasses.

"I'm so glad you liked it. I thought you might like a

small taste of the Bay." It was the least she could do to show her appreciation for Rachel bailing her out. "You got the spa gift certificate too, right?" Cecily had done her research to find a reputable place with good reviews that wasn't too far away from where Rachel lived and worked.

"Yes. I'm looking at my calendar to schedule a day. It's on my to-do list." Something about the way Rachel approached a spa day, something that should be fun and relaxing in a systematic way really spoke to her. Perhaps this friendship truly was meant to be.

"Great. Let me know how it goes. So you want to just get started?"

"Sounds good. Let's start with the profit and loss statements from two years ago."

"Give me a sec to pull it up."

They were plowing through the files when Cecily heard a door open. Seconds later, she heard the bathroom sink. *Crap.* She sent up a silent prayer that Jeffrey would be quiet and inconspicuous. She should've left him a Post-it note so he'd know.

"Hey, Cecily, you there?" She whipped her gaze back to the screen where Rachel looked confused.

"Yes, I'm here. Sorry, where were we?"

"Are you okay?"

"Yes. Why do you ask?"

"Because you look distracted. And your voice got really high at the end there just now."

"No, no. I'm fine." She was so not good at the covert and stealth. It was lowering to realize how obvious she was.

"If you say so…" Rachel's tone was skeptical, but she let it alone. Thank God.

"Right. Let's go back to the SEC files from last quarter."

"We finished with that ten minutes ago." Now Rachel was clearly amused and enjoying herself. Damn it. She fumbled with her notepad for a few minutes to get her bearings. She was making a valiant comeback when it all went to hell.

"Hey, where's the coffee?" Jeffrey strolled out into the living room, and she bit back a curse. Emerging fresh from bed, he was shirtless, but to her relief, had pulled on some gym shorts so he wasn't parading around her apartment naked. In other circumstances, she'd probably appreciate said nakedness, but this was definitely not the time and place.

"Who's that?" Rachel piped up.

Knowing the jig was up, Cecily closed her eyes. Hearing the voice from her laptop, Jeffrey walked around behind her couch so he could investigate. Great. This was getting better and better.

"Sorry, are you working? You should've told me. I could've just gone for my run and came back after you were done."

"Not your fault. I should've told you."

Jeffrey leaned down to wave to the camera. Rachel's eyes grew wide as saucers as recognition dawned. "Hi there," she choked out.

A pleased grin curved his lips. "Rachel? Is that you?

How are you?"

"I'm good, but obviously not as well as some other people."

"Well, I'll get out of your way. I'll be back in about thirty minutes?"

"Sounds good."

"But seriously. Where is that coffee?"

"I didn't have time. You can hit the Starbucks around the corner."

"That works." He leaned down to kiss her on the cheek. Then waved to the camera again. "Bye, Rachel. Good to see you again."

"Same here." The door closed quietly behind him as he left.

Cecily knew she was in for a world of pain when she saw the Cheshire cat grin on Rachel's face.

She pasted a bright fake smile on her own face. "Sorry about the interruption. So, where were we?"

Rachel crossed her arms and shook her head. "Oh no. You aren't seriously trying to pretend that didn't just happen."

Damn. She really had no skills at this. It didn't work on Adrienne when Jeffrey had surprised her a week ago by showing up early and crashed her and Adrienne's movie night, and it wasn't working on Rachel either.

"Well, I had to try," Cecily replied with a sigh.

"How long has this been going on? And no wonder you were looking disheveled."

"Hey! I was cleaning."

"I'm just saying." Rachel shrugged innocently but Cecily wasn't fooled.

"It's the truth," she insisted.

In response, Rachel held up a hand. "Whatever you say. Besides it's really none of my business if Jeffrey got you all mussed up."

"Oh my God," Cecily groaned.

"If you're calling him God, he must be pretty damn good. Is he a sex god?"

How did she never know that Rachel had such a sly sense of humor?

"Is there any chance you're going to let this go?"

"Did our mothers teach us to leave our shoes on indoors and track the nasty outside into the house?"

"For heaven's sake."

"Spill. You're the one who was swearing up and down nothing was going on between you two."

"It started when we were back in Brooklyn for New Year's," Cecily explained as quickly as possible. "We're taking it slow, and we're not telling anyone," she continued with a significant look.

"I knew it! I knew I saw something at the community center. You were with him weren't you? That's why you needed me to cover for you."

In for a penny in for a pound. "Yes," she confessed. "So you understand why I didn't tell you then. And why I want to keep this quiet for now."

"Fine. I'm sworn to secrecy. Besides I owe you. I wouldn't have gotten an eyeful of some damn fine man

LISA LIN

chest if it wasn't for you. And it's not even noon here back East."

"Rachel!"

"I'm an analyst. That's my analysis."

Cecily groaned. "Can we please get back to work now?"

"You're no fun."

An hour later they were finally finished slogging through the files.

"Thanks again so much for this, Rachel. You have no idea what a lifesaver you are."

"Not a problem. This is what I do, after all." Rachel pushed up her glasses again and shifted in her seat. Cecily frowned. It wasn't like Rachel to be fidgety.

"Is everything okay?"

"No, it's just…" Rachel's voice trailed off as she took a breath, as if to gather her courage.

What the hell was going on?

"So, I have some vacation time coming up I need to use or lose. And your gift basket got me thinking. I've never been to San Francisco and thought it'd be a nice place to visit. And if you're available it'd be great to meet up. No pressure of course."

"Absolutely! This will be great. Just let me know the dates and I'll prep my guest room." Despite herself, Cecily began to get excited. What a fun and great way to get to know Rachel even better and strengthen their bond. Cecily started to make a mental list of things to do and buy. She could put together a small toiletry and spa kit with a big fluffy robe and sleep mask and lay it out on the bed in her guest room with a small box of Ghirardelli chocolates to officially welcome Rachel to the Bay Area. Plus a map and guide to San Francisco where she could mark off the best places to see and go eat. And of course she would need to put some fresh flowers in the room and make sure the blankets and sheets were fresh. Also talk to the front desk to add Rachel's name to the approved visitors list. She grabbed a pad to write it all down when Rachel spoke and poured cold water all over the proceedings.

"I appreciate the offer, but I'm going to find an Airbnb and do my own thing. I think that'll work out better for everyone, and besides, I don't want to impose on you."

"Are you sure? It's no trouble at all, really." She hated to sound desperate or pushy but part of her was baffled at Rachel turning down her invitation. And okay, hurt. This was another peace offering and she'd been rejected. Rachel would rather spend good money to find her own accommodations than stay with her for free. That stung.

Was it something she'd said? Something she'd done? She'd thought the two of them had made such good progress at the diner and buried the hatchet. They'd even conspired together in a cover-up for heaven's sake. But apparently not.

"Positive." Rachel's voice made it clear the decision was final, but she softened the blow with a small smile. "I promise I'll let our parents know so you don't get in trouble. And I would love to get together for dinner."

"Okay, great." Cecily gulped. Getting blowback from the parents had been the furthest thing from her mind, but she appreciated Rachel's gesture there at least.

"I'll keep you posted. Do you have any last-minute questions? If not, I'm going to log off and go grab some lunch. I'm starving." Clearly the conversation and bonding were over.

"No, I think we're good. Thanks again and enjoy the rest of your day."

"In that case, I'm going to go. It was great to talk to you," Rachel said, with a small smile. She even gave a wave.

"Bye."

"Bye."

Rachel disconnected first. Cecily let out a breath and leaned back on her sofa. Perhaps she hadn't made as much headway on making a new friend as she'd thought. Maybe she'd have to revisit Resolution 4.

Chapter Eleven

"WHAT ARE YOU doing? I thought we were going to watch that baking show you liked together." Cecily and Jeffrey were stretched out on the couch after lunch, and Cecily was trying to put the morning's Skype episode behind her.

She looked up from the top of the book she was reading. "Sorry I can't. This is for my book club. I only have two days left to finish before we meet to discuss. I don't have time now."

Jeffrey peered over at the cover and raised a brow. "*Sister Wives of Nantucket*? I remember this. The studios were practically throwing money at the author to make it into a movie two years ago."

"Well hurrah for the author. It was either this, or *The Jane Austen Book Club*. I love Austen as much as the next girl, but this seemed more my speed. *Sister Wives* is good, but I'm having a hard time getting into it because I'm so busy and I keep starting and stopping. I need to focus."

"A book club book about a book club does seem overly meta. Very *Inception*-y," he mused.

"Exactly."

"But on the other hand, *Cinema Paradiso* is an awesome movie about movies. So meta isn't always bad. We should watch that."

With a huff of exasperation, she batted his hand away. "I told you, I don't have time. I have two hundred fifty pages left and I need to get it done by Thursday."

Without warning, he plucked the book from her hand and tossed it over his shoulder.

"Hey!"

"Listen, I have the solution to your problems. Let's just watch the movie. That way, you'll be done in about two hours, and we can get on with our lives."

"Are you kidding? I can't do that—that'd be cheating." The idea was unthinkable.

"Why not? Consider it more as maximizing efficiency. Think of all the other stuff you could be doing instead. Or all the billable hours you could be racking up." More tempted than she'd care to admit, Cecily crossed her arms.

"Hey, I'm helping you problem-solve here. And I'm offering to watch a chick flick with you. Don't I get any points for that?"

"How do you know it's a chick flick?"

Jeffrey rolled his eyes. "It's called *Sister Wives of Nantucket*. What else could it be?"

Men. Ugh.

"I take strenuous objection to you using the term chick flick. It's insulting, patronizing, and dismissive."

"To quote *Jerry Maguire*, 'Help me, help you.'" To add insult to injury, Jeffrey said it complete with the Tom Cruise hand gestures. Cheeky bastard.

"How do I know the movie adaptation is any good? What if there's a scene that's in the book that's not in the movie or vice versa? What if I miss something important?"

Jeffrey shrugged. "Fake it. You're a lawyer. Aren't you supposed to be able to bullshit for a living?"

"Are you seriously suggesting I do something mildly unethical? Then hurling insults at my profession?"

At that he rolled his eyes. The jerk.

"If the shoe fits. Besides, a lawyer worrying about ethics? What are you, a unicorn?"

Outraged, she threw a throw pillow at him as a matter of principle. With a dramatic groan, as if she'd used a rock instead of a teal decorative pillow, he flopped onto the couch beside her.

"You left yourself wide open on that one. You can't blame me for taking my shot," he pointed out reasonably.

Despite herself, Cecily just couldn't stay mad. And judging by the gleam in his eye, Jeffrey knew it. Dammit.

"Come on," he coaxed. "You know you want to. Plus, once we're done with the chick flick we can watch *Cinema Paradiso*. I'm going to need a palate cleanser."

For that, he earned a punch in the arm. "Fine. But just so we're clear. If I get caught by the book club, I'm blaming you."

With a triumphant smile, Jeffrey threw up his hands in victory. "Bring on the chick flick."

Not even ten minutes into the movie and Cecily was ready to strangle him.

"Are you sure this isn't a WASP version of you and

your mother?"

"Some people can't pull off accents and they shouldn't try."

"This bit really feels like cultural appropriation."

"That kid really is a little shit."

Enough was enough. Cecily grabbed the remote and hit pause. Jeffrey turned his head and blinked innocently. "What? I thought we were enjoying the movie."

"Are you kidding me right now?"

"No. This is fun. And not as painful as I thought it would be. Also, why are you taking so many notes? You're not studying for a midterm."

"For the book club!" This is what she got for trying to find a new hobby.

Jeffrey's brows creased in confusion. "You're acting like you're going to be quizzed on this."

"I have to be prepared."

"Now correct me if I'm wrong, but did you or did you not join this book club as a hobby? A fun activity."

"Yeah. So?"

"Then why are you treating it like homework? Like another item to be checked off the to-do list? Shouldn't you be, I don't know…having fun?"

Now it was Cecily's turn to be confused. "What are you trying to say?"

"So what if you don't finish the book, or if you don't know all the answers to the questions? Will the world collapse? Will someone die?"

She rolled her eyes. "Don't be silly."

"No, you're the one who's being silly. Stop taking everything so seriously."

"I'm sorry if that doesn't come as easily to me as it does for you," she snapped without thinking. Looking at his face she realized she'd crossed the line and it hadn't come across as she'd intended.

"I'm sorry, that wasn't fair, and I didn't mean it that way. I'm doing this the only way I know how. Not sure if I'd even know how to just relax and have fun."

Jeffrey raised a brow. "Does that include taking cheap shots at me?"

Cecily winced. "No, not at all. Again, I apologize. It wasn't about you, I swear."

"Then what is it about? Because I'm just trying to help, but if this is your reaction, I'll know better than to do that next time."

Oh Lord. How had this conversation gone so off the rails? Jeffrey was absolutely right: she shouldn't have said what she did. "I think it just reminded me of how my mother would react and it triggered an automatic response. It made me think about all the times she told me I was doing something wrong or not good enough," she admitted.

At that Jeffrey's eyes lit with understanding. Then he shook his head ruefully. "So I'm just collateral damage?"

"Something like that." Cecily took a breath and laid her hand on top of his. "But you are right: that's no reason to take it out on you. I'll work on it, I promise. Next time I go too far, please let me know. I'll listen, explain, and if necessary, apologize."

Jeffrey paused and looked at her thoughtfully. "You apologizing? That could be a sight to behold."

Cecily resisted the urge to stick out her tongue. But fair was fair and she was relieved they were able to talk it out. And she was glad Jeffrey understood that she hadn't meant to hurt him. She vowed to herself that she would work on being better at listening first.

"And in that spirit, I will try to relax and enjoy this book club thing. It's supposed to be stress-relieving."

"My point exactly. So calm down. You will not bring shame to the family if you are not the perfect book club member. You already put in seventy hours a week at work, it's okay to have a little fun and blow off some steam. Dial down the Asian guilt will ya?"

With a shaky sigh, Cecily replied, "You do realize you're asking me to ignore and overcome more than thirty years of programming, right?"

"I believe in you. We're all works in progress."

With a laugh, she settled back on the couch and rested her head in the crook of his neck. "Okay. You're right."

Without missing a beat, Jeffrey whipped out his phone and punched a few buttons. "Can you repeat that? I'd like that preserved for posterity."

"Stop it, you jerk."

Dropping a kiss on the top of her head, he suggested, "So what do you say we skip the chick flick and watch *Cinema Paradiso* instead? I promise you'll love it. It's way better."

"And if I don't like it?" she asked with an arch of her brow.

"Name your terms."

Cecily thought for a minute, then whispered in his ear.

A wicked grin crossed his lips. "You're on. Though this sounds more like a win-win to me."

CECILY WALKED INTO Simmons' Bookshop with no small amount of trepidation. It was her first book club meeting and she was clinging to her copy of *Sister Wives of Nantucket* like it was a lifeline.

Mentally she gave herself a pep talk. "In the list of tough things you've faced in your life this doesn't even crack the top hundred," she told herself. "You've gotten food poisoning twice, and moved across the country where you didn't know anyone. If you can make it through a reception with a room full of federal judges, you can survive this. This is a book club. You decided to do this as a hobby, so you're supposed to be having fun for God's sake."

She took a fortifying breath and entered the store. After asking the cashier behind the front desk where the meeting space was, she walked up to the second level of the store, and found the closed-off area for the book club meeting.

Immediately, she was accosted by a perky woman in her early forties with glasses and a short blond haircut.

"Hi, I'm Becky Gardner."

"Cecily Chang, nice to meet you."

"Are you here for the book club?"

Cecily flashed her book like a shield. "I guess so." Becky gave a small squeal and clapped her hands.

"Well, welcome! We're so glad you're here!" She took Cecily's hand and led her to the other side of the room where a refreshment stand was set up. There was a wine bucket filled with ice and three bottles of wine chilling. So far so good.

"We have a meat and cheese tray, and hummus and veggies if you're vegetarian or vegan. There's gluten-free and dairy-free cupcakes if you'd like one too. We all take turns bringing food. There's a list of forbidden ingredients. Just making sure we cater to any possible allergies and dietary restrictions," Becky said with a big smile.

Shit. Not only did she have to read a book every month, now she had to be Betty Crocker too? A vegan, sugar-free, gluten-free, nut-free Betty Crocker to boot? She was so not here for this.

"We'll be getting started in a few minutes," Becky informed her. "Why don't you take a few minutes to settle in, get your bearings?"

Cecily found a seat in a far corner and sat and observed, minding her own business. She saw a bunch of women mingling, mostly white, who all seemed to be slightly older than her and all married. She was hearing snippets of conversations about soccer practice, essential oils, minivans, and chaperoning field trips.

She had nothing in common with these women. The

next two hours were going to be hell. Cecily began to look for an exit strategy when Becky called the book club to order. She bit back a curse. Too late.

"So, ladies. Tonight is very exciting. We have a new member here with us today. Everyone, this is Cecily Chang." There was a round of polite applause.

"Cecily, why don't you tell us a bit about yourself?" What was this, an interrogation?

"Uh, not much to tell. I'm a lawyer, and I work for Harmon Burke. I don't get a lot of downtime, so I thought I'd join this book club as a way to relax, have fun, and meet some new people."

Was it just her imagination or was she getting some side-eye?

"Are you from the area?" one of the other ladies asked. Cecily thought her name might have been Patrice.

"No."

"Oh, where?"

"New York," she answered shortly. From the looks around the room, Cecily could tell that wasn't the answer they were expecting. Or wanting.

"Like oh my God, I don't think I've ever met anyone from like New York City. This is totally cool. Like seriously the coolest thing ever. I've heard New York is like so much more intense or whatever than San Francisco."

Cecily's ears bled as the Valley Girl speak kept coming out of Gretchen's mouth. First, she was put under the microscope like a moth and now Valley Girl speak. Was there no end to the indignities?

"Okay let's get started. Who wants to go first?"

"I gotta admit, I didn't finish the book. I only made it about halfway through," another blonde, Alycia, admitted with a sheepish shrug. To Cecily's shock and surprise, Alycia's confession was waved off as no big deal.

For heaven's sake, what was the point of coming to a book club discussion if you weren't prepared to discuss the book? This would be like if she walked into a meeting with a client when she'd never bothered to read the file and know why the client was there to see her in the first place. But instead of being fired, and possibly disciplined by the state bar, book club incompetence was just fine.

Unbelievable.

Becky finally got the discussion started and after a few minutes, Cecily actually began to enjoy herself. She reminded herself that Jeffrey was right: this was supposed to be fun. This wasn't a client meeting. Some of the other book club members were making smart, insightful comments. Getting into the spirit, she raised her hand.

"Yes, Cecily?"

"Just to follow up on what Holly said about the water imagery, I thought it was a good example of the author using the water to represent the theme of self-reflection. As you can see on page 85, when Jocelyn takes a walk by the lake, she's trying to figure out whether or not to accept Oliver's proposal, and wondering if she has what it takes to be a politician's wife."

"What a fascinating observation," Becky managed.

Cecily beamed, preening at the compliment.

"How did you come up with that?" Alycia asked. Then her eyes bugged out as she saw all the color-coded sticky notes poking out from Cecily's book.

"Are all those the notes you took?"

Cecily shrugged.

"Wow, you're so…organized."

"Hazards of being a lawyer, I guess." She refused to be embarrassed or make apologies to make the Mean Girl wannabes feel better. Their insecurities were not her problem.

"I guess we need to start upping our game, ladies, if we want to keep up with Cecily."

There were twitters of laughter. For once, Cecily blessed her thirty-plus years of experience of dealing with a tiger mom. If these women thought these pathetic attempts to tear her down were going to work, they had another think coming. Her skin was way too thick for that.

"We're just more relaxed and informal than you're probably used to," Becky explained.

"My fault for trying to take it seriously I suppose."

She started thinking to herself this was two hours of her life she was never getting back.

Ninety excruciating minutes later, the discussion was finally over, and the meeting was wrapping up.

"Great discussion, ladies. I hope everyone enjoyed themselves tonight," Becky said with a meaningful glance in Cecily's direction. "See you all next month."

Cecily was trying to make a beeline for the doorway when Becky stopped her. She gave a longing glance at the front door. So close, and yet so far.

"Did you have fun?" Becky chirped. "I know it can be intimidating to be the new person, but I hope we've made you feel welcome."

"I'm glad I came," she said honestly. Oftentimes it was just as important to know what didn't work as much as finding out what did work.

"I hope you'll become a regular," Becky hinted.

"I don't know," Cecily demurred. "My work schedule is so busy and unpredictable. We'll see." Falling back on the lawyer standard of vague non-committal answers, she picked up her bag and jacket.

Alas, Becky didn't get the hint. "Be sure to find us and join our group on Facebook."

"Facebook?"

"Yes. That's where we vote on the next month's book selection, then Simmons puts it on their newsletter and website. We have a nice online community going on there. I can find you and send you an invite. And be ready for some friend requests."

She would rather redo all three years of law school and retake the bar exam.

"I'm actually not on Facebook that much, but if I can I'll check it out."

"Feel free to just jump in. We'd love for you to suggest what we should read next. Maybe a legal thriller!"

Sure. That was exactly what she was looking for in a new hobby. An opportunity to talk more about her work.

"I have an early morning meeting tomorrow so I need

to get going. Thank you for letting me join you tonight."

"Of course! Happy to have you and hope to see you next month," Becky called out as Cecily walked down the stairs.

Walking out the door, Cecily took a deep, gulping breath of fresh air.

That had been...something. She couldn't wait to get the hell out of Dodge and back home into her pajamas.

Resolution 6—a total flop. The search for a new hobby continues.

"So what do you want to do today?"

"I don't know." Cecily stretched and yawned. It was already 10 a.m. and she and Jeffrey were still in bed. It was glorious. This was the first weekend she'd had completely off in almost six months and she was going to take full advantage of it. "I'm feeling lazy. I think we should just stay home today. We can read, watch TV, hang out. Do you have work?"

"Nothing that can't wait."

"Good." She snuggled closer. "I have frozen pizza, and some chicken and vegetables in the fridge. We can whip up a curry with that."

"Ohh I get to see you channel your inner June Cleaver."

She threw him a look. "Yeah no. You will never catch me cooking or doing chores wearing pearls and heels."

"Damn. I guess that's one fantasy of mine that'll never come true."

She studied his face, unsure whether or not he was joking. But damn if his poker face wasn't on point at that moment. Then he smirked.

"You are a sick twisted man, Lee."

"I must be—I'm with you." He took a look over at her night table, which had a stack of books on it.

"What's that?"

"Oh, just books I checked out. Need to return them to the library actually."

He leaned over her to examine the titles. "These don't look chic lit-y. Which one is your next book club book?"

"None. These were just some I picked up for fun."

"Fun," he mused. "What a novel concept for you."

"Hey, I'm trying here. It's a work in progress," she protested. She had picked up some John Grisham thrillers, and some Sweet Valley High books for the nostalgia factor.

"I know, honey, and I'm very proud of you," he patronized. He lessened the sting by giving her a kiss.

"You know, I can have fun on my own. I don't need you for that. Maybe I'll read in bed and you can find something else to do out in the living room."

"All right all right, I give." He rolled his eyes. He peered at the books again. "So what is your next book club selection?"

Cecily cleared her throat. "Actually, I don't know. I maybe sorta left the club."

He turned to her in surprise. "You what?"

"Well, it was taking up a lot of time and it was stressing me out. Besides, most of the people there are suburban soccer mom types and I just had nothing in common with them. It was weird and awkward." She would rather do anything than go through another night like that. Becky had indeed sent a ton of friend requests her way but so far she was standing strong and ignoring them.

"I'm proud of you," he said, beaming. Even though it shouldn't, his support and understanding made her feel warm and fuzzy inside. "But what are you going to do instead? You need to find a new hobby?"

She looked at him under her lashes. "I had an idea as a matter of fact. I was going to make up a list of classic movies. Watch one or two every month. I think it'd be fun and it'd be a lot less stressful and time-consuming than a book club."

"I love that idea. And I can give you suggestions for movies you could watch. You loved *Cinema Paradiso*, remember?"

"Yes, I do. That's what gave me the idea. I can do this at my own pace. Besides, I'd rather do something by myself. Guess I'm not really a team player."

"I could've told you that," he teased.

"Hey!" She punched him on the shoulder.

"Remember when we were ten? Joanne Petronski had a birthday party and everyone was playing Clue. You got mad because people weren't following the rules."

"I don't remember that," she sniffed. Joanne was a low-down lying cheater, and deserved to be called out.

"Anyway," he stressed, "I'm just glad you decided to change course and find a different hobby instead of feeling like you had to stick it out. Life's too short to make yourself miserable."

"A good attorney always readjusts and reevaluates strategy in light of new facts," she said loftily.

He chuckled. "Was the book club really that bad?"

"I had to Marie Kondo the book club. It did not spark joy."

With a mischievous gleam in his eye, Jeffrey snaked his arms around her, pushed her back onto the bed and leaned down to capture her lips.

"How about we spark some joy together right now?"

She smiled up at him. "Bring it on."

Resolution 6—a draw. She wasn't going to expand her horizons with the book club, but film appreciation had definite possibilities as a new hobby.

Resolution 5—triple check. She was making up for lost time, because she wasn't missing out on sex anymore, that's for damn sure.

Two hours later they were sitting on her couch with plates of reheated frozen pizza, sodas, and a big bowl of popcorn. Jeffrey had insisted the experience wouldn't be complete without them.

With great ceremony, he turned her TV on. He turned to her and said seriously, "Are we ready?"

She laughed and rolled her eyes. "Just start the movie already."

"I'm making sure you're prepared for what you're

about to see. *Charade* is a cinematic masterpiece. We're talking 1963, the end of the golden age of Hollywood. We got MGM, the studio system, the glitz and glamor. Cary Grant at his best and Audrey Hepburn is luminous." He was such a film geek and it was beyond adorable.

Charade was his first suggestion for her movie appreciation club of one. A fun, accessible movie that would ease her in. And Grant and Hepburn were legends after all.

"You're playing the expectations game all wrong you know," she drawled.

He frowned and tilted his head. "What are you talking about?"

"You're hyping *Charade* really hard, increasing my expectations. The more you talk, the better I expect it to be. It's like the *Seinfeld* finale. Everyone talked about it for months leading up to it, expecting it to be the best, funniest hour of TV ever. It got great ratings but everyone hated it because no matter what, whatever Jerry and the writers came up with would never live up to expectations."

Giving her a look, knowing she was messing with him, he deadpanned, "Okay. I take it all back. This movie sucks and is a waste of your time."

"That's better."

"All right, let's do this."

After the credits rolled, he looked at her like an earnest puppy. "Well?"

Cecily sat back and considered. "It was fun. I really liked it. I can't believe that was Walter Matthau though."

He kept looking at her. "And??"

"I don't believe Cary Grant. He's not Brian Cruik-shank. He's still pulling a scam on her. Audrey should have run. She deserved better."

"You have no romance in your soul," he muttered.

"He lied to her the whole entire movie!"

"That's all you got?" he asked, throwing up his hands.

She finally relented. "It was a good film. Really fun, kept me interested and engaged. Hepburn and Grant had great chemistry, though the age difference made me a little skeevy." She held up a hand before he could protest. "Beyond that, I'm not knowledgeable enough to go into the details on the lighting, camera work and all that. You made a good choice, and I'm glad I saw it."

He beamed. "Your film education is off to a great start."

"Let's not get crazy now. It's not supposed to be homework, remember?"

"You know what I meant. Okay. But I'm warning you, if corpses aren't your thing, you should brace yourself for the next movie selection."

"What is it?" she asked suspiciously.

"*Ran*. A Kurosawa classic. There's a number of dead bodies and probably a decapitation or two."

She wrinkled her nose and grimaced.

"Hey, it's partly inspired by a Shakespearean tragedy so what do you expect?"

"Seriously?"

"Yes, *Ran* is a great mix of East and West. And we'll see if you can figure out what Shakespeare play it references.

Expect a quiz after."

"Ha ha, very funny."

"Essay only, no true or false, or multiple choice. And I don't grade on a curve either." He had to be kidding. But hell, if he was going to expect in-depth discussion and analysis she could Google and do her research ahead of time. This was one of those times when it paid to be an anal, detail-oriented overachiever. Why not let her natural instincts play themselves out?

"Okay fine. Whatever you say. I need to defrost the chicken for dinner." As she got up, she caught the gleam in his eye. "No. Don't even think about it. I already said no heels and no pearls."

"Bummer."

Revised Resolution 6—so far so good.

Chapter Twelve

JEFFREY RUBBED HIS hands together in anticipation. It was time for another movie, and he couldn't wait to introduce Cecily to his new pick. They've been doing this for a few weeks now and so far it'd been going great.

"You ready?" he called out.

She walked over holding a bowl of popcorn, looking adorable and rumpled in sweats, leggings, and fuzzy socks.

"Actually, could we have a slight change of plans?"

He gave her a suspicious look. "What sort of change?"

"Can we watch a cheesy mindless rom-com today instead of one of your films? I've had a hellacious week at work and I want to turn my brain off for a couple hours. I'm not even working this weekend. I deserve a treat."

"But I was really looking forward to *Raise the Red Lantern*."

She raised a brow. "Is it fluffy and angst-free?"

"Well, the main character is a poor young woman who is forced to become a concubine in 1920s China and ends up living in a big rich mansion, but is driven to madness by the psychological mind games between her and the other wives. If that's your idea of a good time, then yes, it's fluffy and angst-free. If not, maybe not so much."

"Ha ha."

"I'll make you watch it eventually."

"Please?" she wheedled. She rained kisses on his face.

"Fine, fine. We can watch a rom-com. But I'm warning you, *Raise the Red Lantern* is next." Then *12 Angry Men.* He figured Cecily would appreciate the legal angle.

Cecily pumped her fists in victory. "Excellent. I have the perfect film. *Monster-in-Law.* J.Lo at the height of her rom-com powers."

Jeffrey caught himself from making a face just in time. "What's the movie about?"

"J.Lo dealing with her awful mother-in-law is my best guess. But I found it on Amazon and it looked fun. Let's watch it."

As much as he hated to admit it, it wasn't as painful as he thought it would be. It was over the top but managed to have enough teeth to not be saccharine. In fact, he was enjoying the escalating war between J.Lo and Jane Fonda's characters.

"You know, this was a good idea. This is kinda fun."

"Hush," Cecily ordered, not taking her eyes off the screen. But he couldn't resist.

"You better not show this to your mother," he commented. "Let's not give her any ideas."

"Please." Cecily snorted. "Neither of them are a match for my mother. She'd have both of them begging for mercy."

"You'll get no arguments from me there. My mom, too."

"Now stop talking over Wanda Sykes. She's the best part."

The two of them laughed their way through most of the movie, but then Cecily got eerily quiet. He had a feeling that there may be a wedding scene coming up, most rom-coms did after all, but he was hoping it wouldn't be a sort of trigger. Besides there was wedding stuff mentioned before in the movie, and she'd been fine with it.

"Hey," he said quietly as he hit pause on the movie. "What's going on?"

"Nothing, it's nothing."

"It's obviously not nothing."

Cecily squeezed her eyes shut. "It was stupid to let it get to me like that. Forget it."

"Not a chance. Spill." He had a feeling he wasn't going to like what was coming next, but he had to face the music sometime.

"That wedding dress. It looks almost exactly like the one I picked out."

Oh crap.

"Do we need to talk about this?" he asked hesitantly.

Cecily took a long moment before she responded. "You know, my first instinct is no, I would rather not revisit one of the worst moments of my life, but what the hell. Let's clear the air once and for all. You said you left because you were trying to protect me and you were working through some stuff. Which you never even tried to tell me about before you cut and ran." When she saw his hesitation, she continued. "Let's just face the music and get it over with.

You know we'll never really be able to move forward until we deal with it. It'll keep lingering like an ugly dark cloud."

Jeffrey took a deep breath. Part of him was convinced that no good could come of revisiting the past—some things were better left undisturbed. But on the other hand, maybe leaving the issue unaddressed would be like leaving a wound untreated, allowing it to fester and infection to brew. Perhaps sunlight was the best disinfectant and they could finally move forward with a clean slate. The look on Cecily's face told him he really didn't have a choice in the matter anyway. So it was time to bite the bullet.

"I'm going to preface this once again by saying I was young and stupid," he warned. "Not an excuse, just an explanation."

"Stop stalling."

"It was right before I decided to leave medical school. Remember that day you came back from wedding planning? And I told you how I was thinking about leaving medical school? You made it clear you were not on board."

"Wait. Hold the phone," Cecily said with dramatic slices of the air with her arms. "That is not how it went down."

"That's exactly what happened, Counselor. I remember that conversation quite distinctly."

"No it didn't. You told me you were thinking about leaving school, yes."

"And the prospect of dealing with the drama and fall-out was too much for you. I get it. Can't say I blame you."

"I never said that!" she said heatedly. "I asked if you

were prepared for the shitstorm, but obviously I would be behind you no matter what you decided. I had your back."

"You never said that!"

"I shouldn't have had to say it. You should have known that I'd support you."

"How was I supposed to know that?" he retorted. "Like I'm supposed to be some kind of mind reader." But the look on Cecily's face told her he was greatly mistaken. And perhaps about ready to die.

She shook her head. "I can't believe you. I can't fucking believe this. That's why you broke off our engagement? That's why you left without any warning? Because you thought I wasn't willing to stand by you?"

He shrugged defensively. "What else was I supposed to think? You said you had no way of seeing this coming and you were shaking your head. I couldn't blame you for bailing and deciding this wasn't what you signed up for. I didn't know what I wanted to do with my life but I knew I needed to figure it out and it wasn't fair to make you wait until I got my act together."

"Ohh," she steamed. "I could hit you. I could actually hit you right now." Cecily clenched her fists. He may be wrong, but he thought he saw her count to twenty before she spoke again.

"I can't believe this. You idiot, of course I didn't see you wanting to quit medical school coming. You didn't tell me what you were thinking, or feeling. I had no idea what was going on. How the hell was I supposed to know? That doesn't mean I wouldn't have stood by you."

"Like I said, I was an idiot. I fully acknowledge this."

"Do you have any idea what it was like the weeks after you left? I had to call the venue and vendors to cancel, beg them for mercy so we could try to avoid any penalties and fees and maybe get some money back. Try having to face all the neighbors looking at you with abject pity. You haven't lived until you walk into a room of gossiping aunties and it immediately goes dead silent. It made me want to scream."

Oh God. "I had no idea it was that bad." He grimaced.

"What did you think would happen?" she scoffed. "That it all just magically got fixed? You don't want to know how much money my family lost over the wedding."

"I never thought that far ahead," Jeffrey admitted. All he'd been focused on was leaving Brooklyn as soon as possible. He hadn't really thought about the fallout.

"Typical. Leave it to the woman to clean up the mess after the man barges through like a bull in a china shop and destroys everything." Cecily's tone and crossed arms said everything.

"In my defense, I really didn't mean to wreak so much havoc. I was dealing with my own shit, which had nothing to do with you. I really am sorry everyone got caught up as collateral damage. Again, I plead ignorance and idiocy."

"And the worst part is you thought I wouldn't have supported your decision to leave medical school and wouldn't accept you as anything else but a doctor. You really thought I would prefer you miserable in the name of making me happy, your parents happy, or whatever the hell it was you were thinking? That I could be that selfish, instead of wanting what was best for you? When the truth is—back then—I would have married you if you didn't have a penny to your name. I was that in love. I would have told you you'd figure it out, or we'd figure it out," Cecily said, emphasizing the *we*. "You were the one making all these assumptions, and you didn't bother to talk to me so I could tell you how dead wrong you were. And now I find out you thought so little of me. That's not how love works. That's not how relationships work."

"I thought the world of you," he insisted, staggered by her words. "And you're a hundred percent right—I should have talked to you instead of making those assumptions. It was wrong. I have no excuse."

Cecily took a deep breath and stood up. "I think I'm going to go for a jog to clear my head." She paused. "And I think it would be best if you were gone by the time I got back."

He gulped. "Okay, understood."

"Just to blow off some steam," she clarified. "I need time and space to figure out what to do. I don't want you beating yourself up or anything."

At his skeptical look she admitted, "Okay, maybe just a tiny little bit."

"Your honesty is touching and refreshing," he murmured. And at least Cecily wanted time to think as opposed to kicking him to the curb now. He hung on to that thin shred of hope like a desperate lifeline.

"I'll call you," she offered just before disappearing into

the bedroom.

As he began to gather his things, Jeffrey hoped this wouldn't be the last time he stepped foot in this apartment or saw Cecily again. But as he reflected on how hurt and angry she was after he'd confessed, it could very well be. And the worst part of it was he understood and wouldn't blame her a bit.

CECILY WALKED UP to the Doe Memorial Library with a bounce in her step. She was here to meet with the genealogist she'd hired to do research on her family tree, and she was beyond excited. Operation Anniversary Present, a.k.a. Resolution 7 was well underway and ahead of schedule. There was still two months left before the anniversary. She opened the door, walked in, and made her way to the courtyard. The two of them had agreed to make the courtyard their rendezvous point. Luckily for Cecily, she had arrived ten minutes early so she had some time to get her bearings and extra time in case she got lost. She found one of the seats in the wooden benches and waited.

She'd been on a non-stop hamster wheel at work and while that normally was aggravating but par for the course, this time it may have been a blessing in disguise. It'd been two weeks since Jeffrey had dropped that bombshell and admitted why he'd left her right before their wedding and to be honest she was still reeling a bit. The hurt was still very much present. Jeffrey, wisely, had taken the hint and they hadn't talked since. She needed the time and space to wrap her mind around the new information and what she was going to do about it.

At first, she'd been ready to kick him out of her life forever but she paused and took the time to think. While what Jeffrey did was not okay, she had to admit his reason made sense in a perverse twisted logic sort of way. And he had done it because he thought he was doing what was best, not to hurt her. That had to count for a lot. Even if he had been one hundred percent dead wrong.

But that was ten years ago, and it was clear Jeffrey realized the error of his ways and was remorseful. He was older and wiser now, and people shouldn't be held responsible for their actions when they were young and stupid. Especially if they have shown signs of growth and change. Which as far as she was concerned, she has seen. And maybe she'd been so caught up with law school and wedding preparations she hadn't seen the red flags. So perhaps it wasn't all Jeffrey's fault. More like just ninety-five percent.

Cecily gave a sigh. She needed a little more time, and as hard as it was, she felt she and Jeffrey could work past this. He would have to commit to continuing to work on those communication skills, and she'd have to try to be more attentive and open, but this wasn't a dealbreaker.

He was so lucky she'd had a thing for him since they were six years old.

There was time to stew on that later. Now it was time to meet Kelly. Looking back, this whole thing could have been better planned. Cecily had contacted the history department chair at Berkeley, who had put her in touch with a professional genealogist who had been eager to take on the challenge. And the generous fee Cecily had offered for the work hadn't hurt either. Through their previous correspondence via email, Kelly Parkinson seemed professional, competent, and smart. But she had no idea what the woman looked like. Despite her best efforts, Google had failed her—Kelly Parkinson had turned up too many options. Which is something they should've figured out before deciding to meet.

Behind her sunglasses, Cecily looked around, trying to see if she could figure out who Kelly was. She was also feeling a little out of place among the baby-faced undergraduate students walking past. Thinking quickly, she shot an email to Kelly, telling her she was in the courtyard waiting, and what she was wearing. There. Problem solved.

A few minutes later, a tall woman with sleek chestnut hair in a neat braid appeared. She wore a burgundy button-down shirt and a tweed pencil skirt and had an oversized tote bag slung over her shoulder. With the wedge espadrilles she was wearing, she towered over Cecily like an Amazon.

"Ms. Chang?" She stuck out a hand. "Hi. I'm Kelly."

Cecily got up quickly and resisted the urge to tug at her cuffs.

"It's nice to meet you, and please, it's Cecily."

"Sure, and please call me Kelly. Why don't we go inside? I reserved a private study room for us so we can talk and go over what I found so far."

"That sounds great. I didn't know you could do that."

"Students and faculty are allowed to reserve a room. I'm an adjunct here, so I got a room. I figured you'd rather not discuss this out in the open in public."

"I appreciate that." Cecily followed Kelly as she signed in, got the key, and they walked through the maze of the library until they got to their room on the third floor.

Kelly took her massive tote bag and dropped it onto the chair next to her. She pulled out her laptop and a big, thick manila folder.

"So, where would you like to begin?"

Cecily shrugged. "I'm just excited to see what you found."

"All right. Let me just boot up my laptop. While we do that, let me show you some of what we found." She opened up the folder and took out a photo.

"Do you know who this is?" It was a black and white photo of a handsome man in his thirties standing in front of a sprawling traditional Chinese house with an inclined roof. The whole structure was raised on a platform and there were steps leading up to the main entrance. The man was holding on to a bicycle and he was gazing straight into the camera.

Cecily stared. "I have no idea."

Kelly gave a small smile. "This was your great-great-uncle, Chang Ming Wu. And this photo was taken in 1912."

"I've never heard anything about him. I never even

knew he existed."

"There's probably a reason why. A year after this picture was taken, he left the family home and was never seen or heard from again."

Cecily's mouth opened in surprise. "Why? What happened? Did he get killed? Get kidnapped?"

"Nothing like that." Kelly chuckled. "Your great-great-uncle ran off with a British officer's daughter after meeting her on vacation in Hong Kong."

"No way!" This was the best thing ever.

"It was a huge scandal, yes. Obviously it was not something the family was eager to have publicized, but word got out. Apparently, Great-Great-Uncle Chang Ming fell in love and broke an arranged marriage. His parents were furious, the whole family was in an uproar."

Oh this just got better and better. "Was this in the newspapers?"

"No, we found a letter from your Great-Great-Aunt Pei Ling. Pei Ling was his younger sister. It turns out in order to maintain the family's reputation, and to save face, your great-great-grandfather married the woman Ming Wu was betrothed to. He helped preserve your family's honor." Kelly showed her the original wedding invitation, and the new one with the replaced groom.

"Do we know anything about what happened to Ming Wu?"

"Unfortunately, the paper trail ended."

"Maybe he went to Britain with that officer's daughter." She was tickled at the idea of having such a scandalous ancestor. Who knew she came from such stock? She couldn't wait to see what her parents had to say about this. The next time her mother gave her crap about something she'd be able to answer back: "Hey, at least I didn't run away with a British officer and shame the family!"

But apparently, this need to break away and do your own thing was a family trait passed down through the generations. Maybe this was why she'd felt compelled to move all the way to California.

"Is there any way to see if I have any cousins in the UK?"

"You could probably try one of those DNA ancestry kits," Kelly said, amused. "Send in your spit, who knows?"

The idea had some appeal, but sending sensitive personal data—even in the form of spit—spent her lawyer spidey senses tingling. Who knew who'd be able to get access and what was done with the spit? No thank you.

"This is cool. Let's keep going."

"I want to go to the maternal branch of your family tree now."

Cecily rubbed her hands in anticipation. Kelly opened up another folder and showed her another photograph. This time it was a woman, performing a Beijing opera, in full costume and makeup. Finding out all of these things about her past was like discovering buried treasure. Growing up she hadn't been the most interested in family history, but this meeting was changing that big time.

"Who is this?"

Kelly gave a smile. "This is your great-great-grandmother, Tsai Fa Li. She was a well-known, very popular Beijing opera star in her day."

Cecily's jaw dropped. "Get out. Really?"

"Yes indeed. We found reviews of her performances in some newspapers. Here's one from 1888 from a Peking newspaper. You can read the translation here." Fascinated, she ran her hands over the photo and pored over the image. Her great-great-grandmother stared back at her, her gaze bold and fearless, the jut of her chin defiant. This was a woman with spirit and spine, one who knew how to command the attention of a room. Perhaps it was all just part of the performance, but Cecily liked to think those traits also applied to her great-great-grandmother, and had been passed down through the generations. There was just something in the snap in Fa Li's eyes that told Cecily her great-great-grandmother was no wallflower, no pushover.

"My sister Gillian looks a little bit like her," Cecily murmured. "Around the eyes and the mouth." It was surreal really. Looking at the face of a woman who died over a hundred years ago, and knowing that part of Fa Li's DNA ran in her own veins. History truly was a past, present, and future thing.

Kelly opened up her laptop and tapped at the keyboard for a few minutes. She then turned the screen toward Cecily. "We were able to find an actual recording of one of her performances. Would you like to hear it?"

"What? How?"

"Beijing University has a database and I reached out to a colleague there. They were able to find this recording for us. Want to take a listen?"

"Absolutely."

"This is a song from *The Drunken Concubine*, which is the story of Yang Yuhuan. Yuhuan is known as one of the Four Beauties of Ancient China and was a concubine of Emperor Xuanzong."

Kelly offered a set of earbuds and Cecily stuffed them into her ears and adjusted the volume of the computer. As her great-great-grandmother's voice came through the earbuds, a tear slid down her cheek. If she was honest, she didn't understand the lyrics to the music, but something about the soaring melody spoke to her very soul. As if somehow in her bones, she knew what her great-great-grandmother was trying to convey with the music on some deep spiritual level. As the song ended, she gave a small hiccup, and wiped the corner of her eye. Moved beyond words, she took the earbuds off.

"Shit. Whatever I'm paying you, it's not enough. This is incredible."

"I had fun with this project, so the pleasure was all mine. Really."

Cecily gave a sniffle. "I can't believe you were able to find all this."

Kelly gave a grin. "Oh, I'm not done yet. Let's read on."

"I don't think my heart can take anymore."

"Somehow I think you'll be able to handle it."

Kelly pulled out another folder and showed Cecily another document.

"This is your great-grandfather, Chang Ching Jia. He was the first member of your family on your father's side to come to the United States."

"Yes," Cecily said. "Family legend said he came over when he was twenty, trying to start a new life."

"Well this is your great-grandfather's naturalization certificate. It's dated October 3, 1945."

"I know I keep repeating myself but holy crap," Cecily whispered.

"You're looking at the moment the first ancestor in your family became an American citizen. How does it feel?"

"Like I owe him a great debt," Cecily responded. And it was the truth. This was the man who'd changed the trajectory of her life before she'd even been born. Who'd opened the whole world of possibilities for her. If it hadn't been for her great-grandfather's decision to take that risk to come to America, who knows what her life would have been. Instead of a lawyer living in San Francisco, she could have been a peasant girl living in rural China, working the family farm, like previous generations of her family. She could be speaking fluent Mandarin or a local dialect, instead of Chinglish. Her family could have fallen victim to Mao's regime and she may not even exist at all. Or she could be a high-powered businesswoman in Beijing or Shanghai living it up *Sex and the City*, Asian style. Who knew?

The life she had was thanks to this man, her grandparents, her parents. Everyone who had sacrificed and built a future so she could live the life she had now. She truly stood on the shoulders of giants. It was a humbling realization. And a great responsibility to shoulder.

Kelly looked at her watch. "I think our time is just about up. And I need to meet with a student after we're done here." Both women stood up and got ready to leave.

"Thank you so much," Cecily said sincerely. "You are going to make my parents' year. They're going to love this—I just know it."

"I'm so glad. How about we meet in a few weeks and finalize everything. Then we can talk about how you want to put everything together."

"Perfect." Cecily followed Kelly out of the library, and found her way back to her car. She was patting herself on the back for totally nailing her seventh resolution. There was no way her parents wouldn't love this.

She was feeling so good she decided maybe it was time to make the first overture to Jeffrey. He wasn't out of the doghouse completely but maybe this time out had run its course. And she appreciated that he'd respected her wishes in wanting time and space.

Listen, I've been thinking about the next movie we should watch together.

Do you mean Raise the Red Lantern?

Yes.

I've been hoping to hear from you. Thanks for reaching out.

I'm still not happy, but I can understand where you were coming from. It'll take time but I'll get over it and we can move on. As long as you remember to just talk to me instead of assuming and pressing all those feelings down. And I promise to really listen.

Deal!

Great. Cecily gave a grin, her heart feeling lighter. *I found a new Taiwanese restaurant that opened nearby so maybe we can get food there when we watch it.*

Sounds good to me.

Excellent. We'll figure out the schedule and I'll see you soon. Then she paused.

Does Raise the Red Lantern have a wedding in it?

There was a long pause before Jeffrey responded. *Perhaps we should go with a different movie.*

Let's. Cecily shook her head as she started the car and made her way home. Two steps forward, one step back.

Chapter Thirteen

CECILY WAS FEELING good. She'd had a great day at work, and her zoning hearing had gone off without a hitch. She was ready to let off some steam and celebrate and enjoy the nice spring weather. Walking out of her office, she saw that the bullpen was slowly clearing out, with people shutting down their computers and making their way home. She bit her lip. Priscilla was long gone, having left early to take her kid to the orthodontist, Jeffrey was back in L.A., and she knew Adrienne was tied up in a deposition. So, she was at loose ends.

What was she going to do? She could pop in another movie from Jeffrey's list but she felt the need for some company. Just then she saw a group of young female associates who were chatting as they walked toward her. One of them saw her and came to an abrupt stop, and the rest of the group followed suit. And they all fell silent.

One of them—Jennifer maybe—cleared her throat. "Uh hi. Is there something we could help you with, Cecily?" Never mind that they worked in a different practice group. When a senior associate asked you to jump, the only acceptable response was "how high?"

"Oh no, I'm just on my way out. Are you all done for

the day?"

One of the others spoke up. "Yeah except for these depositions I'm going to read on the way home," she said, lifting her briefcase. Cecily winced in commiseration. "But we're grabbing a drink first."

Oh perfect. Cecily beamed as inspiration struck. This was a group of young female lawyers starting out, who probably were overworked, overstressed and still learning the ropes. What a perfect opportunity for her to reach out and offer some advice and mentorship. She was still a little hurt that Rachel had turned down her offer to stay with her when she visited San Francisco. Maybe this was a way to put Resolution 4 back on track. And maybe making some more work friends (or work acquaintances—Adrienne would kill her if she was replaced as work bestie) could lead to her getting more of a life if that meant more after-work happy hours.

"Oh, would you guys care for some company? I know you all are starting out, so if you'd like you could ask me any questions you might have, pick my brain. Or we could just chill and have some fun. My treat," she offered.

The other associates gave each other a look. Then the ringleader said, "Sure," in a bright, cheery voice.

Even Cecily wasn't oblivious enough to not recognize a pity invite when she heard one. She pretended to answer a ping on her phone. "Damn. I forgot I have some errands to take care of. Guess that drink will have to wait for another time." She tried not to take the barely disguised looks of relief personally.

"For sure, we'll definitely make that happen another time. Rain check." In other words, when hell froze over.

Cecily stood there as the younger associates escaped and made their way to the elevators. No doubt they were talking about her and her spectacular fail at attempting to bond. She gave a sigh and rubbed her head. She'd made a total fool of herself for no reason. That had gone horribly wrong, even though she'd meant well.

Was she really that bad company? She was fun; she knew how to have a good time damn it. She frowned as her phone actually rang. It was Jeffrey.

"Hey." His voice was warm and made her smile despite her recent debacle. He had been making a concerted effort to keep in better touch after she'd reached out to him.

"What's up? To what do I owe the pleasure of this call?"

"I just missed hearing your voice and wanted to say hi."

Awwwwww. "Well I appreciate that. It's nice to hear from you too."

"What's going on? Are you still at work?"

"On my way home as a matter of fact. I tried to invite some of the younger associates out for a drink, but I was roundly rebuffed. They were on their way out and I offered to treat them, and you would have thought I was trying to recruit them into an MLM."

"Rejection's a bitch." The sympathy in his tone made her feel a bit better.

"The biggest."

"But you said they were younger associates, right?"

"Yes, why? I was trying to be nice!" Just like she'd tried to be nice to Rachel and been turned down.

"I know," Jeffrey said in a placating tone. "But it's not about that. You mean well but look at it from their perspective. They've had a long day at work and want to blow off some steam before doing another hour or two of work when they get home. Would you want to hang out with your bosses after work if you didn't have to?"

Cecily bit her lip. He had a point, damn it. "But I'm not their boss. I'm just a senior associate."

"What do your people call it? A distinction without a difference. You're close enough. Let them have their space. Let those poor souls drink in peace."

"Fine, fine." Then she paused. "Did you say distinction without a difference?"

"Yes, yes I did. I thought that would impress you."

"Are you studying up to impress me?"

"In the interest of full disclosure, no. Because you were so adamant about me not Netflix-cheating on you, I'm putting on *Law and Order* reruns while I work. Pretty sure I heard Sam Waterston rattle that off at some point. Anyway, all I'm trying to say is, getting rejected sucks but it's probably got nothing to do with you personally. It's okay."

Cecily had to admit the wisdom of Jeffrey's advice. She'd been focused on her overture being turned down, but she hadn't considered the associates' perspective. Goodness knows if the shoe were on the other foot, she wouldn't be that eager to spend time with the partners if she didn't have to.

And maybe Rachel not wanting to stay with her didn't mean she was rejecting her hospitality. Rachel could just be someone who liked their own space and privacy. Totally understandable.

Feeling lighter, Cecily grinned. "I'm so glad you called. And thank you for the pep talk—it really helped." She hefted her briefcase and made her way to the elevators.

"Anytime. Can I still get points for the legal mumbo jumbo?"

"I'll take it under advisement."

"You're a tough judge."

"Damn straight I am. Though actually I never considered a career on the bench, but maybe that should change. Judge Chang does have a certain ring to it."

She heard him chuckle and fake a wary sigh. "I have unleashed a monster. I'm hanging up now. I miss you, and I'll see you soon."

"Miss you too. Bye."

With a shake of her head, Cecily made her way to the elevator to start her trek home. Perhaps fate had been doing her a favor. Instead of a noisy night at a crowded bar making awkward small talk, she could go home, get into her pajamas, put on a face mask and watch something mindless on TV to decompress. That sounded way more appealing.

Forty-five minutes later, she was back home at her apartment, pajamas on, hair up, face mask on, and collapsed on her couch. For the fun of it, she'd decided to watch a Spanish period drama on Netflix that was so bonkers she was highly entertained even though the plot made no sense and she in fact had no idea what the hell was going on.

Just then she saw her phone ding with a message from Rachel. Well, that was a surprise.

Hey. Hope this isn't a bad time.

No. Not at all. What's up?

I'm just letting you know I booked my flight and reserved my Airbnb for my trip to San Francisco. I'll be there the last week of April. If you're still up for it, dinner would be great. But no pressure. I know how busy you are.

Cecily gave an inward cheer. Yes, tangible proof Rachel didn't actually hate her and maybe did want to be friends. She quickly typed back a reply.

Of course! Dinner would be great. I'll clear my calendar for Friday or Saturday night and check with my friend Adrienne to make sure she can join us. It'll be great.

Sounds like a plan. Looking forward to it.

Same. And let me know if you want a ride from the airport instead of splurging on a taxi or Uber. Cecily held her breath as she waited for a response.

Actually, that would be great.

Rachel then sent a screenshot of her flight details and Cecily dutifully filed away the information.

I appreciate you making time for me. And the ride.

Anytime. If you need any recommendations from a local, hit me up.

Will do. And thanks for understanding about not staying with you. Hope you know it's nothing personal. I just feel more comfortable in my own space.

Well she'd be damned. Jeffrey was absolutely right

about looking at different perspectives after all. But she wasn't going to tell him that. A girl still needed some secrets after all. And a lawyer knew better than to give opposing counsel any advantage.

And besides I really don't want to walk in on anything I shouldn't.

Cecily stared at her screen, her face heating as she guessed Rachel's meaning.

What?

You and the sex god. There are some things I'd rather avoid seeing. I'm better off giving you two your privacy.

Cecily groaned and face-palmed. She was never going to live this down. On the other hand, it was a good sign that Rachel felt comfortable making a joke and giving her a hard time.

How was she supposed to respond to that? Sometimes friends could be the worst because they know how to best roast you. Luckily Rachel saved her from having to form a reply.

I gotta go to bed. I just wanted to let you know my plans. See you in a few weeks. Good night.

Good night.

Cecily sighed but there was a smile on her face. Maybe her earlier attempt to make some more friends had back-fired, but clearly, she and Rachel had made a great headway to developing a strong rapport and she couldn't be happier. And she was looking forward to seeing Rachel in a few weeks.

Resolution 4 was going very well. She just had to re-member to cut herself and others more slack, and realize that sometimes her interpretation of events wasn't accurate.

She'd made progress on her list and had had a grow-ing/learning moment. All in all, not a bad day.

JEFFREY WALKED QUICKLY up the street to his apartment complex, carrying a large bag of Mexican takeout. He was starving and dying to dig into his carnitas tacos. Plus, he was still riding high from how well Cecily had taken to the film club and his selections. He couldn't wait for them to watch the next movie together now that she had come to spend the weekend with him.

He opened the door, took off his shoes, and made a beeline to the kitchen table. He put the bag down, ripped it open, and started emptying the contents, laying it out like a banquet feast from *Eat Drink Man Woman*.

"Hey CeeCee, I'm back," he called out. "I didn't know if you wanted medium or spicy salsa to go with the chips and guac. I think I have some mild in the fridge if you'd rather have that." No response.

He tried again. "This smells delicious, and the tortillas are fresh. We should dig in before it gets soggy. Besides, I'm starving. I'm liable to eat your portion if you're not careful."

More silence. Had she turned mute in the twenty minutes he'd been away?

Baffled and annoyed he walked into the living room to find Cecily. He found her sitting in his armchair, arms crossed, foot tapping. The expression on her face made it clear she was not happy with him and he was in serious shit.

"What's wrong?" They were just finding their footing after the *Monster-in-Law* bombshell, and things were starting to get back to normal. What could he have done to mess up again already?

"You really have to ask? You know what you did."

"I really don't. But clearly you're upset."

"Well, can you blame me? I thought I could trust you. I believed in you."

"Okay, I honestly don't know what the hell you're talking about."

She pointed an accusing finger and announced in a grim tone "I just found out you cheated on me."

"Are you kidding me?" Jeffrey sputtered. "I would never. Where are you getting this from?" This had to be some crazy nightmare he was in. How could she possibly think he'd cheat on her? It was beyond insane.

Cecily pursed her lips. "All right then. Let's look at the evidence." She got up from the armchair, grabbed the remote and turned the TV on. She then pulled up the Netflix app, and logged in. She tapped onto a few more screens and pulled up *The Great British Baking Show*.

"Now, the last time we were together we watched the end of Season Three. Is that correct?"

"What the hell? Are you actually cross-examining me right now? And what does this have to do with cheating?" Now he was confused and hungry.

"Just answer the question."

"Okay. Fine, yes. I guess it was." If this was Cecily in trial lawyer mode, he wanted no part of it. She was scary as hell.

"Now, did we or did we not agree that we would wait and watch Season Four together?"

"If you say so."

"A yes or no answer please."

"Okay fine." Had Cecily gone around the bend? What the hell was even happening right now?

Cecily clicked a few more buttons and brought up season four of the show. "And yet, as we can clearly see here, the first two episodes of Season Four have been marked as watched." She then used the remote as a pointer. "You Netflix-cheated! You watched the show without me!"

"Are you kidding me? Is that what this is about?"

"I take Netflix infidelity seriously. What do you have to say for yourself?"

Relieved beyond belief, he calmed down and saw the glint in Cecily's eyes. She wasn't really mad. She was messing with him.

Son of a bitch.

Shaking his head and holding back a laugh, Jeffrey fixed a penitent expression on his face. "I am so sorry. I promise it was an accident. I was working and I turned Netflix on to have some background noise. It was totally random. I didn't mean it."

"That doesn't make it okay." Her lips were trembling too, obviously struggling to keep a straight face.

"Would it help if I swear it meant nothing to me? It

was a one-time fluke, I promise."

"That makes it worse." Man, Cecily was playing it up to the hilt, trying to channel her inner movie star. But what the hell, he could get into the spirit too.

With a dramatic sigh, he got down on his knees, clasped his hands in a prayer position, and said, "You're right. I am completely guilty, and I have no excuse. I throw myself on the mercy of the court."

Giving up, Cecily giggled helplessly and grabbed his hands to help him up. "You are such a dork," she said with affection.

"I'm just glad you aren't actually mad."

"Of course I'm not mad. Slightly irritated but there are worse things than Netflix-cheating." But she gave a warning look. "Just don't do it again."

"Never, Scout's honor." He even held up his hand and gave the salute.

"You were never even a Boy Scout, this means nothing to me."

"Okay fine. I'll swear a blood oath if that's what it'll take. Now can we please go eat? I'm really starving." His stomach was rumbling, and while he was more than willing to go along with the silliness, getting between a Lee and their next meal was never a good idea.

"Yeah. Me too, and you're right. Those tacos and the guac do smell amazing."

"I'm blaming you if everything's gone soggy," he warned as they made their way back to the kitchen.

"That's on you. Your Netflix transgression had to be

addressed." She shrugged.

He really must be sunk when even her pain-in-the-ass moments made him laugh instead of wanting to tear his hair out.

"Let's eat."

An hour later, the food had been demolished, the table cleared, the leftovers put away, and now he was doing kitchen cleanup. He was elbow-deep in soapsuds when his phone rang. He swore mildly. He turned to Cecily who was trying to "help" by rearranging the canned goods in his cabinet. Apparently it was unacceptable that it wasn't arranged alphabetically and by expiration date.

"Would you mind getting that for me?"

"I charge $350 an hour to deal with phone calls."

He threw her a look and she relented.

"Fine, fine. I can play receptionist." She went over, grabbed his phone, and answered with a perky chirp, "Hello, Jeffrey Lee's line. He's not available to come to the phone right now, but would you like to leave him a message?"

Oh for God's sake.

Jeffrey went back to the dishes without another thought.

"Uh huh… Uh huh… Oh I see. Yes, I'll be sure to give him the message. No, I'm just a friend. It was nice talking to you too. Have a good night."

Cecily hung up the phone and went silent. Without a word, she pulled out a chair at the kitchen table and sat back down.

He grabbed a dishcloth and dried his hands.

"Well, that didn't sound like a telemarketer. Who was it?"

She didn't say a word, just tapped his phone against her palm.

He swallowed nervously. "Why do I get the feeling I'm in trouble again?"

Cecily raised her brow before speaking. "Well, I was speaking with someone named Greg. I believe he's a friend of yours. Someone you've worked with."

"Oh yeah, he directed an indie film I wrote."

"A film you say?"

"Yes, why?"

"Well, Greg was just calling to remind you that he's throwing a party to celebrate this little film that I never knew about. He wanted me to remind you to come, and to bring a case of beer." Her voice rose. "A film that's getting shown at NYC Film Festival, apparently."

Crap. He could tell this time she wasn't pretending to be angry. She was honestly upset. Her face was flushed, and her voice was tight.

"Oh, that movie."

"Yeah. That movie." The look on her face told him he better start explaining, fast.

"It was a small movie Greg made last year, and he entered it on a whim. Neither of us expected it to final and be shown. And I was a finalist in the screenwriting contest, but I didn't win. It was cool, but not really a big deal."

"Not a big deal? It's an incredibly big deal! Why didn't

you tell your family? More importantly, why didn't you tell me?" She punched him on the shoulder.

"Well, nothing really came of it. I didn't win. We got some good reviews, and we got to meet some cool people, but I figured no one would really be interested. I don't really get why you're mad I didn't tell you."

"I'm mad because that is an incredibly huge accomplishment! I'm so proud of you I could burst!"

Now he was confused. "But I didn't win. And it's not like I won a million-dollar settlement or something like you do at work."

"So what, who cares? Getting your work out there is huge. And landing a prestigious film festival is totally something you should've told all of us about. You should have told your parents, I'm sure they would have bragged to the neighbors for weeks! I'm not in a creative field, but I imagine it takes a lot of courage and hard work to put your work out into the world like that."

"It can be terrifying," he admitted.

He hadn't expected her to be so understanding and insightful. He assumed Cecily wouldn't take his work seriously, and wouldn't be impressed at all. Instead she was beaming and pride was radiating off of her. Then her expression turned thoughtful.

"But why didn't you tell me? I freely admit I know nothing about your industry, but I could have listened, I could've been there for you. Why didn't you let me?"

Her question stumped him. "I don't know," he admitted. Her reaction told him he had been wrong to assume she wouldn't understand or take him or his work seriously.

"Unless you thought because I'm not in Hollywood I wouldn't understand, which I get. But please know even if that is the case I would still always support you one hundred percent, okay?"

"Duly noted," he responded with a grin, his heart lightening.

"Is this why you didn't tell your family either? You didn't think they'd be understanding or supportive if it didn't work out?" she asked briskly. He gave a silent nod.

"Look, I get why you feel that way. Our parents can be tough. But they're not heartless. And besides, what's the point of you writing these incredible stories if you aren't going to share them with everyone? You don't have to do this alone, you're just choosing to. I think you should really consider inviting them. They'd love it and be so proud." Sensing his hesitation, Cecily went on to explain. "Plus, don't you think letting them see tangible proof of something you've done could help assuage their concerns and help them understand better? You being a bit more open could help get them off your back."

Jeffrey tilted his head. That was an excellent point she'd made. "I'll definitely think about it," he conceded.

"Good. But I'm still mad at you. You should give yourself more credit. Stop making light of all of your hard work, and your accomplishments. I'm so proud of you, but you should be proud of yourself most of all." She framed his face and gave it a gentle stroke.

Her words touched him deeply. It felt so good to know

that she got it, and was supporting him, even if she didn't know everything Hollywood entailed. It boded well for the future. He really should talk to Greg about that Iris Chang project. He'd definitely be up for that.

"Thank you. That means a lot."

She leaned over and gave him a smacking kiss. "Good. Now, to make it up to me, you're going to dinner with me next month."

He started getting suspicious. "What sort of dinner?"

Cecily's grin was swift and diabolical. "There's a bar association dinner at the Hilton. One of the partners at the firm is a keynote so we all have to go. Bring your suit."

"Are there going to be speeches?" he demanded.

"Oh yeah. Quite a few of them. And the requisite banquet rubber chicken meal."

"Boring speeches?"

"I'll nudge you if you fall asleep and start to snore."

"This all sounds horrible: long awful speeches and inedible chicken. Like straight out of Dante's *Inferno* horrible." Talk about swift and brutal vengeance.

"Oh, it will be," she assured him, patting his shoulder. "But that's what you get for keeping things from me. Suck it up, buttercup."

"Isn't this an Eighth Amendment violation? How does this not count as cruel and unusual punishment?" he griped. It had to qualify.

"No, the Supreme Court has ruled it's constitutional, and an acceptable form of deterrence, but nice try. You're coming with me. April 12th. Mark it on your calendar."

"You're evil, you know that?"

"Lawyer," she reminded him.

"Fine," he grumbled.

"Now, you're going to sit down and tell me everything about this movie. And don't leave anything out."

"I NEED GINGER and garlic." Without a word, he went to a fridge and brought out the requested items. Cecily had completely taken over his small kitchen. The wok was on the stove, and every inch of counter space was used up.

This was an unprecedented side of Cecily. But now, the prospect of having dinner with Greg and Gina was throwing her into a tailspin. After telling Cecily about the movie the night before, it had been decided that it was time for the four of them to meet and have dinner. But now he was having second thoughts.

"Cornstarch."

"In the cabinet over your head," he said. "Are you sure you want to do this?" he asked again. Cecily's hand froze, the cleaver in her hand mid-chop.

"Are you trying to say I can't cook?"

"No, I'm just saying the party is tomorrow, and you've been saying how swamped you are with work. You don't have to do this."

Cecily huffed a breath. "Of course I do. I'm meeting your friends tomorrow. I need to make a good impression."

"In that case, you should just bring a case of wine." He

held up a hand in surrender when she hissed. "Okay, okay. Bad joke, bad timing." He had to remember there was a time and place for this sort of thing and clearly this was not one of them.

"I need a pot for this," she demanded. "Where is it?"

"Where do you think it is? Where it's supposed to be."

With a grunt, she put down the cleaver, took a quick look around, and made a beeline toward the oven. Where any self-respecting Asian stored their pots and pans. Yanking the door open, she rattled around trying to find the right pot for her needs.

"Hey, careful. I'm going to need my security deposit back," he complained.

"You're going to need medical attention if you don't stop getting in my way," she growled.

"If making mapo tofu makes you this aggravated, maybe you shouldn't be making it." He threw up his hands again. "I'm just saying." She was acting like this was life and death. *What gives?*

"Of course, I'm making it. It's my mother's recipe. It's foolproof. Easy to make ahead of time and perfect for a buffet. They're going to love it." Was she trying to convince him or herself?

"I need the tofu and ground pork."

Understanding his place now, he went and got her the requested items.

He watched as she made short work on the tofu. He started to tell her that the pieces were uneven, but then thought better of it. Cecily put the tofu in a bowl and turned her attention to the pork. She ripped open the package and dumped the pork into the sizzling wok. Unfortunately, the hot oil splashed back and hit her hand. Swearing ripely, she ran to the sink to run it under cold water.

He was over in a flash. "Are you okay? Did you burn yourself? Let me see."

"I was stupid and not paying attention. Damn it, I'm okay though."

Without another word, he turned to go to the bathroom, and grabbed the aloe and Band-Aids. Over her protests, he took care of the small burn to make sure it didn't get infected.

"I told you, I'm fine. Stop fussing."

Jeffrey wanted to shake her until he saw the look in her eyes, and suddenly he got it.

"You're nervous," he murmured. How could he have missed it? The shortened temper, tightened voice, the anal-retentiveness. It wasn't impatience, it was panic.

"Of course, I'm nervous," she burst out. "I'm meeting your friends tomorrow. What if they don't like me? Nobody likes lawyers."

He walked over behind her and wrapped his arms across her waist.

"Hey," he protested. "I like you and I'm not nobody. Besides, people may not like lawyers, but we all acknowledge they serve a useful function in society. You know, like alarm clocks. No one likes them, but everyone still uses one to get up in the morning. Annoying, but necessary."

"Is this you trying to make me feel better? Because if so you really suck at it." She leaned back against him, and they ended up sitting on the floor, with his back against the dishwasher.

"You're not a bedbug at least," he persisted. "They're just straight-up evil and have no positive purpose. Feel better now?" For that he earned a half-hearted slap.

Cecily gave a sniffle. "A little." He gave her hand a pat.

"Anyway my friends are going to love you. If anything they're going to give me crap for dating way out of my league."

"Well they're right about that."

"If you want to really be popular, you can lie. Don't tell them you're a lawyer, say you're a kindergarten teacher. That should be safe and non-threatening enough. Or maybe a librarian. You'll be the belle of the ball."

"Stop making me sound like an idiot." She was sounding more like herself. Thank God.

"Just trying to help. We good?"

"Yes."

"Good, because you left the burner on and the pork is almost burning." With a curse, Cecily jumped up and ran to the stove. She turned the burner off immediately, and moved the pot away from the heat. Then took a few deep, calming breaths.

"It's okay," Jeffrey reassured her. "Mapo tofu is so saucy no one will notice if the pork is a little dry."

"Not helping," she muttered. She concentrated and

pulled up her mother's recipe on her smartphone.

Jeffrey peered over her shoulder. "I have the chili oil and bean paste."

"You want to help me with the rest of this?"

He gave her a grin. "Sure." Working together in harmony, the dish came together in no time. Half an hour later, they were putting the last touches on their masterpiece, throwing some fresh scallions on top. The firm tofu cubes were swimming in a bright red spicy sauce speckled with the ground pork, and the chilies were hitting them right in the face, just like they were supposed to. Cecily grabbed a teaspoon from the drawer next to her and dipped it into the wok for a taste test. She put the spoon in her mouth and tasted the sauce.

"Hhmm, I think it needs a dash of vinegar. What do you think?" She held up the spoon to Jeffrey. He promptly swallowed the remaining contents.

"It's really good." Without another word, he reached overhead to grab a bowl.

"What are you doing?"

"Having a snack before dinner." He grabbed a serving spoon and prepared to dig in.

Without compunction, she slapped his hand away.

"No you don't. This is going into the fridge for the party tomorrow. Besides, you know this stuff gets better the next day, though I've never understood why."

"But I'm hungry," he complained.

"How about I make you a sandwich?"

"You have a pot of mapo tofu here that I can just dig

into, but you expect me to settle for a measly sandwich instead?"

Cecily put the lid on the wok with a resolute snap. "Do not touch this under penalty of death. If you don't want a sandwich, I'll make you something else."

"Just for the record, I don't like this Stepford wife side of you."

"Do you want a sandwich or not?"

"Fine. If that's how you're going to be about this."

JEFFREY WALKED INTO the outer office at the production company and tried to not turn around and run right back out. The receptionist behind the front desk looked up from the computer screen and gave him a smile. "Can I help you, sir?"

"Hi, I'm Jeffrey Lee. I have a two o'clock meeting?" After a few clicks at the keyboard, she looked back up.

As fun as last weekend with Cecily, Gina, and Greg had been, the dreaded day had finally come. It was his High Noon. He was meeting with the producers about the Ian Grey series.

"Yes, they're running a few minutes behind, but you can have a seat right over there," she said, pointing over to a set of white sofas and two armchairs. "They'll be right with you."

"Thank you…I'm sorry, what's your name?"

The receptionist blinked in surprise. "Sarah. Uh, my

name is Sarah."

"Thank you, Sarah."

Sarah's smile warmed a few degrees. "Would you like some water? Can I bring you some coffee?"

"No, I'm good. Thank you." He sat on the couch, and grabbed his stack of notecards from his pocket, trying to rehearse and memorize the points he wanted to make. His heart was pounding; his palms were sweating.

Jeffrey tried to remind himself this was a Hollywood meeting. It wasn't like he was going off to war. The stakes were high, but not life and death. No one ever died from doing this. The worst that could happen was they said no. The rejection would be devastating, and he would want to die, but life would go on.

However, if the adrenaline spike was any indication, his body thought he *was* about to enter a war zone.

"This is it. Don't throw away your shot. Your one big chance to level up. It's no hundred-million-dollar deal but it's not nothing either." He sat for a few more agonizing minutes as the clock kept ticking.

Mercifully, Sarah came over and led him down the hallway to a meeting room where three executive suits were sitting, leaning back in their chairs, ready to play judge, jury, and executioner. They got up and introduced themselves as Glenn Campbell, Tom Vernon, and Carl St. James.

Carl spoke first. "We're excited to meet and talk with you. Heard great things."

Oh great. No pressure there.

"You ready to get started?" Tom asked. He saw the look on Jeffrey's face and gave a slight chuckle. "Don't worry. This is more of a get-to-know-you thing. You can relax. I promise, no one has ever died from doing this."

The other two men chuckled as well. Which was such a comfort. Not.

Jeffrey fumbled for his stack of notecards, but Glenn put his hands up.

"No, no, put those away—you don't need them."

"I'm sorry?"

"Let's not use the note cards. We want you to be more natural. The notecard makes you seem too stiff and rehearsed. Just be yourself."

Just then the magnitude of everything crashed down on him. The room spun and he stopped breathing. He felt crowded and suffocated. His ears were ringing, and his adrenaline was spiking. He didn't know what was going on, but all he knew was that his fight-or-flight instincts were kicking in.

He had to get out. Now. He tugged at his collar, and croaked out, "I'm sorry. I'll be right back. Need to use the restroom." He all but sprinted out of the room and back down the hallway. As he made his way out of the entrance of the production company, he heard Sarah calling after him, "Sir? Sir?"

The next hour was a blur as he got in an Uber and made his way back to his apartment. He yanked open his front door, kicked off his shoes, and blindly made his way to his bedroom. He slammed the door shut, pulled all the blinds and plunged the room into darkness. That's what he needed right now. Darkness, silence, and oblivion. He had just bombed big time, and most likely committed career suicide. Forget being able to write any more blockbusters or small critically acclaimed indies in the future. He'd be lucky to get a job writing commercial jingles. A man needed privacy at a time like this.

But it was not to be. Soon enough, his phone rang insistently. He saw the name on the screen and groaned.

"What happened in there?" Marty demanded. "You imploded."

"Yeah I know," he admitted. "I just lived through it. I don't need a reminder."

"Not good enough. Start explaining," Marty barked.

"I'm sorry. I just panicked, and I left before I made an even bigger ass of myself. I know how bad this is, trust me. No need to get into the details."

"Do you know how this looks? Do you know how this makes me look?"

Jeffrey squeezed his eyes shut as the guilt landed on his shoulders like a giant boulder.

"I know, I'm sorry. I don't know what else to say."

Marty harumphed and heaved a sigh. "Well, what's done is done. Let me see what I can do to salvage this mess. I'll be in touch."

"Thanks."

He made his way to the kitchen, and grabbed a beer from the fridge. He didn't care that it was three in the afternoon. This was an emergency.

Just then he got a call from Cecily. He closed his eyes. Great.

"Hi," she said in a bright, bubbly voice as soon as he answered. "I just wanted to see how the meeting went. I'm on a break from my CLE so I wanted to check in."

He took a deep breath as he tried to figure out what to say. Part of him now wished he hadn't told her about this meeting during the dinner with Gina and Greg.

"Hey. Is everything okay?" The concern in her voice almost killed him.

"I'm fine." Then after a pause he came clean. "No actually I'm not. The meeting didn't go well at all."

"Oh no what happened? Were there some sort of technical difficulties? Were those producers jerks?"

"Nothing like that." He had to laugh a little at Cecily's indignant tone. She sounded like she was ready to kick some ass for him. Bless her heart.

"Then what happened?" Her voice became totally puzzled.

"I had a panic attack and walked out before the meeting even started," he confessed.

"Wait. What?"

"I think it all hit me at once and I couldn't handle it, I guess. I totally blew it."

The phone was silent for what seemed like forever. Just when he thought she'd hung up, she finally spoke. "You know what? I've had bad days in court and messed up. I remember the night before my first hearing, I was sick to my stomach and I almost threw up before I went into the courtroom. So I get it."

He let out a breath he hadn't known he'd been holding. She understood and didn't think he was an idiot.

"But the important thing is to pick yourself up and keep going," she continued. "I took the ten minutes to get myself together and remember that my client was depending on me, and that I was as ready and prepared as I could be. You can ask if you can have a redo, see if they'll let you give your pitch again."

"I don't know if that's possible," he began.

"You don't know unless you try," she pointed out. "Ask your agent. That's what he's there for, right? And we can make sure you're super prepared for the next meeting. You can practice and rehearse with me. That way it'll cut down on the nerves. You can totally do this."

"That's incredibly kind of you to offer," he managed.

"Of course," she said warmly. "Everyone suffers setbacks. The important thing is how you bounce back. And I know you can. This isn't the end of the world."

One the one hand, the fact that Cecily was being so supportive was wonderful. On the other hand, he had no idea if he could bounce back from this. There was no guarantee Marty could convince those producers to give him another meeting. He had to have a plan for what to do next.

"You're right. I'll talk to Marty and see what he says. But it may just be a better idea for me to work on something new and start fresh."

"But Jeffrey, if this is something you want, you should

fight for it." Cecily's voice was intense now. And part of her sounded baffled as well. Which made sense. Cecily would always attack a problem and wouldn't stop until she'd solved it and wrestled it into submission.

"I understand what you're saying, but this is Hollywood. It may not be up to me," he pointed out. "I'm just trying to keep my bases covered. If it works out great. If not, I got other irons in the fire. It's how we were taught after all. Hope for the best but prepare for the worst." He really was intrigued by Greg's idea of a movie about Iris Chang and he could feel the ideas bubbling.

"Well, I think you shouldn't give up on landing this gig quite yet. But I have to admit I don't know or understand the workings of Hollywood, so do what you think is best. I'm here to support you. And my offer still stands. I can so help you kick ass and impress those producers."

"That means a lot," he said sincerely. He knew Cecily meant what she said, but it was clear she would prefer he fight to write for the Ian Grey franchise. Part of him would love to, but that depended on way too many factors out of his control.

"Good, I'm glad."

"So what else do you have going on?"

"Well Rachel is coming out to San Francisco next week so Adrienne and I are taking her out to dinner. Maybe some sightseeing if she's up for it."

"Well that's a recipe for trouble." He chuckled. Then he gave a slight frown. "I got tortured by a horrible bar association dinner two weeks ago and Rachel gets the red carpet treatment? How's that fair?"

"I'm sure I have no idea what you're talking about," Cecily said with a sniff.

As they continued to chat, Jeffrey could feel the weight leave his shoulders. Maybe this whole day wouldn't be a complete disaster and he could find a way to fix things. Maybe.

Chapter Fourteen

CECILY LOOKED UP from her phone to Adrienne's expectant face.

"Rachel's on her way. She should be here any minute. Be nice," she warned.

Ever since she and Rachel had confirmed their plans, she'd been looking forward to this dinner, and for her two friends to meet.

"Girl, I'm always nice," Adrienne said with a wave of her hand. She took another sip of her old-fashioned.

"I mean it, Adrienne. Rachel is shy. I don't want to scare her off."

"All right. I promise I'll be a Stepford friend."

"Ha ha."

"I never heard you talk about her before," Adrienne commented.

"We grew up in the same neighborhood. Weren't really close. We reconnected over New Year's."

"Seriously? First you get back with your ex, then you made a new friend? And you tried to keep all that from me?"

Cecily frowned. "I thought we'd already covered that. I paid my penance." She'd spent two miserable Saturday afternoons in a row helping her best friend with trial prep. The slate had to be wiped clean by now.

"The jury is still out on that." Fantastic.

Rachel walked up to the table and blinked. "Um sorry. Am I late?"

"Oh, not at all." Cecily climbed out of the booth and gave her a hug, which Rachel awkwardly returned.

"This is Adrienne. Adrienne, this is Rachel Bai."

Adrienne also got out of the booth to hug Rachel. Once they all settled back in, they pored over the menu.

"Do you want to get something to drink?" Cecily asked. "I ordered a Bellini and it's delicious."

"I think I'll stick with water, thanks."

Adrienne raised a brow. "So, I've been looking forward to meeting you. CeeCee has told me a lot about you."

"Oh."

"All good things," Cecily rushed to clarify.

"That's good to know. She mentioned you, and that grew up here and you're a lawyer too. I don't think she said much else about you."

The way Adrienne's eyes drilled into Cecily's told her she was about to spend a few more weekends paying penance. Crap.

"Have you been having fun on your vacation?"

Rachel gave a small smile. "Actually yes. I visited Alcatraz today. It was fascinating. I went to the Ghirardelli factory, rode the cable cars."

"Ticking off all the big touristy items." She'd lived in San Francisco for years and still hadn't made it to the

Ghirardelli factory. She made a mental note to put it on her schedule.

"What do you have planned for tomorrow?"

"I think I'll walk the Golden Gate Bridge."

"Can't visit San Francisco without doing that," Adrienne said with approval. "Make sure you wear comfortable shoes."

"I don't have any that aren't," Rachel replied wryly.

"How's your Airbnb?"

"Fine. Adequate for my needs. Close to public transportation and I can walk to a lot of places."

"You aren't staying with CeeCee?" Adrienne asked in surprise.

"No. She offered but I preferred my own space."

Cecily raised her eyebrow to say, *See?*

"Besides," Rachel continued. "I didn't want to walk in and see something I shouldn't have. Especially if the sex god was around."

Cecily groaned as Adrienne burst out in peals of laughter. She was so lucky Jeffrey wasn't here to hear this conversation. He'd stayed home this weekend to work. She'd never hear the end of it, and his ego would swell to insufferable proportions.

"Sex god?"

"Yes, Jeffrey."

"You call him a sex god?"

"Absolutely not! She came up with that." Cecily pointed an accusing finger at Rachel, who shrugged unrepentantly.

"It was an understandable mistake. You should've been more clear."

"That is not what happened and you know it!"

"I need details."

"It's a long story. We don't have time for that."

"I have time. Do you?" Adrienne asked Rachel.

"Sure. I don't have anything planned for the rest of the night. Just going back to my Airbnb to rest. My feet are starting to kill me."

"Spill." When hell froze over.

"No. But I'm warning you now if either of you uses that phrase in front of him, I'll kill you. Got it?" She tried to infuse as much menace into her tone as possible, but her efforts fell flat. Neither of them were taking her seriously at all.

"I think I just received a death threat," Rachel said, eyes wide.

"No worries," Adrienne replied. "I'm a witness. If she ever goes through with it, I'll testify for the prosecution at her murder trial. It'll prove premeditation and intent—that way she won't be able to plea down to manslaughter. I got you. Assuming she doesn't decide to off both of us at the same time."

"Ditto. And for the next while, we should be careful to not eat or drink anything she's personally handled. You know, just to be safe."

"Good call," Adrienne said with a nod.

"Are you two done?" Exasperated but amused, she couldn't help but be happy that the two of them were hitting it off. Even if it was at her expense.

"You started it," they replied in unison.

"I need another drink," Cecily grumbled.

"Nope. Not until we toast." Adrienne raised her glass. "To Rachel and her first visit to San Francisco. May she enjoy everything our fair city has to offer. And to friendship. Even when one of us is threatening to commit a felony against the others."

Rachel and Cecily also held up their drinks and the three women clinked glasses. "Cheers!"

IT WAS NOW mid-May and, once again, Cecily found herself sitting at San Francisco International waiting to board her flight. And once again, she was heading home back to Brooklyn. This time it was to celebrate her parents' fortieth anniversary. She had been lucky that she'd been able to get the time off. Lucky meaning she'd had to say goodbye to that spa weekend in Napa. Filial piety really did suck sometimes. But in this case it'd be worth it.

The good part was Jeffrey was also heading home the same weekend to celebrate Bethany's graduation, so this time they could be a support system for each other.

She sent him a quick text to check in and got a quick reply.

I'm getting ready to board. See you in a few hours.

Safe travels. See you soon! She sent a kissy-face emoji before she could think better of it. There was a big smile on her face as she hit send.

What a difference a few months could make.

As promised, Jeffrey gave her excellent directions on where to find him in the baggage claim area. She couldn't help it—her face lit up when she saw him. Sneaking up behind him, she covered his eyes and whispered in his ear, "Guess who?"

"Keira Knightley," he said without hesitation. She pinched his arm.

"Just kidding," he murmured as he lowered his lips to hers for a kiss.

"I missed you," Cecily confessed when they came back up for air. His face broke out in a grin as he hugged her close.

"Same here. You ready?"

She hitched up her overnight bag and carry-on suitcase. "Yup. Let's call an Uber." They both looked at each other for a moment, until Jeffrey got the message.

"You mean let *me* call an Uber," he said ruefully.

"Will you look at that, beauty and brains," she teased.

"I ordered the Uber last time," he pointed out.

"Some traditions are meant to be observed and respected."

He shook his head. "Fine. Then I expect you to pay your half tomorrow."

"Absolutely. We just need to factor in the girlfriend discount, which says I don't pay. Meaning I owe you zero."

He threw her a look, and she smiled unrepentantly.

"It'll be here in three minutes," he grumbled. But he put his arms around her waist as they walked out of baggage claim together.

"Great. That'll give us plenty of time to discuss your Keira Knightley fixation."

"It was a *joke*."

SITTING NERVOUSLY AT the edge of the couch, Cecily laced her hands together as she watched her parents open their present. So far, her parents' anniversary celebration was a complete success. The food at the banquet hall was delicious and roundly praised. One of her uncles had even smuggled a bottle of Kaoliang liquor to the party. As expected, Owen was perfect in his role as MC, keeping the crowd laughing and entertained. Her parents were eating it up. While still maintaining proper Asian levels of decorum and modesty as they soaked in all the attention and praise. Meaning they spent the whole time pretending they were embarrassed and hating it.

Now they were back home for the private family event.

Gillian, Peter, and Owen had gone in together to surprise her parents with a five-day Caribbean cruise. Her mother had been excited even as she put up token protests about how extravagant it was, and how they shouldn't have wasted their money. "Too expensive!" But now it was her turn.

Her mother frowned as she tried to remove the gift wrap and unscroll the tree. "This is so heavy." Once it was removed, she stepped back to look at it.

"What is this?"

"This is our family tree, Ma. I hired a genealogist to research out family history and she put this together for you and Dad. Isn't it cool? You can hang it up on the wall."

Judith's scowl deepened. "You hired someone to dig into our family business?"

Was she kidding with this? Cecily threw a look at her siblings. Gill, bless her, spoke up.

"Ma, look at this. The genealogist traced our family all the way back to the 1600s! That's incredible."

"It's so big." Her mother, always ready to find the flaw in every situation.

"Well, that's what happens when the family tree goes back ten generations," Cecily said through gritted teeth.

"It's very nice sweetheart," Paul said with a soothing pat on her back. "This must have taken a lot of work."

Ever the peacekeeper, her father. Bless him for trying.

"Yes, Kelly spent months putting all this together. And there's more." Reaching behind the couch, Cecily presented the scrapbook she'd had professionally done too.

"Kelly also found letters, newspaper articles, photos, and I put it together in this book."

With great reluctance, Judith sat down and opened the book.

"I don't know who any of these people are," her mother complained.

Growing desperate, Cecily flipped forward a few pages. "Look at this. This is our great-great-grandmother Fa Li.

She was a famous Beijing opera singer."

Judith's eyes opened in surprise. "Great-grandma Fa Li? Is that her?"

"Yes. Kelly found this photo and this newspaper article about a performance she gave at one of the most famous theaters in Beijing."

"I had no idea." Gillian whistled.

"Are you talking about that high-pitched screeching stuff Mom makes us listen to sometimes?" For that, Owen received a smack in the arm from Judith and an elbow to the ribs from Cecily.

"Show some respect," Judith scolded. "Great-Grandma Fa Li was famous. People said she had a voice like an angel."

Cecily gaped. "You knew about this?"

Judith shrugged. "Sure. Your grandmother remembered her, and she told me about her concerts."

"Why didn't you say anything?"

Judith looked at Cecily as if she was crazy. "You never asked."

Un-freaking-believable. Seriously?

"Thank you, CeeCee, this is a lovely gift," her father said. Gillian nodded in agreement.

"Yeah, gotta admit, sis, pretty cool. You did good," Owen said through a mouthful of food.

Gillian kept flipping through the book, then laughed. "Look at this. Here's a list from the palace. Chang Kai Ping. Our great-great-great-great-great-grandfather took the imperial exams and failed. He had to take it three times before he passed."

"Sounds like you," her sister said, glancing at Owen.

Owen took immediate umbrage. "I only failed pre-calculus once. And I still don't know why I needed to learn that crap." He crossed his arms.

"Owen, watch your language," Judith warned. She took the book from Gillian and looked for herself. She studied it for a moment and looked at her husband.

"He was a Chang. Should have known it was from your side of the family, not mine."

As always her father just shrugged it off.

The family spent the next few minutes looking through the book. Cecily wasn't going to lie, she was feeling pretty damn good right now. Mission accomplished. And then some. She'd kicked ass on Resolution 7.

"Ma, if you want, I can take you to a shop and get a nice custom frame for the family tree."

"Custom? Sounds expensive."

"Consider it part of my way of showing how much I appreciate you both." Cecily felt the smile screwed to her face. It was legit starting to hurt. But she took a deep breath and reminded herself that her mother didn't mean to be cutting or dismissive. It stung like hell that Judith couldn't say anything nice, but just kept picking at the flaws like she always did. But there was nothing for it but to take a deep breath and suck it up. She shouldn't ruin the day for everyone else.

Judith gave a considering frown. "Maybe you're right— it would look nice if it was framed and displayed." There was a flint glimmer of hope before she asked her next question.

"Maybe you can have it remade in ten years? Maybe Owen and Sonia will be married and have more grandkids. Or maybe you'll finally find someone to marry and we should add that too."

"Sure. Why not?" Cecily tried to keep her tone light, though the effort was monumental. Once again, she had fallen short in her mother's eyes.

"What's the matter? The family tree will need to be updated to make sure it's accurate." Now Judith sounded confused, as if she didn't realize the backhanded nature of the comments.

"Nothing. I just wish you could have been as appreciative of this gift as you were of the other one. I didn't hear you complaining about going on a cruise, but this you have problems with," she said as calmly as she could.

The room became deadly silent.

"Who said I was complaining?" Judith demanded. Her voice was also calm but made it clear that Cecily was skating on thin ice. The rest of the family, except for her father, looked braced for impact.

"My mistake I guess. As usual. Sorry, let's carry on." Sometimes there was virtue in picking your battles and living to fight another day. There was no point in trying to wage war if there was no hope of success.

Her father laid a hand on her mother's shoulders. Her mother turned her head, and they had a silent conversation. But after a brief moment, Judith gave a small nod.

"Okay. Time for cake." There was a palpable release of tension in the room as Judith clapped her hands. As everyone made their way to the kitchen, Cecily let out a shaky breath. That had been a close call. But if experience was anything to go by, this wasn't the last she'd hear about this. Not by a long shot. The pitying look she got from Gill, and her father's supporting squeeze all but confirmed it.

Maybe the resolution about the anniversary gift wasn't such a slam dunk after all. And she had definitely broken the resolution on no drama and not letting her family get under her skin. Once again—two steps forward, one step back.

BETHANY'S GRADUATION PARTY was in full swing. Cecily had spent the whole day yesterday busy with the anniversary celebration and he missed her. The house was packed to the gills with people who were roaming all over the place. Per Bethany's request, the music was blaring, and their father was manning the grill out in the tiny backyard. The food was plentiful, and the drinks were flowing. Jeffrey barely recognized twenty percent of the people in the house right now.

He wondered if he should go back upstairs and lock the door to his room. He did not want strangers wandering in. He stood at the top of the stairs, looking down. There were too many nosy aunties and uncles around. He didn't trust them for a second. Turning on his heels, he walked back down the hallway and turned the lock on his door.

Satisfied that his belongings and privacy were properly secured, he went back downstairs to enjoy the party. Jeffrey decided to search out Cecily's parents. Ever since New Year's, the Lee and Chang parental units had declared a détente of sorts, so they were at the party today too. He had Bethany to thank for that. So now was as good a time as any to try to mend fences with his hopefully future in-laws.

He grabbed a beer from the ice tub and wandered around, trying to find Judith and Paul. But before he could find them, he saw Cecily and some random man talking. They were sitting too close for comfort to his mind, and whoever the man was it looked like he was trying to make a move on his girlfriend. Who was apparently not trying to do anything about it.

Cecily caught his eye and with a big grin waved him over. Proceeding with caution, he walked over and sat down.

"Jeff, this is Matt Lu. You remember him, don't you?"

"No, can't say as I do." He couldn't claim that his tone was the most polite but it was civil.

With a confused frown, Cecily sent him a look. *I don't know what's crawled up your ass but stop being a jerk and behave.*

"Cecily has been telling me all about San Francisco and Los Angeles," Matt said, shaking his hand enthusiastically. Cecily dug into her bag and pulled out a business card, which she handed over to Matt.

Okay, clearly he had misread the situation so he took a breath and reset.

"I know the Bay Area housing market is ridiculous but I'm sure you and your husband will be able to find something," Cecily continued, giving Jeffrey a significant look. He gave an apologetic look back. *I will eat my full serving of crow later. Promise.*

"Between that and daycare for our daughter I don't know how we're going to afford living there but we'll make it work." Matt gave a rueful laugh and shake of his head.

"Well you want to be closer to Brad's family," Cecily said with a shrug. "Give us a call when you get settled in." Normally Jeffrey wouldn't be thrilled at having dinner with yet another couple, but this time he'd make an exception. Matt seemed like a good guy.

"Good luck," Jeffrey said sincerely.

"I see my mom waving, I better go see what she wants." With a final smile, Matt got up and left the couch. Immediately his girlfriend turned to him and gave him a look.

"Feeling sufficiently stupid?" Cecily asked archly.

"Yes, I shouldn't have assumed," Jeffrey admitted.

"Good," Cecily replied with a satisfied nod. "Now, how are you doing?" she asked, patting him on the knee.

"Fine. Just made sure my room was locked up so no one snoops."

"Can't say I blame you." With a good-natured roll of her eyes, Cecily tossed her hair back. "So, have you talked to your agent?" Her voice was bright with anticipation.

"About what?"

"Setting up a new meeting so you can redo your pitch, of course!"

Oh that.

"Well, I think he was able to talk them into giving me a second shot at it."

"That's fantastic! This is so exciting."

"Well let's not get ahead of ourselves here," he warned.

Cecily's bright smile dimmed slightly. "I get it, you're nervous but you can do this. And this time, you have me. If you want, we can practice until you have the pitch memorized and can rattle it off in your sleep, whatever you need."

"That's very kind of you, but I don't know if that will be necessary."

"What do you mean?"

He gave a shrug. "No guarantee that he'll be able to pull off getting me another meeting. Either way it'll be okay."

Her look was sympathetic. "I get not wanting to get your hopes up but no reason not to help fate along a bit. You know what they say, the harder you work, the luckier you get."

Now he began to squirm a bit. Cecily was definitely getting ahead of herself. "I appreciate the support but it's never wise to put all your eggs in one basket in this business. If it doesn't work out, I'm sure something else will come along." Maybe nothing of this magnitude but he'd deal. Besides, he wanted the freedom to do more projects that appealed to him, not just those that made the big bucks.

"I don't understand this," Cecily replied with a shake of her head. "How could you be so blasé about this? This is your life, your career you're talking about here."

"I told you before, Hollywood is nuts. Why obsess about things that are out of your control?" Now he was getting confused. Why was she getting worked up about this?

"But what's the point if you aren't even willing to take a risk, put yourself out there?"

"I'm doing the best I can," he protested.

"Are you? Are you really?" she tossed back.

Taking a glance around the room he realized they were starting to attract looks. Making an executive decision, he took Cecily's hand and led the way upstairs back to his bedroom. He noticed Cecily's mother watching them with narrowed eyes but at that moment he had bigger fish to fry.

He unlocked the door, rushed them both in and shut it again.

"What's all this for?" Cecily demanded.

"I figured if you were going to ream me out it should at least be in private."

Her scowl softened. "I'm not reaming you out. I'm trying to understand. What you're doing, how you're acting is making no sense. I told you before, and I'll say it again. If you want this opportunity, fight for it and give it all you got! Maybe you won't get it but you have to at least try. Get up off the mat and get in the ring! Why are you just giving up?"

"That's not what I'm doing at all!" Was it?

"Maybe you don't see it that way, but from where I'm standing it's looking a lot like you've already tossed in the towel before you even begin."

"You are certainly fond of the sports metaphors today," he said.

"Stop joking and talk to me!"

So much for trying to ease the tension—it just seemed to be making things worse. But he had some things to say too. "Just so I know, is this what it's going to be like for us from now on? Anytime I make a decision about my career," he said, emphasizing the last two words, "that you don't agree with, you're going to question and criticize?"

"The fact that you see this as me attacking you is part of the problem here. I keep telling you I'm not, I'm trying to understand and asking you to talk to me so I can get on the same page."

"I'm sorry if you and I just don't have the same instincts and act the same way," he said, beginning to get frustrated himself.

For a few long moments Cecily just stood in front of him, arms crossed. When she finally spoke, her voice was low and firm. "You know I've wanted to be a lawyer since I was little, right?"

"Yes, ever since you watched those old *Matlock* and *Perry Mason* reruns." Where was she going with this?

"I loved the idea of getting up in front of a courtroom and using my skills and knowledge to persuade people with my arguments. I worked my ass off to get good grades, go to a great college, law school, to make law review, the whole bit." Her arms fell to her sides as she kept trying to make her point.

"When I graduated, I had to take the bar exam. I took a bar prep course and it sucked so hard. It was quite possibly the most miserable two months of my life. I did basically nothing but eat, sleep, and study—literally." Then she turned to him, eyes flashing.

"But then I made it to the other side. I passed the bar, found a job I'm good at and have a career I love. It was all worth it, all the blood, sweat, and tears."

"What are you trying to say?"

"That I was willing to do whatever it took to achieve my dreams. Why the hell aren't you?" she tossed back.

Her words struck him to the core. But Cecily wasn't finished.

"This is your dream, or isn't it? Do you even want to be a screenwriter? Why are you just content to coast? It seems like every time things get a little hard or you face an obstacle or setback, you retreat. You decide it's no longer worth the effort. Maybe it was okay ten years ago when we were all younger and stupider, but that doesn't cut it now. Grow up," she snapped. "You deserve better. Hell, I deserve better. If this is going to keep being your M.O. I'm out."

"CeeCee, stop. We can work this out," he pleaded. How the hell had it gone so off the rails so quickly?

With a sad smile, Cecily shook her head. "I don't think we can. You have some things to figure out. I know for damn sure I'm worth the effort, and I deserve to be with someone who knows that too. And you have to decide if you have what it takes to fight for what you want, and to fight for me."

"But you're what I want!" How much more obvious could he be?

"I need you to show me. And I wouldn't take too long, I'm not going to wait forever, no matter how much I care about you. This year has shown me that it's time I stop messing around and take charge of my life. I know what I want and that's someone who loves me, makes me happy, and is strong enough and willing to stand by me and with me no matter what life throws at us. My equal in every way. I deserve nothing less." Cecily gave a last squeeze of his hand and without another word left the room and closed the door behind her with a quiet click.

With a deep sigh, Jeffrey plopped back down on his childhood bed. He dealt with words for a living, but he'd underestimated a lawyer's ability to verbally slice and dice with the precision of a scalpel. Given the choice between Cecily furious and livid or the way she had just carved out his heart with her words, he would take Cecily yelling at him and calling him names all day every day and twice on Sunday.

The hardest part was he couldn't find fault in anything Cecily said. Was screenwriting truly what he wanted if he wasn't prepared to commit all the way and go ham? Was he ready to totally put it on the line, for his career, for her? Because at base the problem wasn't that he didn't want his career or want Cecily back. The problem was he didn't know if his best would be good enough.

And that above all else was what was killing him the most.

Chapter Fifteen

CECILY WOKE UP in her childhood bedroom, groggy from her nap, and a headache brewing from the crying jag from earlier. Normally she hated to cry, because it usually happened only when she was really angry and upset, usually at the worst and most inopportune times. She was a firm subscriber of the Tom Hanks philosophy of "There's no crying in baseball!" but this time she felt different. She felt hollowed out, like she'd purged all of the emotions, got it all out of her system. It felt so cathartic. She wasn't ready to face the world yet, but she was definitely feeling more steady and even-keeled.

The door flew open and Judith walked in. Great, just great. Her mother's timing was impeccable, as always. On the best of days she needed to be in top form to deal with Judith and obviously at this moment, she was nowhere near her best. But she started with an apology.

"Ma, I'm sorry. I know I made a scene at Bethany's party." Cecily gave her best penitent look and hoped that would be enough.

"I'm not talking about that!" Of course it couldn't be that easy.

Once again, Cecily took a deep breath and reminded

herself of that conversation she'd overheard at New Year's. Her mother could be overbearing, yes, but she meant well.

"Then what did I do wrong this time?" She tried to rack her brain about what could possibly be stuck in her mother's craw, but came up short.

"You're with that boy again," Judith accused.

Crap. "I was, but I'm not anymore, so you can save your lecture."

Judith's eyes narrowed dangerously. "Watch your tone."

"I know you want to say I told you so, and I deserve it, but can it please wait?"

"Is that what you think I want to do?"

Cecily just gave a helpless shrug. Judith continued to stare at her and size her up. Then she gave a resigned sigh.

"You still love him." It was a statement, not a question. "That's stupid."

At that she bristled. "So now I'm stupid?"

"No, I said what you did, getting back together with him, was stupid." Well, that was a hell of a hair to split.

"You know, Ma—I love you, and I know you want to help and mean well. But that doesn't mean the things you say and do aren't hurtful as hell."

Judith looked poleaxed. "Hurtful? How could you say that?"

Cecily gave a snort. "Like when you ask why I haven't gotten promoted yet, or telling me that sweater I love makes me look fat. Or when I was a kid, telling me how Vivian Wu got a gold medal at piano recitals when I didn't." On a roll now, Cecily couldn't help but keep going. "You love to tell me how to do everything, and to point out everything I'm doing wrong. I rack my brain to come up with an amazing anniversary gift for you and Dad, something to showcase our family, but you just tell me it's a waste of money and an invasion of privacy. I know you think that's helping but did you ever stop to think how that would make me feel?" She almost referenced the conversation she'd overheard at New Year's but stopped herself in the nick of time.

"And yes, maybe getting back together with Jeffrey was a mistake, but it was my mistake to make." Cecily finally took a breath. She had to admit it felt good getting that off her chest.

Her mother meanwhile stood there silent for a few long torturous moments. When she managed to speak again, the response was vintage Judith Chang. "Why didn't you say something sooner? What makes you think I'm some sort of monster who doesn't care about your feelings?"

Cecily shook her head and squeezed her eyes shut. God she was so tired.

"Judith, leave the girl alone." Thank God her father was there. He gave her a small smile over her mother's head.

Judith whirled to face her husband. "How can you say that? You know what she's done. Stop making excuses for her—you've always been too soft on her." Then she turned back to her daughter. "I never criticized your anniversary present. I said it was nice, didn't I? I was just worried about you spending too much money on us while you're living in San Francisco. It's expensive there. And as for the other thing, family business should stay in the family. But it was a nice gift."

"Judith." Her father's voice was low, but firm. When Cecily was growing up, he'd let their mother take the lead when it came to discipline, but when necessary, he would intervene. Judith frowned. But she didn't stay quiet for long.

She pointed an accusing finger at Cecily. "Did you hear what she said about me?"

"Yes. Cecily, I told you before, you may not understand her, but you know she cares and just wants what's best for you. Next time, just talk to her instead of bottling it all up until you explode."

Suitably chastened, Cecily just mumbled, "Yes, Daddy." She sat back down on the bed. Clearly her efforts to be a better listener and communicator still needed work.

Then he turned to his wife. "Give our daughter credit to know her own mind."

"But we're her parents, we know more."

"Do we?" He raised a pointed brow. Cecily looked at her parents, fascinated. What was this about? Clearly her mother knew because she pouted.

Her father continued. "If our parents know so much better, you would have married Russell Yang instead of me."

Russell Yang? Who the hell was Russell Yang?

Paul turned to Cecily and explained. "I was a poor

graduate student. Your grandparents wanted her to marry Russell instead. He was a businessman. Managed his parents' restaurants. Considered very rich and successful."

Cecily looked at her mother, bug-eyed. "Ma?"

"That's not fair. That was completely different. Russell's parents were horrible. His mother was a witch. No one liked her. I wouldn't have been able to live with them! Besides, he was short and ugly with a hairy mole." Her chin at a defensive tilt, Judith crossed her arms.

"Then let CeeCee make her own decision. Trust her," he whispered in his wife's ear. Judith's face was still mutinous. Finally, she spoke.

"Okay. I don't like it, but I'm outnumbered." Then her expression softened. "But I am proud of you. Always have been. Don't you ever forget that."

Cecily's eyes got misty. "Thanks, Ma," she choked out. It was moments like this that made up for the times her family drove her bat-shit crazy.

Her relationship with her mother may never be easy, but she still needed to do her part. Yes that meant being more patient, but she also had to be more open about what she was thinking and feeling before misunderstandings and assumptions got in the way. It would require effort from both sides.

But then, naturally, Judith returned to form. "About you and Jeffrey."

"Judith," Paul warned.

This time, she waved her husband aside. She got straight up in Cecily's face.

"If he's who you want to be with, fine. But don't let him off the hook. He needs to make up for what he did, and make sure he's good enough to deserve you. Understood?"

Cecily bobbed her head. It was all she could do. Satisfied, Judith gave a nod of approval. Then she reached out and held Cecily's face in her hand. Her eyes narrowed as she scrutinized every inch.

Judith shook her head. "That boy must be very good in bed." She let go of Cecily's face.

"Ma!" Horrified and embarrassed beyond belief, Cecily tried to hide her scalding cheeks.

"It's the only explanation," her mother insisted. "And I understand. Good sex is important. Trust me, I should know." She smirked.

"Oh my God, I think I'm going to hurl," Cecily moaned.

"Judith, stop embarrassing our daughter," Paul admonished.

"You're the one who keeps saying she's grown up now. She shouldn't be so squeamish. She wouldn't be here if it wasn't for sex. It's natural. What's there to be embarrassed about?"

"Ma!" she squawked, unable to bear it any longer. She grabbed a pillow and put it around her ears. "La la la la la."

Thankfully, Paul managed to usher his wife out the door, and closed it behind him, giving Cecily some much-needed recovery time.

"I'm going to need so much mind bleach," she grumbled as she flopped back on the bed. But her heart was light, and there was a smile from ear to ear.

JEFFREY COULDN'T HELP but have bad flashbacks as he walked back into the same room where he crashed and burned just a month and a half earlier. There was the same group of white guys, and unless his brain was seriously screwing with him, they were sitting in the same exact places they were sitting in last time, wearing the exact same outfits.

He may have decided to change his career priorities but that didn't mean he wanted to embarrass himself and bomb. Again. He reminded himself of the pep talk he'd given himself five minutes ago when he was trying to resist the urge to cut and run for a second time. He'd been in the bathroom, splashing water on his face and calculating how badly Marty would kill him when he suddenly looked at himself in the mirror. A voice in his head told him to stop.

You've gone over this presentation with Greg; he thinks the changes are great. You believe in this story, so fight for it. You can do this. Marty thinks you can do this. Greg thinks you can do this. The only person who seems to think you can't do this is you. That's got to stop. Not this time. You're better than that now. You can do this. So what if you're terrified? Get over it. Cecily deals with hundred-million-dollar deals and she doesn't lose her nerve. She'd get in there and do it. So that's what you're going to do. You're going to show her, and yourself, that you are capable of rising to the occasion. No more excuses.

Sarah quietly closed the door behind her, and he tried not to compare it to the sound of a jail cell slamming shut.

"Hey, Jeffrey, have a seat."

"Thank you for seeing me and giving me another shot at this."

"Marty was very persuasive." Tom's tone made it clear this was strictly a courtesy to his agent.

"Well, let's get started," Glenn said.

"Yes. Okay." He reminded himself to breathe. "I know the studio is looking for a fresh new perspective for the franchise in the next movie. So what I propose is…" He took in the unblinking stares looking back at him and began to lose his nerve.

"Yes?" Carl said, slightly impatient.

Okay. It was now or never. Do or die time. He reminded himself of that pep talk again and suddenly, somehow, a calm came over him. He opened his mouth and just spoke, his voice clear and confident.

"I think we should shake things up. Have more diversity in the cast, and the locations."

Tom frowned. "But there are certain elements to the franchise that need to stay. Ian has always been British. The audience has certain expectations. If we veer too far off course, we risk turning them off. Especially the die-hard fans. We don't want any negative backlash."

"But does that mean the lead needs to be white? The last time I checked, Britain was not all white. Or is Idris Elba a figment of all of our imaginations? David Oyelowo? Or Carmen Ejogo, Thandie Newton, Indira Varma, Dev

Patel, Naveen Andrews, Parminder Nagra?" He took a breath and went on. "Listen, I grew up in New York City, one of the most diverse places in the world. You can get on the subway and hear at least ten different languages and accents. It was amazing. But as a kid, whenever I turned on the TV, or went to the movie theater, seeing someone like me on the screen was like spotting a unicorn. I just want to increase representation for the next generation. We all deserve to see ourselves reflected on the screen."

Glenn, Tom, and Carl stopped glancing at their phones and paid attention.

"Look at the movies that have been coming out the past few years that have diverse casts. They've all done incredibly well in the box office, and Netflix has been raking in the money with their new projects. Audiences are hungry for the content. Don't you want to get on board? Why are you leaving money on the table?"

At that the three of them perked up. Typical. You could get anyone in Hollywood to pay attention when you started speaking their language—money.

"You make a good point, but let's put a pin on that and revisit it later," Tom said. There were nods all around.

Okay. So far so good. That wasn't that bad.

"We read your new revised script," Glenn began as he flipped through his notes. "And we have some concerns."

"Oh?" He could handle this, he reminded himself.

"Yes. In your script, you have Ian afraid of heights after suffering a fall from a helicopter while on a mission that happens before the movie starts. He's at a hotel with glass elevators and instead of riding it, he uses the stairs. Isn't the point of the Ian Grey character that he isn't afraid of anything? Isn't that what makes him so successful as a spy?"

"I think it adds depth to Ian's character, and heightens the stakes of the movie. A character who succeeds at everything and doesn't have flaws is boring. Not relatable. I think humanizing him is the right move. Besides, having him afraid of heights makes the scene at the climax of the movie where he has to climb to the top of the Eiffel Tower to complete the mission have more emotional impact. Better payoff for the audience as they see him conquer his fear for the greater good. What's not heroic about that?"

Now the three of them looked impressed. "Well, I guess we never thought of it that way," Carl mused.

"We'll certainly take that under advisement," Tom agreed. "Now if we're going in this new direction, I think we need to revisit the age range we're looking at for this film. I think Ian might need a slightly older sidekick in this one."

Jeffrey shrugged. He could live with that. "That's something I could look into changing in the script."

"I want to talk about this scene you wrote in Fiji. I don't think we have the budget for that," Glenn started.

And on and on it went.

An hour later, Jeffrey walked out of the building, exhausted but exhilarated, adrenaline running high. He was pumped. There was no denying that the meeting had gone well, better than his wildest dreams. Thanks to the Cecily mental pep talk, he'd conquered the fears and doubts to do

THE YEAR OF CECILY

what he needed to do. He had taken barely ten steps when his phone buzzed.

He looked at the screen. Of course.

"What's up, Marty?"

"So I heard it went well."

"Yeah, I think so." He couldn't help the smug tone that had crept in.

"Good job, kid. I knew you could do it."

"Well thanks. I couldn't have done it without you. I know they only gave me a second shot because of you."

"Don't rest on your laurels. It's not a done deal yet, and from what Glenn told me, there are a lot of changes to make. You got a lot of work ahead of you."

Just then the reality of the situation crashed down on him. He had this incredible news, and the one person he most wanted to share it with, the one who'd been rooting for him the most, wanted nothing to do with him. Again.

"I know. I don't mind. It's not like I have much going on to distract me. It'll give me something to do to fill the time."

"Hey, I know I said nothing is set in stone, but nothing wrong with exercising cautious optimism. This is a win. You should celebrate."

"Maybe. Don't really feel in a celebratory mood, though." Hard to want to go whoop it up when your personal life was in shambles, a complete total mess.

"I don't know what's going on with you but whatever it is, figure it out. Get your head out of your ass. I'll call you next week." Without waiting for a response, Marty ended the call.

"Thanks, Marty," Jeffrey murmured. He took a deep breath of L.A. congested air and tried to get his bearings.

He didn't mind admitting that he was proud of himself for digging deep and conquering his fears. And the risk had been totally worth it—he'd impressed Tom, Carl, and Glenn. The irony of him channeling Cecily in order to accomplish it was not lost on him. But that was okay. This was a good first step to proving to her, but more importantly himself, that he had what it took to be the sort of man she wanted, needed, and deserved. Now it was up to him to keep the momentum going and figure out his next step. He wasn't quite sure yet what that would be, but this time, he knew he'd be able to figure it out.

Jeffrey whistled as he walked down the street to grab a coffee and some food before heading back home. For the first time in a while, that faint glimmer of hope was shining brighter and brighter.

Chapter Sixteen

LATER THAT EVENING, Jeffrey was trying to work, and to come up with his "How to Show Cecily He Finally Got His Shit Together And Woo Her Back Plan". Unfortunately, he wasn't making any progress on either front. His phone buzzed. A FaceTime request from Bethany. He ignored it.

Two more requests.

Then his phone pinged with a text. *I swear to God if you don't pick up the phone, I'm booking a flight to L.A. to kick your ass.*

His baby sister wasn't screwing around. He picked up the phone and engaged the FaceTime app to call Bethany back.

Her irate face filled the screen. "What the hell did you do?" she demanded without preliminaries. Her tone bordered on the openly hostile.

"I have no idea what you're talking about."

"Mom and Auntie Judith are talking again. They were in the kitchen drinking tea and gossiping. Then things took a turn. Mom was yelling and carrying on about her stupid stubborn son. So again I reiterate, what did you do?"

Great, so now he was on the outs with all the women in his life. Batting a thousand.

"Why do you care? They're pissed at me, not you."

"Wow. You really are that stupid."

"Watch your tone," he warned.

"You know what? I take back my earlier threat. I'm gonna convince them to go visit you in L.A."

Oh no she didn't. He narrowed his eyes. "You wouldn't dare."

"Try me." They engaged in the age-old battle of the Lee sibling standoff. Jeffrey blinked first. He decided to chalk it up to work fatigue.

"Cecily and I had an argument at your graduation. She decided to call things off until I get my act together. Which I would love to do but I'm coming up short on ideas on how to prove myself to her." Part of him couldn't believe he was confiding in Beth like this. It must be a sign of how desperate he was to figure this out.

Bethany heaved a weary sigh and stared up at the ceiling. "How could I possibly be related to someone who is so dumb and such a...*man*?"

"Did you FaceTime me just to verbally abuse me?"

"No, loser. I'm here to help. Duh." The eye roll was oddly comforting.

"You have an odd way of showing it."

"My services come at a price."

"I'm hanging up now."

"Fine. Okay. What stupid man thing did you do to upset Cecily?"

"I don't want to talk about it."

"How am I supposed to help you if I don't have all the

information?"

He narrowed his eyes again. His sister was looking a tad too innocent. "You just want the gossip."

"You want my help or not?"

"Long story short, she accused me of giving up too easily and not going for what I want."

"So, go after her and what you want. This is easy." His baby sister threw up her hands and gave an eye roll.

"It's not that simple, Beth," he retorted.

"It is if you want it to be," she insisted.

"Not all of us are as single-minded and ruthless as you." Unless he was mistaken, Bethany preened.

"Look, there's not enough time for me to teach you all of my ways. Not that I would anyway—I can't give up all my secrets, you know," she mused.

"Beth."

"Even the most cunning of us need time to come up with a plan to take over the world. So, she wants you to show her you've changed, right? To be the kind of man who's not afraid to go after her, what you want. Someone who deserves her. The best way to do that is to come up with a plan for how you're going to go after what you want. A plan that shows her you're no longer scared. It doesn't have to be big monumental changes. Slow progress is lasting progress, after all. Just show her you listened to her and are committed to working on getting to a newer and better you."

Something in his sister's words struck a chord. Come up with a plan. Who knew his baby sister was so insightful and would be the one to give him the kick he needed? The wheels started turning and Jeffrey grinned. He rubbed his hands together.

"Hello! Where are you?"

"Thanks, Beth. I can take it from here."

"What are you talking about? I'm not done yet!"

"Bye." He pressed to end the call but not before Bethany had the final word.

"I'll send you my invoice."

After putting away his phone, Jeffrey opened up his email and a new blank document. He had work to do.

CECILY SAT AT La Tulipano across from her dining companion and wondered what the hell was wrong with her. Here she was, eating a delicious plate of shrimp and clam pasta, drinking a crisp and refreshing glass of white wine, and the man sitting across from her was witty, handsome, urbane, charming, smart, and funny. A fellow attorney, Luke Trudeau was the complete package. As Paul Hollywood would say, he ticked all the boxes. They had interests in common, mutual work acquaintances, and his dark wavy hair, piercing blue eyes, and chiseled jawline would make any woman's heart flutter. Add to that a slight Texas twang, and Luke was the dream date.

And yet, Cecily felt nothing. Not a flutter, not a pang, not a single butterfly in the stomach. She appreciated a fine specimen of manhood as much as the next gal, but there was not one spark of interest. Zero. Zip. Nada. She was dead inside.

She blamed Adrienne for her current predicament. After two weeks, her best friend had decided Cecily's allotted time to mope and wallow was over, and in her words, it was "Time to get back on the horse. You told him you weren't going to wait around for him, so prove it." This blind date had been arranged over Cecily's strenuous objections. But Adrienne had come over the minute Cecily got home after giving Jeffrey her ultimatum. She'd provided ice cream, tissues, pizza, and everything else the Girl Code required. The least she could do was give this date a chance. Though even that was proving to be impossible.

So here she was, with a smile pasted on her face, trying not to feel bad that she was wasting this perfectly nice man's time because as far as she was concerned, this date was going nowhere, fast. She was swearing off all men indefinitely, and poor Luke had no idea.

"Then Judge Tompkins rules my key piece of evidence is inadmissible. And tosses out the corroborating witness statement. My client looks ready to fight so I have to practically put him in a headlock to get him to keep his mouth shut. Opposing counsel is smug as can be, and I'm already pissed because it was 10 a.m. and I hadn't even had any coffee yet." He paused dramatically.

Cecily tried to muster up the requisite amount of interest, as if she had been paying attention instead of letting her mind wander. "Sounds like a bad day."

"Oh I haven't even gotten to the best part," he said

with a mischievous smile. "I was trying to calm my client down when I heard the loudest shriek I've ever heard in my life."

Now that was unusual. "What happened?"

"The court stenographer saw a mouse scurry out from the jury box."

"No way!" she gasped, horrified.

He held his hand up, Scout's honor style. "I swear it's true. I couldn't make this stuff up, even if I tried. We couldn't figure out how it got up there. I mean, we were on the tenth floor. We were nowhere near the cafeteria or anywhere with food. The court officer called maintenance, and we adjourned for the day. I couldn't wait to get out of there."

Cecily shuddered. "I don't blame you. I would have freaked out too, if I were the stenographer. I do not like critters."

"Can't say I'm a fan either. But that was definitely one of my more memorable court experiences. I've avoided Judge Thompkins's courtroom and chambers ever since."

She chuckled. She looked at Luke again. It really was a damn shame she was currently soulless and couldn't summon any emotions because in another time and place, she would have been all over it.

Luke, bless his heart, was still trying to impress. "But enough about me, tell me more about you. Any courtroom war stories to share?'

"Nothing as exciting as that," she replied wryly. "But I did have a zoning board hearing that went awry. I was setting off the metal detectors at security and we couldn't figure out why. So I was incredibly late and almost didn't make it. The city attorney is a total ass and told the judge I looked like I needed to go back to law school for a refresher. Then to top it all off, I spilled my coffee and it went all over my files."

Luke's eyes widened in horror. "Oh God. What a nightmare."

She scoffed. "Tell me about it. It was my second year at Harmon Burke. Not exactly the way to impress the senior associates or the partners." She rolled her eyes.

"So what did you do?"

Cecily was about to answer as something caught her eye. She saw a man walk in—tall, jet-black hair, glasses, with the same nose and sculpted lips and cheekbones. She couldn't breathe, and her heart started jackhammering. No. It couldn't be.

Seriously. What was he doing in San Francisco, and what cruel twist of fate would have him walk into the same restaurant she was dining at? And with another woman to boot? It sure didn't take him long to move on. Look how quickly he'd jumped on the chance to find a rebound.

The man walked closer, and she realized her mind was playing tricks on her. This guy was at least ten years older than Jeffrey and bore only the slightest resemblance. Damn it.

"Shit," she whispered to herself. With a start, she realized she'd let a good minute lapse while she rode that rollercoaster of emotions, and her date probably had written her off as a certified nutjob.

Luke had a wry look on his face. "I would ask if you're all right, but you know the first rule of our profession. Never ask a question you don't already know the answer to," he drawled.

Cecily winced. "I'm sorry. I just had a bad moment when I thought I saw someone I recognized. But it was just a false alarm." She smiled and tried to refocus on the date.

Luke signaled the waitress for the check.

Oh yeah. She'd blown it big time. So much for moving on.

"I am so sorry, Luke. I've been horrible company, and totally wasted your evening. But please don't blame Adrienne for this. She meant well, and it's not her fault I'm such a crappy date."

"Not at all," he replied gallantly.

She threw him a look. "You're too kind. I'm usually not such a hot mess, I swear. I haven't been myself lately."

The waitress dropped off the check, and Cecily opened her wallet. When she looked up, she saw that his credit card was already in the folder.

"No. It's the least I can do," she insisted. She reached for the folder, but he grabbed it away.

"Where I come from, a gentleman always pays," he says with a wink.

"At least let me split the bill."

"Absolutely not." The matter settled, he handed it over to the waitress.

"Well now I feel horrible. Let me make it up to you.

Do you want to meet for coffee next week or something?" Despite everything, he was a nice guy, and she wouldn't mind getting to know him as a friend. There was nothing in her list of resolutions that said a new friend couldn't be a man.

"Don't worry about it." Double ouch.

They sat there in awkward silence while waiting for the waitress to return.

Finally, he spoke. "But maybe you can do me a favor."

She pounced. "Absolutely."

"Let me know how it works out with that guy you can't seem to get over."

Damn, she was that pathetic and obvious.

His lips quirked. "I saw the guy who distracted you and Adrienne told me you were looking to move on. Didn't take much to put two and two together. But now I feel invested. Perils of our profession—we're too nosy for our own good."

Cecily shook her head. "You are way too kind. And clearly you have the patience of a saint."

Luke signed the credit card slip and they both got up and put on their coats. He raised a brow. "I can assure you it's the first time anyone has ever accused me of that."

She continued. "I'm sorry things didn't work out tonight, but I hope you find the perfect person for you. You deserve it."

"Thank you." With a brief handshake they exited the restaurant and made their separate ways.

An hour later, she was on the couch in her sweats,

watching *White Collar* on streaming. As the episode ended, she gave up and groaned.

It was time to face facts. There was a reason why she didn't feel any sparks with Luke, and why she was almost hyperventilating when she saw that man in the restaurant.

It was Jeffrey. It'd always been Jeffrey. She'd been in love with him since they were six years old, when she'd kicked a bully in the shins for him after the bully pushed him down in the playground.

She'd lost her heart to him decades ago. It was time to accept that. For better or worse, right or wrong, she loved Jeffrey Lee and she always would.

White Collar and the prettiness of Matt Bomer totally forgotten, Cecily threw off the blanket, went to her tiny kitchen, and got herself a bowl of ice cream. The leftover ice cream from her emergency girls' night with Adrienne two weeks ago. She shuffled back to the couch, shoveled in ice cream, and pondered the problem.

She was still pissed at Jeffrey, no doubt about it, but she also wanted to see him and talk to him, so what was her next step? She bit her lip. She wasn't exactly ready to put it all on the line again. She'd basically said her piece at Bethany's party and put her heart on her sleeve. If Jeffrey didn't believe in himself, in her, in their relationship, the whole thing was a non-starter. It would never work otherwise. The next step was going to have to be his.

Cecily just hoped he didn't take too long. Jeffrey better get his act together, pronto. Patience had never been her strong suit. She was going to give him another week or two tops. If she didn't hear from him by then, she'd have to take matters into her own hands. Issue him a subpoena or something.

Okay fine, she would have no grounds for a subpoena. It would probably be unethical and illegal. Unless it was made clear it was a fake subpoena. Maybe he'd think it was cute. And funny.

"For God's sake. Get a hold of yourself. You're talking like a crazy person," she muttered to herself. "A fake subpoena? Seriously? What the hell are you thinking?"

SO MUCH FOR a work-life balance. Cecily took a look at her watch and gave a sigh. It was 9 p.m. on a Saturday night and here she was sprawled on her couch trying to get some work done. And failing spectacularly. She had a thirty-page contract to review and she was pretty sure she'd been staring at the same paragraph for the past fifteen minutes. Screw it. It was time to call it a day.

It had been a week since her disastrous blind date with Luke and her stunning (or maybe not so stunning) revelation that despite the ultimatum she'd given to Jeffrey and her warning that she was not going to sit around and wait for him, her heart was and always would be his. And she'd been going slightly insane waiting for him to come to his senses.

He'd always been such a stubborn pain in the butt. But then again, so was she. That was why they were so perfect for each other. She was more than ready to get on to the next portion of the program, but she was determined to wait him out.

Just then her phone pinged. With a raised brow, Cecily picked it up. It was a text from Bethany.

You're welcome, in advance. I swear you two are such idiots. Don't make me have to actually knock your heads together. Also, I assume this has cemented my place as your maid of honor.

What the heck was this about? Something told Cecily to be on her guard, because there was no telling what Bethany had set in motion. Almost on cue, there was a knock on her door. She closed her eyes. This was too freaky to be a coincidence. She knew, deep in her bones, who was there on the other side of that door. It was about damn time.

Taking a deep breath, she made her way to the door and yanked it open. Her heart was beating so fast she was surprised it hadn't escaped her chest.

"What a surprise to see you," she managed as she drank in the sight of him. He looked like he hadn't slept in ages, and he was wearing worn jeans and a T-shirt, and he had a backpack slung over his shoulder. But to her he'd never looked better.

"I have some things to say," he said, with a determined glint in his eye and jut of his jaw.

Without another word, she ushered him in and made her way back into the living room while he took off his shoes and joined her. Making herself comfortable on the sofa, she gave a sweeping, *go ahead* gesture. "By all means, don't let me stop you. Go on," she said grandly. She couldn't wait to see where this was going.

Cecily had indulged in imagining possible sweet romantic sweeping gestures that Jeffrey could employ to woo her back. Given the man's line of work, it wasn't unreasonable to assume he'd go for the dramatic. Instead, he reached into his pocket and took out a sheet of notebook paper.

Well, that was…a choice, to put it mildly. But despite his bravado earlier, Cecily could see the nervousness underneath. She gave an encouraging smile.

Jeffrey cleared his throat and began reading from his sheet of paper. "Jeffrey's 'Get His Shit Together and Win Back the Girl List'." At her surprised look, he explained, "I know you're a big proponent of coming up with a list of goals and plans to achieve them. So that's what I decided to do."

At that, she became utter putty. Romantic gestures were great, but in reality, Cecily was a practical woman. Having the love of your life understand you so well and show that was more romantic to her than a room full of red long-stemmed roses. He truly knew her and what made her tick. What was not to love about that?

Then Jeffrey's face became a bit sheepish. "Okay, in the interest of full disclosure, and because she'd kill me if I didn't give her credit, Beth was the one who helped come up with this idea. But the execution is still all me," he insisted earnestly.

Which explained Bethany's random text. Cecily laughed and tears formed.

"I haven't even started yet," Jeffrey protested. "At least

let me do this. You can kick me out but let me have my say first."

"I am one hundred percent not kicking you out," she assured him. "Carry on."

"Number one. Get a second meeting and rework the pitch so it's a winner." He looked up. "Done. The meeting went well by the way. The producers seemed on board and gave Marty good feedback. And that's thanks to you. I faltered a bit before I walked in the room but I asked myself WWCD."

WWCD?

"What would Cecily do? I told myself you would never give in to fear. You would push through and do what you needed to do, so that's what I did," he said with a crooked smile.

My heart.

"Number two. Set up regular twice-monthly meetings with Marty. We're now talking on the first and fifteenth of every month. It helps keep me on track with the script rewrite and keep me on his radar when it comes to new work."

Damn it, she was not going to cry.

"Number three. Do some preliminary research with Greg about setting up our own production company. We're working on a movie about Iris Chang," he explained. "We're trying to see if we can somehow make it happen ourselves if we can't get someone on board. But I have to admit, the paperwork is scaring the hell out of us and we have no idea where the money would come from but we're working on it," he admitted with a grimace.

"I think I know someone who can help with the paperwork." Her face was starting to hurt the smile was so big. Holy crap he was stepping up big time. He'd heard her and was delivering. He wasn't just giving her pretty words, he was backing it up with action. The fact he'd mentioned paperwork and money told her he actually was trying to do his homework. She wasn't asking for perfection—a good faith effort was all she asked. And this was it in spades.

"Number four. Go find Cecily and show her that she is the most important person in your life."

She started to beam then hesitated. What? "Wait. Why am I number four? I should be first!"

He gave a small laugh and shook his head. "That's what I love about you. Only you would be competitive about where you ranked on a list."

Well, it was the damn principle of the thing. But then he explained. "You told me to only come after you once I figured out what and who I wanted, and had the guts to go after it. I had to do that other stuff first to prove to myself that I had what it takes. That was the only way this was going to work. I have to believe in myself before asking anyone else to believe in me, right?"

Oh. In that case… "I'll allow it."

"Number five. Since Cecily pushed you to achieve your dreams, help her achieve hers." He opened his backpack and pulled out a sparkly tiara and a copy of Marie Kondo's book. "You said that you figured out this year that you needed to focus on making your life the best it can be, and what makes you happy. So I thought these could help." At her confused look, he gave a small grin. "Things that spark joy." At that she gave a watery laugh. This was beyond perfect. Then he gave her a look. "I'm still not introducing you to Daniel Henney. I will do just about anything for you, but that's a bridge too far." Jeffrey's eyes sparkled with humor, and she just shook her head.

"Number six. Try to convince Cecily she needs a roommate." Looking up, he explained earnestly. "For the next while I'm still going to need to be based in L.A. to take meetings but eventually, I want to be in a place where I can move up here to San Francisco if that's what you want. I can drive or fly down to L.A. or take virtual meetings instead of having to be there in person all the time. That will be easier if I get more established."

"When," she corrected. Seeing this Jeffrey, at his best, left her no doubt he could do it. "And we can figure that out. Maybe I can transition my practice down to L.A. or we can find somewhere between the two places," she suggested.

"Next, come up with ways to make Cecily's life easier and show you know her better than anyone else." Jeffrey went into his backpack again and pulled out two small objects. One was a pink rubber ball with Mom written on it in black Sharpie marker. "This is for when you're talking to your mom or family on the phone. You can use it as a stress ball if they start driving you nuts."

"Now why didn't I think of this before?" she asked with a laugh. Then he stuck a small stack of paper stapled together. It was a coupon book. "And if the stress ball doesn't work, or if you just had a bad day at work, use these. Each coupon is good for a ten-minute neck and shoulder rub."

Cecily gave a slight shake of her head. "This is no good," she said with a mock frown. "Ten minutes is so not going to cut it. This is my mother we're talking about. I say it's got to be at least thirty." She gave a cheeky grin.

Jeffrey narrowed his eyes slightly. "I'm willing to split the difference and make it twenty but that's it," he said, his lips quirking.

"Deal." Good God. They really were tailor made for each other. No one could piss her off like Jeffrey, but no one else could make her laugh like him. Only he could think of a fun way to turn her "issues" with her family into something that could make her laugh and not take it deadly seriously. And only he could step up and come up with a creative way for them to face the issue together.

His face got serious and he cleared his throat. "I have one more item on my list." His eyes darted and his hands balled up.

She raised a brow. She couldn't wait to see what else he had up his sleeve. "Go on," she encouraged. "You've been doing great so far."

"Show her that you will spend the rest of your life making her as happy as she makes you if she's willing to give you the chance. And that you have always loved her and will always loved her. She's the one and has been since you were both six."

He got down on one knee and took out a black box and opened it up. Inside was a beautiful two carat emerald-cut diamond ring. And at that, Cecily gave up. The tears began flowing and her hands covered her mouth.

"I know I still have a lot of work to do and I don't deserve a second chance. And I'm not asking you to say yes now, but if you think you could get there someday, that would make me the happiest man in the world. This can be a new start for both of us and we can do it right this time, finally. And I promise I will do my best to make sure you never regret saying yes."

She was going to kill him. This was possibly one of the most romantic moments of her life, and here she was in sweats and a tank top, exhausted from work. Her hair was in a messy bun, and she didn't have a stitch of makeup on. Plus she was pretty sure she could feel a pimple emerging on her forehead like some sort of obscene ridiculous bull's-eye. Seriously. Would a heads-up have been too much to ask for? How could she face telling any possible future grandchildren this story when she'd have to confess to looking like this? She could already picture Adrienne rolling her eyes as she gave all the details.

Oh who was she kidding? Right now she was so happy her heart was ready to burst. Of course it didn't matter what she was wearing or what she looked like.

Sometimes actions spoke louder than words. Cecily threw herself at Jeffrey and kissed him, hard. She threw her arms around him and wrapped her legs around him. Reeling a bit, Jeffrey was surprised but he got over his shock soon enough. The force of Cecily's lunge landed them on the couch and kept them occupied for several minutes.

Finally Jeffrey came up for breath, with a dazed goofy grin. "I'm going to take that as a yes."

Cecily lifted her head from his chest. "I'm still so pissed at you, you know."

He hummed and traced her lips with his fingertip. "It's okay. I have the rest of our lives to make it up to you."

"This is true. But your list is perfect. I love it, and you." She was so happy, she was more than willing to give him credit for a job very well done. But then she saw his expression and made a face. "You are like my Kryptonite or something. Why can't I ever hate you or stay mad at you? Even when you're being an ass?" She poked his chest jokingly.

Jeffrey just smiled smugly. "Because you love me."

"I must have been dropped on the head as a child," she muttered.

"And I love you too," he said seriously. "And I'll try not to be stupid and ruin things again."

She smiled brightly. "If you do, I'll just throw things at you until you come to your senses," she said sweetly.

He shook his head. "I don't know if I like this violent streak you've developed. But fair warning, I've gone through some lean times and probably will again. You know how capricious Hollywood is."

"That's okay. You don't want to be a sugar daddy but I may not mind being a sugar mama."

He turned serious. "I mean it, CeeCee. I lost you once. I'm not about to do it again. I want you to know what you're setting yourself up for. Especially if we decide to have a family."

Her expression turned sober too. "Of course I do. I told you, no matter how hard I tried, I never hated you. You screwed up, but I realized I'll never be happy unless I take that leap of faith. We have work to do, but what couple doesn't? As long as we face it together, we'll be fine. And I told you I believe in you. We'll figure it out. I'm done fighting my heart, and fate. You're the one," she said simply.

His eyes sparkling with joy, he leaned down and gave her another lingering kiss.

A few minutes later they lay sprawled together on the couch, Cecily beaming and admiring her ring. "And this time, we're going to do it right," she murmured.

"Absolutely."

With a glint in her eye, she whispered in his ear, "What do you say we get started on those 2.6 kids?"

He smirked. "Our parents would be scandalized, but what the hell. They insist on grandkids. The ends justify the means." He quickly scooped her up and led her to her bedroom.

A few hours later, they were in bed, Cecily breathing hard and waiting for her heartbeat to come back to normal. Cecily looked at Jeffrey expectantly.

"What?" he asked.

"I feel like I should inform you that Bethany has already staked out the position of maid of honor for the wedding. And you have to admit her assistance was invaluable."

He gave her a look. "Remember how we said parents were a taboo subject when we're naked in bed together? Add siblings to the list."

Cecily snickered "Fine. But still. We owe her. Big."

"Whatever you decide is fine. Just as long as we both say I do, I don't care if we do it in a huge church, or with a justice of the peace at the courthouse during lunch."

"Aaww you sure know the way to a girl's heart. But our parents would kill us if we don't go all out and invite the entire neighborhood to the wedding."

"Didn't we just discuss the parental ban?" He gave a shudder.

"All right, all right," she acquiesced. "But I want to get married before the end of the year."

"Works for me." His hand traced the graceful curve of her spine.

"The Year of the Pig is going to be awesome."

"It's shaping up to be the best year yet."

Her gaze turned mischievous. "Especially if you take your fiancée to the Ian Grey premiere. I really, really want to meet Daniel Henney on the red carpet if he shows up. Experience that handsomeness and sexy up close and personal." She saw the sham outraged look in his eye. "Don't worry. To me, you'll always be sexier than him." She gave him a consolation kiss.

"That's better," he muttered. "But just so you know,

I've been thinking of trying my hand at writing a romantic comedy next. Women can't get enough of them, I'm told." He saw her brow rise. "What? You don't think I can write a good rom-com? Just because I'm a guy?"

"No, I have no doubt you have the chops for it. You can bring the romance when you want to. I just have to make sure you stay in the right mind frame." She slithered on top of him and lowered herself onto his cock, her entrance stretching to accommodate him. They both groaned in pleasure as she began to rock. Her new diamond ring caught the emerging dawn light, and sparkled. Her eyes sparkled brighter with laughter, love, and burgeoning arousal.

"Game on," he murmured as he fused his mouth to hers.

"MORE CHAMPAGNE?" WITH an ear-to-ear smile, Cecily grabbed the Dom Pérignon from the ice bucket and prepared to pour.

Jeffrey adjusted his bow tie, slightly nervous. The August heat was horrible, and he thanked God for A.C. He and Cecily were in a limo with his parents, heading to a special screening of *Xiao* at the new L.A. Museum of Asian American Art and History. The museum had turned the grand opening into a red carpet gala event, and thought a screening of the movie would fit in perfectly. He'd flown both his parents in for their first red carpet event and he was hoping to show them an amazing time.

Martin gave the champagne a skeptical look. "That looks expensive."

"I think this occasion calls for it, don't you?" Cecily's tone was syrupy sweet but the edge underneath told him she was ready to throw down for him if necessary. Which warmed his heart.

Then his mother chimed in. "Of course! Who knew I'd ever get to go to a red carpet event?" Pam had spent all afternoon at the salon getting ready and had fussed over her outfit, a lovely deep navy suit with some beading on the jacket, and low pumps. Jeffrey had to drag his father to a J.Crew to get him a suit made in this decade and a matching pair of shoes. Martin had grumbled the whole time.

"Hollywood people are so strange," his father said, even as he held out his flute to be refilled. "Your movie is already out, why is there all this fuss?"

"This is for our son," Pam scolded. "Enjoy this."

"Greg and I worked with the museum to pull this event off. It's a great way to get publicity for the museum and the movie. They got a lot of people to agree to come and press to cover it. I should warn you the attention is going to be on the actors and director. People probably won't even notice me or make a big fuss. Just so you know."

Pam frowned. "That makes no sense. If you didn't write the movie there would be nothing for them to do!" Fair point.

"I agree with your mother. But I suppose we'll have to get used to this. Maybe this suit isn't such a bad idea," his father conceded. "Now that Jeffrey is writing these big movies, we'll be coming to more of these movie openings." Martin's eyes brightened in hope. "Can you get us tickets to the red carpet for Salma Hayek's next movie?"

Pam rolled her eyes. "You always had a crush on her. Forget about it. You'll just stutter and drool and make a fool of yourself." She elbowed her husband slightly. Then looked back at her son. "But if you know Tom Hanks, you can arrange an introduction, right?"

"He needs to introduce me to Daniel Henney first," Cecily informed them.

His mother paused for a moment, then gave a nod of approval. "He's a nice-looking boy. Cute butt." She and Cecily clinked glasses.

Oh God. What had he started?

Jeffrey frowned as he watched his father aiming his phone around. "What are you doing?"

"Trying to take a picture of the limo. I need to show the neighbors. This is so fancy."

"Can you save me some movie posters? I promised to bring some back to New York for the family." The unspoken *and to rub it in everyone's faces* was understood.

Jeffrey gave a rueful grin and shook his head. "Sure, Ma. I'll see what I can do." Feeling good he turned and took in the stunning view of his fiancée.

"Did I tell you how amazing you look?" Cecily was wearing a one-shoulder figure-hugging purple satin dress with her hair in a sweeping updo, dramatic makeup, and matching jewelry. For his money, the diamond ring on her left hand was still his favorite accessory.

"I was waiting for you to notice. This is my first time on a red carpet. I'm pulling out all the stops. Besides you never know—I could run into you know who. I have to look my best," she teased.

He just rolled his eyes. But she was not to be deterred. "Kidding aside, I hope you appreciate the sacrifice here. I'm wearing shapewear for you. And these shoes," she said, gesturing to her high strappy heels, "are going to murder on my feet." Jeffrey wasn't fooled. Her cheeks were flushed—not just from the champagne—and the joy and pride in her eyes was unmistakable. He gave her hand a quick squeeze.

"You're lucky to have such a supportive fiancée," his mother lectured.

"Believe me I know." For that he was rewarded with a big smacking kiss.

His parents exchanged a look and frowned. "Enough of that. You two aren't married yet," Martin said, his voice full of disapproval. Jeffrey looked over at Cecily and they exchanged an amused look of their own.

Pam delicately put her champagne flute down. "Now that you two are here, there are some things we need to talk about," she said, clearing her throat.

Alarm bells began ringing in his head. "About what exactly?" he asked suspiciously.

"Don't be like that. We just want to know how the wedding plans are going."

Oh, boy. "They're going fine." To the best of his

knowledge. It was made clear to him early that his only job was to make sure his tuxedo fit, and to show up at the right place at the right time. The rest was Cecily's show that she was coordinating like a pro.

"Actually, since you're here, how about we go to Rodeo Drive tomorrow and look at some mother of the groom dresses for you?" Cecily interjected, smooth as silk.

"Just try to keep the budget under the national debt," he grumbled. His father just snorted.

"Good luck with that. Which brings us to our other point."

Jeffrey crossed his arms and waited for the other shoe to drop.

"You're getting married soon, and you need to start thinking about the responsibilities of providing for a family. We know this premiere is a big deal and everything, but have you thought about what's next? Do you have other jobs lined up?"

"Maybe you need to talk to your agent about getting more work," Pam suggested.

Jeffrey closed his eyes and tried to stop a groan. "That's not how this works, Ma. That's not how any of this works." He appreciated his parents wanting to help, but sometimes it was a double-edged sword.

Cecily gave his hand a squeeze and leaned over. "I have it on good authority from my mother that your parents bought up multiple magazines with articles about the film and have been insufferable. Just remember they are incredibly proud of you. So breathe and smile." And he did just that.

Nevertheless, his parents persisted. "You need to think about the future, son. How can you expect to provide for my grandchildren on an inconsistent salary?" His father threw up his hands.

"Judith and I have already talked. When the time comes, we'll both come out to California after the baby's born to help you." Pam was beaming, but the prospect of that was enough to terrify them both. Taking a big gulp of champagne, he desperately tried to change the subject.

He saw Pam whispering and elbowing his father. "What's wrong?"

Reaching into his wallet, Martin took out some money. "This is for the dinner we had last month," he explained as he handed over the wad of bills.

"Dad, put that away," Jeffrey protested. He and Cecily exchanged a look as they remembered the incident. The two families went out to dinner and it turned into a whole debacle. Both sets of parents started arguing over who was going to pay when the check came, and the shouting match got loud enough to attract the attention of the other diners. Thankfully, they had gone to a Chinese restaurant so this was par for the course and no one batted an eye. It got so bad Judith had chased Martin all the way to the cashier to pay, but luckily, Cecily had already given the waiter her credit card when they arrived, which put an end to the spectacle.

Or so they had thought. "You can pay next time," he suggested.

The mulish look on both of his parents' faces had him sighing and meekly accepting the money. He'd have to figure out a way to give it back before they returned to New York.

"Maybe you can use it to buy a new laptop for work," Pam said with a smile.

"That's a great idea," he agreed.

It was nice to see his parents show their approval and support, even if it also came with a dose of nagging. It was how they showed their love, after all. He had to give himself some credit. Not even six months ago, his parents asking questions about his work and money would have bothered the hell out of him. He thought that meant they didn't approve of or believe in him. But now, he realized this was them showing support. But most of all, the important thing was he believed in himself. With his family and Cecily by his side there wasn't anything he couldn't do.

Soon enough they arrived at the event and got ready to get out of the limo. As the lights flashed, Jeffrey had to admit at this moment in time, life didn't get much better than this.

Epilogue

New Year's Eve

"DO YOU HAVE the champagne ready?" Cecily asked.

"Of course I do." He lifted up the two flutes and bottle of Veuve Clicquot. He gave a startled look when he saw her.

"I know it's some girl beauty ritual thing that I shouldn't comment on, but it's so creepy when I see you with that."

"It's just a sheet mask," she responded with a roll of her eyes. "I'm hydrating my situation here. Leave me alone."

"You look like an extra from *The Mummy*." He set the champagne and flutes back down on the living room table.

"I don't believe in messing with tradition. I think it brings good luck, so I'm doing it."

"Tradition?" he asked with a bit of a scoff. "I don't re-member sheet masks as part of the New Year's tradition. Is looking like an evil spirit supposed to ward them off?"

"I really don't know why I put up with you some-times," she grumbled. She passed by him to the kitchen to grab some snacks. The mask had to stay on for another six minutes, but she wanted to be prepared.

"You know you love me anyway," he said smugly.

317

"You're so lucky it's true."

But Jeffrey was like a dog with a bone. "Why good luck?"

She gave a sigh. "Okay, last year on New Year's Eve I was home alone and watching the East Coast coverage. And avoiding my family's calls and texts."

"That sounds like you."

"I was getting bored and channel surfing."

"Can we get to the part with the mask?"

"I had a sheet mask on during that whole time. Satisfied?"

He made a go-ahead motion. "Carry on."

"Anyway, before I was so rudely interrupted…"

"Don't be overdramatic."

"I decided that my life needed a reboot, so I made a list of resolutions. It was going to be the Year of Cecily."

"Oh right," Jeffrey said with a snap of his fingers. "The book club. Was all that on your list?"

"Yep. Considering how well this year has turned out, I thought if it ain't broke, don't fix it. I'm even wearing the same pajamas I was wearing that night."

"Knowing you, I'm not surprised." He tilted his head. "What else was on that list anyway?"

"I sense mockery," she sniffed.

"None, just genuine curiosity."

"Fine. I have three minutes left before I need to take the mask off. I'll dig out my planner and show you."

"I can't wait," he drawled.

"Turn the TV on, and find something to entertain

yourself. I'll be right back."

"Maybe one of your new resolutions should be to be less bossy. Let's work on that."

She stuck her tongue out at him, then went to the bathroom to take care of business. By the time she came back out, the blanket was spread on the sofa, snacks were on the table, and the champagne was waiting to be poured. She went to the bedroom to grab her planner then joined him on the couch.

She plopped down beside him and rested her head against him. She gave a small yawn, then opened up her planner. She flicked her eyes up to the TV to see what Jeffrey had picked. He hadn't turned on any of the Times Square coverage. He'd put on a virtual fireplace.

"Awww, how cozy and romantic." She snuggled closer, and he ran a hand through her hair, combing through the strands.

"Yeah, yeah, quit stalling."

"Fine. Ugh. Resolution one was, *Avoid drama. Not your circus, not your monkeys.*"

They looked at each other. "Let's call that a work in progress," he suggested with a twitch of his lips.

"Let's. Number two was *Better Work-Life Balance— don't spend all your time at the office.*"

Cecily gave it a few moments' pause as she evaluated. "I'm calling this a win," she declared.

"Sure. You barely work on the weekends anymore, now that you got another paralegal in your department. And you usually get home before eight. I'll allow it," Jeffrey said generously.

"Thanks so much," she replied drily. "Number three—*Remain calm with family. Don't let them get under your skin.*"

"Yeah, that was never going to happen." He smirked.

"I say it's a draw," she insisted, brows furrowed. "You know how my family is. I plead mitigating circumstances."

"Sure, honey." He looked like he was half a step away from giving her a patronizing pat on the head.

"Don't," she warned.

"You're no fun. What's next?"

"Make new friends. Major check. I love Rachel." She beamed.

"I still don't like you spending too much time with her and Adrienne," Jeffrey grumbled. "The three of you together is bad news."

She whacked him in the stomach and he doubled over and wheezed.

"Don't insult my squad," Cecily warned.

"Okay, you get a gold star for that one. Satisfied?"

"Yes!" She looked at the next item and blushed beet red.

Jeffrey instantly got suspicious.

"What was number five?" He asked, raising a brow.

"Never mind, let's just skip it and move on," she mumbled. She tried to slam the book shut, but his reflexes were too quick. He plucked it out of her hands and opened it back to the same page.

Knowing what was coming, Cecily just dropped her

head and covered her face with her hands.

Get out there more. It's been too long since you've had sex.

He slid a look at her. She refused to look up, but she could sense it. And she knew, could perfectly describe, the expression that was on his face right now.

"Don't, just don't."

"I'm happy to have done my part to help you achieve this particular resolution."

"If you could dial down the smugness like ninety percent that would be really appreciated."

"Too late." He whispered in her ear, "Wanna fool around later? We can ring in the New Year. Literally."

"Keep this up, you may never get sex again, I'm just saying."

"No, I'm pretty sure regular sex is a condition in our prenup."

"I read that thing front to back three times. It absolutely isn't."

"I could've sworn it was. Your loss. *I'm* just saying."

Enough was enough. Cecily picked up her head, and grabbed the book back.

"Moving on," she gritted out.

"Can we revisit the sex thing later?"

"Next up was: *Expand your horizons—join a book club or something.*" Cecily looked at him. "Thanks to you, that's a big check too. Book club sucked, but I've really liked the films you've suggested. Who knew I'd like the Marx Brothers so much? I even got to meet Daniel, which was the best. You are an awesome fiancé," she said with a kiss on his cheek.

"Since when are you two on a first-name basis?" he grumped.

"Don't be like that! Besides, he agreed to be in that Iris Chang movie you and Greg are working on, right?"

"I just don't think this obsession you have for him is healthy."

She chose to ignore that. "The next one is: *Come up with an anniversary present for Mom and Dad that she'll actually like.* It took a while but we got there. I get a check for this too." Last she'd heard from Gillian, her mother was complaining/humblebragging to the neighbors about how much the custom frame for the family tree had cost. The family tree had pride of place on the mantel in the living room.

"That reminds me, I'm going to need the contact info for the expert you hired. I think I want do something similar for my parents."

"No one likes a copycat, dear." When she saw the look he threw her, Cecily relented. "I have Kelly's email somewhere. I'll give it to you. Just warning you now, she doesn't come cheap. But she's worth every penny."

"If I end up being descended from some emperor, I'm going to totally rub it in your face."

"Good luck with that. Oh wait, I nearly missed one. Eight was: *Get out of your comfort zone.*" She held up her left hand, and let the diamond catch the lamplight. "I think that's a yes too."

"Love's always the riskiest game in town."

"But in our case, it worked out." She waggled her fingers, showing off the ring.

"I'm lucky you can be bought off with bling," he joked.

She couldn't help but pout a little. "I resent the implication that I'm shallow."

"I was kidding, obviously. You are the epitome of grace and forgiveness. And a woman of exceptional judgment and heart. I'm the lucky one here." He gave her a kiss in consolation.

"That's better."

"So what else is on the list?"

"That's it."

"Well it seems to me you kicked ass. I would consider The Year of Cecily a great success."

"I can't help but agree. I kicked ass this year. I'd give myself a solid A."

"Of course you would. But this also means you have your work cut out for you next year. How are you going to top this?"

"You make a good point." Cecily bit her lip.

"But that's okay. I'm here to help. The year of Jeffrey and Cecily will be even better." He patted her knee.

"The Year of Cecily and Jeffrey," she corrected.

He frowned. "How come you go first?"

"Alphabetical order. It's easier that way," she said breezily with a wave of her hand.

"Fine, whatever. Have more sex. I think that should be your first new resolution. Begin as you mean to go on, I always say."

"That was my resolution last year. You pig." She rolled her eyes.

"You can never have too much sex."

"One-track-minded pig," she amended.

"Just so we're clear, sex is still on the table for later right?"

"If I say yes, will it shut you up? This list is serious business. You need to focus."

As they continued to bicker, Cecily couldn't help but marvel at how much her life had changed since she made her list of resolutions last year. For the better. The love of her life was back in her life, she'd made a new friend, picked up a fun hobby, and her relationship with her family was improving. She was happier than ever.

As much as she hated to agree with Jeffrey and add to his enormous ego, he was right. The Year of Cecily had been awesome. A total success.

She could hardly wait to see what next year would bring.

The End

Don't miss the next book in the From Sunset Park, With Love series, *The Rachel Experiment*!

Join Tule Publishing's newsletter for more great reads and weekly deals!

Acknowledgements

SO many people have been instrumental on my journey to publication I hardly know where to begin. But here goes:

My amazing agent Courtney Miller-Callihan has been a saint dealing with me and holding my hand throughout this process. Thank you for believing in me and Cecily, and for being such a zealous advocate for me. I am so grateful and lucky to have you in my corner! Not only that, this full length incarnation of the book (including the title!!) would not exist if not for you. I am beyond grateful for your incredible foresight and guidance that got us here today.

Thank you to my editor Sinclair Sawhney for walking me through the editing process with patience, sensitivity, and understanding. Thank you for your great insights and working with me to make this book shine! You have helped make this book so much better, while keeping the heart of the story, and characters, intact.

And thank you to the team at Tule for seeing the potential in Cecily and Jeffrey's book and giving me the opportunity to share their story.

Massive love and thanks to the other 2/3s of the L-Squad, Liana De la Rosa and Elizabeth Bright. Liana and Lizzie, thank you for cheering me on, having my back, keeping me sane, believing in me when I didn't believe in myself, and always being more happy and excited for me than I am for me. I couldn't do this without you two! You have both talked me off too many ledges to count. *mwah*

Heartfelt hugs and thank you to Tessa Dare for all the reasons and all the things. You are the reason I started this journey and I will be eternally grateful to you. Like the Avon marketing team once said I am a Tessa Dare superfan for life! <3 You are the bestestest!

My utmost gratitude and admiration to Courtney Milan, the best Romancelandia big sister anyone could ask for. You look out for me, inspire me, and answer my random questions out of the blue. CM, I can't tell you what it means to me to know you're in my corner and rooting for me. I am beyond lucky and I know it! The mooncakes are coming, I promise! 謝謝你!

Thank you to Lenora Bell who ALWAYS believed this day would come, even when I didn't. Like we said back in 2015, friends for life! <3 (Even when we were living on opposite sides of the world!) Thank you for telling me I was on the right track when I shared Cecily with you, and to keep going.

Thank you to Susannah Erwin for reading an early version of this book and not hating it. I appreciate your help in getting the Hollywood industry aspect of the book right. (All errors are mine). Thank you for telling me I don't suck, even when I don't believe you.

Thank you to Word Count Sherpa Sarah MacLean for cracking the whip so I actually get the words on the page. 50 words!

Thank you to Sally Kilpatrick for always blessing hearts

and dissing heffas with me, and who listens to me whine about revisions and edits. You are the best!

Thank you to Adele Buck and Jayce Ellis for being their awesome badass selves and being willing to smack sense into me if I need it. I appreciate the tough love ladies!

Thank you to the ladies in the Tule Group chat for the pep talks, encouragement, and info sharing. I appreciate all of you so much! We are all in this together.

Thank you to Camryn Garrett who gave me a quick crash course and answered my questions about Jeffrey's career as a screenwriter. Of course, any errors are my own.

Thank you to Felicia Grossman and Stacey Agdern for being so kind and supportive. Extra special shoutout to Felicia for taking a look at Cecily to make sure the legal things were as accurate as possible. Yep, once again, all mistakes are mine.

Thank you to Julie James for teaching me the importance of vino when writing *those* scenes. I will always remember our annual wine dates. You have been part of the journey since the beginning and I so value your encouragement and kindness!

Thank you to Alexis Daria for always cheering me on and giving such great advice. I appreciate when you bring the honest and blunt straight talk. We've both come a long way since those LJS days, huh?

BIG thank you to Priscilla Oliveras, Ally Carter, Theresa Romain, Anne Marie Rivers, Jennifer Iacopelli, Jayci Lee, Maya Rodale, PJ Ausdenmore, and countless others who extended much needed kindness, support, encouragement, generosity, and friendship along the way.

Thank you to ALL the Asian/SE Asian romance writers out there who put cracks in that ceiling and helped pave the way for me. And a huge thank you to Ms. Bev who helped pave the way for us ALL. I know I stand on the shoulders of giants.

Thank you to Elysabeth Grace who answered some genealogy research questions for me. Again, all errors are my own.

Thank you to my parents who instilled in me a love of reading and books by taking me to the library regularly as a kid. It shaped me into the reader and writer I am today. You helped me see reading as a joy, a fun hobby, not a chore like eating my vegetables.

Thank you to my mom and sister, who despite not being well versed in the publishing industry, do their best to be helpful and give support and advice.

Finally, to anyone and everyone who reads this book— from the bottom of my heart, thank you.

If you enjoyed *The Year of Cecily*,
you'll love the next book in the…

From Sunset Park, With Love series

Book 1: *The Year of Cecily*

Book 2: *The Rachel Experiment*
Coming in May 2023

Available now at your favorite online retailer!

Enjoy an excerpt from

The Rachel Experiment
Lisa Lin
Book 2 in the From Sunset Park, With Love series
Keep reading below or pre-order now!

T HE MEETING HAD been going so well. Generally speaking, as a financial analyst, Rachel Bai's days were spent collecting data and research, and presenting her findings at meetings. However most of her days were spent working alone, which was her preference. And frankly it was probably better for all involved. Today was not her lucky day.

"Well, thanks for meeting with me," Tricia Watkins said with a grateful smile. Tricia was the new liaison from Caffrey Pharmaceuticals, one of her major clients. Tricia had suggested they grab a quick lunch to get to know each other. So now they were seated at Townsend Bistro where she was eating a delicious Cajun salmon salad and drinking mineral water. Expensive brand-name mineral water. Rachel had agreed reluctantly because she was always afraid she'd do something to make it all go to hell. Today was no exception.

"I should be the one thanking you. You're the one who paid, after all," Rachel pointed out reasonably. Then she paused. "So, thank you."

"My pleasure," Tricia assured her. Tricia was exactly the type of person who intimidated her and made her nervous. Tricia carried herself like she was born to wear her tailored blazer, blouse, pencil skirt, and high pumps, while Rachel was wearing flats and an off-the-rack generic suit from Ann Taylor. Tricia was the epitome of calm, polished, and poised. Someone who was confident and wouldn't be thrown by a simple conversation over lunch because of course she'd know what to do and what to say. Unlike Rachel.

"I'm looking forward to getting to know you better as we work together the next few months," the other woman continued.

Rachel frowned as a pit settled like a boulder in her stomach. More lunches? More interactions? More opportunities to show how inept she was at this sort of thing? "Hopefully we'll both be too busy for all that." Seeing the look on Tricia's face, Rachel scrambled to backtrack. "I mean, assuming the reports and everything are positive and everything works out, that means more work, and more money for all of us. Win-win, right?" she added desperately.

"Definitely." Tricia got up from the table though her smile had cooled several degrees and was more wary now.

Rachel groaned inwardly. She had screwed up again. Even though she didn't mean to. "Anyway, I will get this paperwork to you as soon as possible." She was much more comfortable when things were on a business footing. At least she knew what to do. Most of the time.

"That sounds great. But you're right about the increased workload if all this takes off. I barely see my husband and kids these days. What work-life balance, right?" Tricia said with a laugh.

"I wouldn't know," Rachel said with a shrug. "I spend most of my days at the office. I don't have a husband and kids so I don't have that problem. Though there are times I wonder why I bother having an apartment when I'm hardly ever there. Maybe I could consider giving it up," she mused. "It would save money, and there may be some tax benefits. What do you think?" she asked Tricia. "Though it would be awkward to find a place to store my clothes and shower and wash up if I did just live at the office full time. Maybe I can find a nearby gym?"

The look in Tricia's eyes told her she had way overshot the mark in trying to relate. Crap.

"Anyway, it's time I got back to work. Thanks again for lunch." Rachel pushed up her glasses and stuck out her hand. Then saw Tricia hesitate. Surely she hadn't gotten this part of it wrong. To her relief, Tricia returned the handshake. After a brief goodbye, the two went their separate ways.

With a sigh, Rachel shook her head and started the ten-block trek back to her office. She should be used to it by now, this inability to carry on a decent conversation over a simple meal. Somehow, at birth she seemed to be missing that particular socializing gene that everyone else seemed to have received. While everyone else seemed to have an intuitive sense of how to act in these situations, she had the uncanny ability to never know the right thing to say, and whatever she did say always ended up making things a thousand times worse and more awkward.

Despite her best efforts, she never possessed the easy ability to connect with people and it always made her feel like the odd woman out. She wished she could be like everyone else—make friends, execute small talk easily, act normal. Be normal.

But, as a person who dealt with numbers and reality, Rachel knew that such wishes were useless. For better or worse, she was who she was. And the fact that she was a weirdo didn't prevent her from being good at her job. She always believed in focusing on her strengths and maximizing them. Maybe someday she could work on making new friends and find someone who didn't mind her awkward ways. She thought back to New Years. She and Cecily Chang had made headway into a friendship of sorts. So perhaps she wasn't a total lost cause after all.

But for now, work called. In that arena at least she knew what she was doing. Rachel clung on to that thread of hope all the way back to the office.

LATER THAT AFTERNOON, Rachel knocked on her manager's door with no small amount of trepidation. Out of the blue, her manager Jake had emailed her to tell her to be in his office at four thirty—a demand not a request. That was all the two-line message said. Rachel had no idea what to expect—a promotion, termination, or an ask for her assistance to head up the recruitment/hiring committee. There was no way to know.

She hoped she wasn't getting fired. Had Trish called and lodged some sort of complaint?

Jake Clyburn gestured for her to enter and take a seat. But he kept her hanging by taking another five minutes to finish writing his email or whatever it was he was doing.

"Hey Rachel, thanks for coming by."

"Sure." It wasn't like she really had a choice in the matter.

He steepled his hands on the desk and gave her a direct look. "I'm just going to cut to the chase. How do you feel about California?"

"California, sir?"

"Yes, the Golden State, home of Hollywood, beaches, palm trees, wine country?"

"I'm familiar. I'm just not sure what you're asking. I have no particular feelings about California. I visited a friend there recently, it was nice." At least she knew now this had nothing to do with her disastrous lunch today. Thank God.

"Well you're about to. We're sending you to San Francisco."

"Excuse me?" What the hell?

"There's an opening in our San Francisco office," Jake

explained. "We want you there to head up a new team."

"I'm flattered sir, but there wasn't anyone who already lives there available for the job?"

"You did hear me say you'd be heading up the team, right?"

"Yes, but I'm still confused."

"We think you have a lot of potential, so we're giving you this chance to step up and take on a more managerial role. I know you've wanted a chance to move up the ladder for some time now, and here is your opportunity."

Rachel's palms began to sweat. It was true, she had been maneuvering for a promotion but didn't think it would happen this soon. "I'm going to need some time to pack, find a place to live. When would I start?"

Jake smiled. "Don't worry about that. I'll have the office manager in the San Francisco office get in touch with you and they can help you organize the logistics from their end. They can help you find a new apartment, etc. But we want you there within the next sixty days."

Well, that wasn't a lot of time. And she was probably picked because she was still single. Transplanting her across the country was a less daunting endeavor than someone who had a family and had to juggle school, daycare, and their spouse's career as well.

What the hell. She could use a new change of pace and California could be interesting. If nothing else, it would give her an excuse to get away from her sister Claudia's wedding madness for the next two months while she prepared to move. Talk about a silver lining.

"How long will I be there?"

"We anticipate six to nine months, with a possible extension. It all depends on how things go. If the team is successful and becomes permanent, we may relocate you there permanently."

"I see."

"Will that be a problem?"

"No sir." At least she wouldn't be alone in a city full of strangers. She could reach out to Cecily and let her know she was coming back to San Francisco. She could get insider info on which neighborhoods would be best to live in, and closest to the office, where the best restaurants were. The essential things. She and Cecily were almost friends, right? It wouldn't be weird for her to reach out and ask. When she visited San Francisco a few months back, Cecily had offered to let her stay at her place. Surely she wasn't misreading the signs.

Jake cleared his throat, interrupting her racing thoughts. "There is one other thing I wanted to bring up though."

"Of course, sir."

"I know you've been with Kirkwood Young and Sloane for almost ten years now, and your work has always been exemplary."

"I assume that's why you picked me, and why I'm being set up for a promotion."

"Yes, of course. Your evaluations have always been top-notch. However, there was one thing that stands out."

"What's that?" What could she possibly be doing

wrong after all these years? Jake was right, her evaluations had always been high, and she'd always taken the constructive criticism to heart and strived to constantly improve.

"You tend to work alone, and your new position will involve much more teamwork."

"I understand," she said boldly. "That shouldn't be a problem."

"In addition, you'll be meeting with potential clients, taking many more meetings, and going to events where you'll be expected to network and bring in new business."

Now this was a problem. Anxiety balled in her stomach. Normally, her job consisted of her sitting behind a computer for most of the day and that suited her fine. Having to interact more with co-workers and clients would be putting her out of her comfort zone, to put it mildly. As evidenced by today's lunch.

Seeing the look in her eyes, Jake nodded, but there was a sympathetic gleam in his eyes. "I know networking and people skills aren't your strengths, but I'm confident you can work on it and get where you need to be. In fact, you're going to need to. Because by the end of this trial period, if you don't recruit the clients we need, we may need to reevaluate."

Rachel gave a hard swallow. "Would I be allowed to come back to the New York office?"

Jake gave a slow shake of his head. "Unfortunately, because you'll be gone so long, we'll have to find a replacement for you. There should still be a lateral analyst position in San Francisco, but that's no guarantee. We'd have to find another branch office to send you to."

Rachel had never been good at subtext, but even she could read between those lines. Either she proved herself and earned the promotion, or she'd be out on her ass. Or relegated to the Omaha office. Neither of which were acceptable options.

Jake looked at his watch. "I think I've taken up enough of your time, and I have another meeting." Taking that as her cue, Rachel stood. Jake extended his hand, and she shook it, gingerly.

"Congratulations, and good luck." Though his smile was encouraging, Rachel couldn't help but detect a note of doubt in Jake's voice. Meaning he too wasn't a hundred percent sure if she'd be up to the challenge.

In a slight daze, Rachel nodded, murmured her thanks, and made her way back to her office. Part of her was excited and thrilled at this opportunity. But part of her realized she was facing a daunting challenge not unlike climbing Mt. Everest. With no proper equipment or prior training.

No matter what, she was determined to succeed and make this work. She'd figure out a way. Somehow.

Find out what happens next...
Pre-order now!

Reader Discussion Questions for
The Year of Cecily

1. *The Year of Cecily* starts with Cecily coming up with a list of resolutions for the New Year. But as the book progresses, the resolutions evolve and Cecily makes progress and suffers setbacks in fulfilling those resolutions. Do you think that's realistic and what do you think of Cecily's motivations to make those resolutions? How do you go about setting your own goals and resolutions?

2. What lessons do you think Cecily and Jeffrey learn about themselves, each other, their relationship, and their relationship with their families? Are they the same people as they were when the book started? Do you think they have worked everything out, or are they still works in progress? Which do you think is more realistic?

3. Cecily loves her family but her feelings about them, particularly her mother, are complicated. Do you agree with her that absence makes the heart grow fonder? Why do you think some people love having family close by and others are happier with some distance?

4. When Cecily goes home to celebrate Lunar New Year, a lot revolves around food. What are your favorite

holiday traditions and recipes? Why do you think food is such a powerful connector?

5. Do you think Jeffrey deserves to be forgiven for what he did ten years ago? Were his reasons understandable? Has he done enough to make amends?

6. Cecily and Rachel were nemeses growing up, but discover they have more in common than they expect and become friends. How do you think their parents affected their perceptions of each other? Has there ever been a time in your life when your impression of someone ended up being totally wrong or skewed?

7. The book focuses on the love story between Cecily and Jeffrey, but also discusses other types of love and relationships between friends, parents, siblings, etc. Why do you think the author made this choice? What roles have these types of relationships played in your life? Why do you think romantic love tends to get elevated and discussed more than these other types?

8. Cecily relies on Adrienne and Rachel at various moments throughout the book. Discuss the ways that friendship between women are unique and the role it plays in the book. Do you have your own squad and what role have they played in your own life?

9. Throughout the book, Jeffrey struggles with self-doubt and believing in himself. But with some help, he finally summons the courage to go after who and what he wants. Do you relate to his struggle? Have you had times when you doubted yourself? How did you overcome it?

10. Both Cecily and Jeffrey were born in the Year of the Pig. What is your Chinese Zodiac Sign? Discuss the traits of your animal and if you relate/think it's accurate.

11. Cecily discovers some fascinating tidbits about her family when she meets with Kelly the genealogist. How do you think Cecily is impacted by what she learns and how does it change how she views herself and her family? Are you a fan of genealogy shows like Who Do You Think You Are and Finding Your Roots? Have you ever researched your own family trees and discovered any secrets?

12. Being a screenwriter, Jeffrey is obviously a huge film buff. Have you seen any of the films mentioned in the book? What do you think of Jeffrey's film choices for Cecily and what significance do the films have? If you had your own "film appreciation club" what films would you pick?

About the Author

Lisa has been an avid romance reader and fan since she read her first Nora Roberts novel at the age of 13 after wandering the aisles of her local bookstore. Lisa loves that romance has the power to inspire, and believes that HEAs are for everyone.

Lisa writes light contemporary romantic comedies with a liberal dash of snark and banter. She enjoys delving into the complexity of Asian and immigrant family experiences, and celebrates female friendships in her trademark dry, witty style. As an Asian-American author writing own voices Asian American stories, Lisa hopes that her books will show the diversity of the Asian-American experience, and the importance of every reader being able to see themselves represented on the page.

Having grown up in Pennsylvania and helping out at her parents' restaurant, Lisa has never bothered to learn to cook. She has two liberal arts undergraduate degrees and a J.D, and in her former life she was an intern, then Legislative Assistant for a PA State Representative. She also worked as a paralegal at a boutique law firm. Lisa is a politics junkie (don't get her started on the wonder that is The West Wing!), indulges in naps whenever possible, and believes Netflixing in her pajamas and ordering take out qualifies as the perfect weekend.

Thank you for reading

The Year of Cecily

If you enjoyed this book, you can find more from all our great authors at TulePublishing.com, or from your favorite online retailer.

9 781957 748900